More praise for

The Song Remains the Same

"Scotch has drawn a fully three-dimensional heroine in Nell, and the story's pacing perfectly mirrors the protagonist's increasing rate of self-discovery. Scotch peppers her chapters with a number of pop-culture and musical references, giving the story a modern and lively feel. With shades of Sophie Kinsella's *Remember Me?* and Liane Moriarty's *What Alice Forgot*, this novel is a breezy yet introspective examination of one woman's newfound history."

—*Booklist*

"Winn Scotch vividly illustrates the confusion, frustration, and anger of not being able to remember or trust. She particularly shines in creating secondary characters—especially Rory and Anderson—flawed but engaging. Readers will love Nell and won't be able to put the book down until they know how much of her past she wants to bring into her future." —*Publishers Weekly*

"Scotch . . . crafts a plausible story, complete with a capable and prickly protagonist, that doesn't resort to any movie-of-the-week amnesia clichés. A dry-eyed, modern take on healing and forgiveness." —*Kirkus Reviews*

"Readers who appreciate women's fiction that investigates serious themes will enjoy Scotch's fine novel. Reading groups will find much to discuss as well." —*Library Journal*

Also by Allison Winn Scotch

The Department of Lost & Found

Time of My Life

The One That I Want

The Song Remains the Same

Allison Winn Scotch

BERKLEY BOOKS, NEW YORK

THE BERKLEY PUBLISHING GROUP
Published by the Penguin Group
Penguin Group (USA) Inc.
375 Hudson Street, New York, New York 10014, USA
Penguin Group (Canada), 90 Eglinton Avenue East, Suite 700, Toronto, Ontario M4P 2Y3, Canada
(a division of Pearson Penguin Canada Inc.) • Penguin Books Ltd., 80 Strand, London WC2R 0RL,
England • Penguin Group Ireland, 25 St. Stephen's Green, Dublin 2, Ireland (a division of Penguin
Books Ltd.) • Penguin Group (Australia), 250 Camberwell Road, Camberwell, Victoria 3124, Australia
(a division of Pearson Australia Group Pty. Ltd.) • Penguin Books India Pvt. Ltd., 11 Community
Centre, Panchsheel Park, New Delhi—110 017, India • Penguin Group (NZ), 67 Apollo Drive,
Rosedale, Auckland 0632, New Zealand (a division of Pearson New Zealand Ltd.) • Penguin Books
(South Africa) (Pty.) Ltd., 24 Sturdee Avenue, Rosebank, Johannesburg 2196, South Africa

Penguin Books Ltd., Registered Offices: 80 Strand, London WC2R 0RL, England

This is a work of fiction. Names, characters, places, and incidents either are the product of the author's
imagination or are used fictitiously, and any resemblance to actual persons, living or dead, business
establishments, events, or locales is entirely coincidental. The publisher does not have any control over
and does not assume any responsibility for author or third-party websites or their content.

PUBLISHING HISTORY
G. P. Putnam's Sons hardcover edition / April 2012
Berkley trade paperback edition / January 2013

Berkley trade paperback ISBN: 978-0-425-25335-9

The Library of Congress has catalogued the G. P. Putnam's Sons hardcover edition of
this book as follows:

Scotch, Allison Winn.
The song remains the same / Allison Winn Scotch.
p.   cm.
ISBN 978-0-399-15758-5
1. Gifted women—Fiction.   2. Aircraft accident victims—Fiction.   3. Amnesiacs—Fiction.
4. Life-changing events—Fiction.   5. Coma—Patients—Fiction.   6. Music therapy—Fiction.
7. Aircraft accidents—Fiction.   8. Amnesia—Fiction.   I. Title.
PS3619.C64 S66   2012   2011049446
813'.6—dc23

PRINTED IN THE UNITED STATES OF AMERICA

10 9 8 7 6 5 4 3 2 1

For Cam and Amelia,
who fill my life with song.

Never forget me, because if I thought you would, I'd never leave.

—A. A. MILNE

The Best of Nell Slattery

1. "Have a Little Faith in Me"—Joe Cocker
2. "Sweet Child o' Mine"—Guns N' Roses
3. "Running on Empty"—Jackson Browne
4. "Every Breath You Take"—The Police
5. "Eleanor Rigby"—The Beatles
6. "You Can't Always Get What You Want"
   —The Rolling Stones
7. "Don't Stop Believing"—Journey
8. "There's a Light That Never Goes Out"
   —The Smiths
9. "Let the River Run"—Carly Simon
10. "Into the Mystic"—Van Morrison
11. "Ramble On"—Led Zeppelin
12. "Forever Young"—Bob Dylan

1

Beep. Beep. Beep. Beep. Beep.

B My eyelids feel like anchors. There is a drill pounding into the back of my skull. My lungs feel as if someone has dumped a sandbox inside of them, then turned on a blender. I inhale and my ribs bark in reply.

Beep. Beep. Beep. Beep. Beep.

My alarm clock is going off. It must be that my alarm clock is going off. I force one eye open, and it just barely complies. The other follows, breaking free from a heavy, cracking crust that coats my lashes. I try to swivel my neck—*where is that alarm clock and how do I get it to stop beeping?*—but discover that it's immobile, swaddled, in a brace, in a pillow of sorts that is holding me together.

No. No. Where am I? I dart my eyes around, my breathing more labored, the beeping increasing with each tightened gasp of air.

In the corner, a tall man with the sloping shoulders of a former football player hovers with a woman whose lines have long ago sunk into her eyes. They are both disheveled, worn, fraying on all sides. His brown hair is tucked under a baseball cap, his three-day-old stubble shadowing his face. His ivory DICK'S DRIVE-THRU T-shirt has two coffee stains on the hem, his jeans marred with a splatter of ketchup. She looks no better in a flowy, used purple dress that could double as a nightgown, her kinky graying hair pulled into a knot on top of her head, reminding me of a mushroom.

"What do you mean she was pregnant?" the man whispers. I want to sit up closer to hear them, lean in and understand, but I am either too sore or too immobile to move. I'm not sure which just yet.

"You didn't know?" she replies.

"No," he says, then sinks onto the arm of a chair wedged next to him. "I didn't know."

She rubs the small of his back and stares out the window to the open landscape of beige dirty rooftops, one of those long stares that betrays her stoicism, that makes you wonder if she isn't about to fall apart entirely.

I try to grunt, to let them know that I am here, that I am watching, but my mouth is too dry, my tongue unused for too long.

"I'll go get coffee," the man says, rising.

Look at me! Look at me! The beeping accelerates. *Beep beep beep beep beep.*

Finally, he does.

"Oh my god, Nell, you're awake!" He rushes over and clasps my hand.

I nod. Or I think I nod.

The woman is by my side in an instant, then just as quickly turns and shouts out the open door, "She's awake! Page Dr. Macht!" And then she is back, crying now, rubbing my forehead, then pressing into me. "Oh my god, thank god, Nell, you're awake."

Before I can understand who she is or what this means, a steady, heady figure appears at the foot of my bed, checking a chart, fiddling with the machines, watching the numbers, the beeping. He nudges his glasses up his nose, smoothing his hair—graying at the temples but thick and wavy all the same—with his right hand. Then he whisks the two of them aside, casting them off like lint, and stares down at me.

"Nell, I'm Dr. Macht. We're very happy to see you. Do you know where you are?"

I glance behind him. A wave of anxious faces—nurses, strangers—have gathered, filling the room and trickling into the hallway.

I don't answer, so he asks me again.

"Nell. You've been in an accident. Do you recognize where you are?" He flits his hand in the air and turns his head abruptly. "If you're not part of the core treatment team, please exit the room." No one moves. *"Now."* Slowly, like the draining of a reservoir, the audience ebbs. A smattering of nurses, the man and older woman, and Dr. Macht remain.

"Nell," he says, and sits carefully on the bed. "Nell, you were in a plane crash. What can you tell me about what you remember about it?"

My eyes circle around, my teeth gnash my bottom lip. I try to search about my memory. *What do I remember?* A plane? Did I get on a plane? *No, no, that wasn't me. I don't think I did.* A crash? How could I not remember a crash? *No, impossible, couldn't have been me.*

"Nothing," I manage to whisper, the air burning the back of my throat. "I don't remember a plane crash."

The older woman who reminds me of a mushroom places a cup with a straw in front of my mouth and nods, so I work my tongue around it, hold it with my teeth, and gulp. *Yes. Like manna in the desert.* The water works its way into me—I can feel its coolness sink down my larynx and into my belly, softening the arid ground within me.

"Okay, this is very normal." Dr. Macht turns to the tall man and the woman. "We expected this. Remember, this is all normal." Then to me, he says, "What do you remember? Let's start there. Can you tell me what you remember about your life?"

I shake my head, as much as my brace will allow.

Dr. Macht ushers the man closer to the bed. He runs his fingers down my matted hair and starts weeping, silently, violently weeping.

"It's okay, Peter," the woman says. "It's going to be okay."

He nods, and sort of yelps—a dolphin call—as a way of pulling it together. The tears abate, though his eyes, red-rimmed and sagging beneath his baseball cap, tell me that he is so far from pulling it together, he doesn't even know what that means anymore.

"Him," Dr. Macht says, pointing up toward Peter. "Do you know who he is?"

I squint and gaze at him and try to remember. I stare at the spread of muscle under his T-shirt, at his wayward brown strands poking out from his cap, at the veins in his arms that announce themselves all the way down to his palms. Something about his generic, looming handsomeness sends a response trigger to my brain, but I can't pinpoint what it means, who he is, how he might be important to me.

A nurse hands Dr. Macht a mirror and he thrusts it in front of me. I see my eyes widen at the sight. *This is me? This is me.* I have no expectation of what I look like, no real map of where my freckles should sit, how my lips should pillow. As it is, there is a purple welt the color of port wine that extends from my left temple down below my eye, and my upper lip has a nasty gash that my tongue flicks over on instinct. My hair is greasy and parted at an angle that illuminates the wan, waxy pallor of my cheeks, and the color of my strands is too close to brown to really be called a natural blond.

"Does this help?" Dr. Macht says.

Does this help what? I want to ask, but instead I stare at myself until my eyes go double. Trying to connect to the face in front of me, the face I've worn my life through but whom I'd never now pick out of a lineup. I am still trying to connect, trying to remember, when the beeping—that damn beeping—creeps back into my ears again. This time louder, more frantically.

Beepbeepbeepbeepbeepbeepbeep.

Remember, goddamn it! Remember!

I am fading. I feel myself fading, the blood throbbing in my temples, behind my eyes, shortening my breath, reverberating in my chest cavity—a headache that feels akin to a small death.

Peter clasps both of my cheeks in his oversize hands, forcing me to stay awake, to focus.

"No," I reply with every last ounce of energy I have. "I'm sorry. No, I don't remember."

"I'm your husband," I hear him say, though it sounds like an echo, a faint echo from so very, very far in the distance, just before I drift away. Just before everything goes silent once more.

When I wake up for the second time, the mushroom woman is asleep in the chair beside my bed. The beeping has slowed now, a mimic of my own heartbeat, such that I barely notice it. It's there, of course it's there, but it's white noise almost, that spot where your brother has pinched you so many times that you no longer feel it.

The TV is on in the corner, low enough so that it won't disturb me, loud enough so that I can still make it out.

The newsreel is spinning in blaring red urgency on the bottom of the screen, and at the forefront stands a man in front of a hospital. An ambulance whines in the background, but either he doesn't hear it or he's too much of a pro to notice it, and he continues without so much as a flinch.

"It was reported earlier today that Nell Slattery, one of only two survivors of the crash of Flight 1715, has emerged from her coma. As viewers may remember, Ms. Slattery was found about two hundred yards from the debris field, still strapped into her seat, next to Anderson Carroll, the actor—we all know his story—and the first and only other survivor found on the scene. Investigators believe that their seats were somehow propelled fully intact out of the plane upon or just before impact. Ms. Slattery has sustained remarkably few physical injuries but suffered a severe concussion and initial brain swelling, and doctors were unsure as to her prognosis until she awoke today. That she woke at all is, they say, very, very good news."

"I am very pleased to announce that what you have heard is true," I hear, and then see, Dr. Macht say on the screen. He is standing at a podium, flashbulbs illuminating, microphones thrust upward from jutting arms. "Nell Slattery woke up for about seven minutes today. I cannot give you the full details of the situation, per hospital policy, but I am happy to say that yes, she is conscious, and someone will keep you posted as to her progress."

Me. They're talking about me. Nell Slattery. I roll my name around in my mind. *Yes, it sort of feels like it fits.* I try once again to remember the crash, of being ejected from a fireball, of being tugged by gravity down toward an inevitable death, but still, it is blank space, a void of nothingness.

I return to the screen.

"As you already know," the reporter is saying, "Ms. Slattery's story—and that of Mr. Carroll—has captivated the nation. That she has finally come to has bolstered spirits around the hospital *and* around the country."

"I just can't believe it! It's like God has granted us a miracle!" a woman cries into the camera. "God bless that girl and Anderson Carroll! They've given us all a reason to believe again!"

"And that," the reporter says, "is what is being said around the nation today. A day of hope, of thankfulness, and of possibility. Nell Slattery, found one week ago in a field in rural Iowa, after the devastating crash of Flight 1715 that left one hundred and fifty-two people dead, has regained consciousness. We'll keep you posted from here. This is Jamie Reardon, happy with the miracle we got today, bringing you more news about it as it breaks."

He nods as a sign-off to the newsroom, and I wish he wouldn't, wouldn't sign off. There is something comforting about his face, about the way he lays out the facts without sounding too factual, about the way he's talking about the most crucial details of my life and somehow not terrifying me.

Jamie Reardon, Jamie, Jamie Reardon, why don't you hear them? A melody weaves through me, a compilation of notes, a made-up song that somehow hums out of my lips. I feel the notes reverberate in my throat and almost laugh from the surprise.

The woman in the chair stirs and, on instinct, glances up at me before even wiping the sleep from her eyes.

"Nell!" She is by me in less than a breath, folding her breasts over me, and I recognize the hint of her honey-smelling soap. It's a fog, a memory of a memory, intangible, ephemeral, but warming, calming, too. "I'm your mother," she says, pulling back, her gold bangles jangling. She holds my cheeks in her hands, her palms soft against me, and then she mimics the melody I'd just created.

Our smiles echo each other's.

"You did that as a child," she says. "Made up songs about anything. Everything. Sometimes, you'd be generous enough to let me join in. Harmonize."

"I'm sorry. I wish I could remember." My smile falls and then my voice cracks, but she just says, "Shhhhh.

"Don't cry, don't apologize, sweetheart. You're alive. You're here. And I'm so thankful for that. Don't waste another second being sorry."

"That news? Is it true?" I nudge toward the TV.

"Oh, let's not keep that on, dear. It's only upsetting."

"But is it? Is it true? All of those people killed?"

She sighs and intertwines our hands. "Yes. You were on a plane flying from New York to San Francisco. Two hours in, it crashed." The blood drains from her face as she tells me this. "They don't yet know why." She waves a hand, the twinkling of her jewelry singing between our silences. "Let's see if I can help remind you of anything. You work in an art gallery. You are thirty-two years old. You live in New York." She pauses. "Does . . . does any of this bring anything back?"

I shake my head no.

"And Peter? Peter is my husband?" I scrunch my face, trying to imagine a world in which I pledged myself to him, that man. I can't see it. More important, I can't *feel* it. *Really?* I think. *Him?*

"Enough for tonight," my mom says, pulling the sheet up to my chest, tucking me in tighter, like I'm a toddler. She leans over and kisses my forehead, humming that same tune, like it might calm me, be the balm to cure me. "Enough for now. Let's put you back together, back to how you were. Then we'll have time to answer all of these questions."

Yes, I think. *Let's put me back together, back to how I was. Then, there will be time for everything else.*

2

A nurse is adjusting one of the tubes in my arms when my eyes drift awake. Though my mother is gone, she hasn't left me alone. The walls are now covered with photos, the nightstand stacked high with albums that must contain remnants of my past, reminders of who I was before I ended up upside down and broken in a cornfield in Iowa.

"Hello, Nell," the nurse says. "How are you feeling?"

"Tired. Thirsty. With about a million questions."

She smiles, nods, and holds the sippy cup in front of me.

"We sent your mother to the hotel to get some sleep. She'll be back in a bit. She left you these at the doctor's request. I'll page him. He'll be in shortly—he can answer some of those questions for you." She places one of the albums in my lap.

She shuffles out of the room, and here I am, alone. Alone with myself, a stranger to my own life.

I turn the first page. Shiny, gleaming faces peer out at me. That man, my husband—Peter—and me, where? In an ocean the shade of blue glass. Him with snorkeling goggles on his forehead, me in a purple bikini and a nose on its way to a sunburn. I turn page after page. Each photo is much the same: a wash of faces that I don't recognize, arms slung around shoulders, hands toting mugs full of beer or glasses of margaritas in bars or beaches or crisp-looking apartments, none of which mean anything to me now. The women are pretty in a common way, in dark jeans and inoffensive tank tops; the men haven't starting losing their hair or putting on too much paunch around their bellies. All in all, this life that I suppose is mine looks solid, content, not a bad one to occupy, if I could just somehow remember it, know that it is mine. I exhale and try to focus on something else—that I am a walking miracle, that I was tossed from the sky, and that the mere fact that I am here—to question these faces, to wonder about this wholly rounded life in the first place—is as much of a blessing that I can ask for right now. I drop my head back a touch. *Who was I? An art dealer. An envied, well-heeled woman-about-town who was admired and revered and who sat on charitable boards and who helped mentor inner-city kids who had a speckle of their own artistic talent. Yes, that sounds right. That sounds simply fabulous.*

Someone clears his throat in the doorway, and I float my eyes open, then shift them lower, to see a guy with a mess of blond-brown hair, the type you can gel into a just-ever-so-slight hipster Mohawk, in a wheelchair sitting in wait. He is wan and shrunken, but his cheekbones are perfect, the kind of facial structure you double-take on the street, and despite everything, I feel myself flush at his handsomeness, at the intensity of his stare.

"Excuse me, Nell, can I come in for a second?"

I nod, confused. A nurse wheels him to my bedside.

"It's okay, Alicia, I can take it from here."

"Press the call button when you're ready for me," she says over her shoulder on her way out, almost like she's flirting with him. I squint. Why would she be flirting with him?

"I've heard that you probably won't remember me," he says.

"I'm sorry, I don't."

"That's okay, it doesn't matter." He waves a hand, and I notice a flash of a tattoo on his inner wrist, a surprise against his skinny frame in a dishwater-colored hospital gown, folded into a wheel-chair. "But I asked to see you when you woke up. It feels impossible that it's been a week since . . . everything." His voice breaks, and he swallows, then sews himself back up. "My name is Anderson Carroll, and even though you don't remember me, you saved my life."

"I'm sorry? I did?" I feel my forehead wrinkle, scanning my brain, but it feels like a muscle that's been unused for too long, flaccid, impotent.

"We were sitting next to each other on the plane," he continues. "I'd . . . well, I'd probably had one too many vodka tonics—I sometimes tend to do that while flying—and I'd zoned out for a few minutes. You woke me up when things starting going wrong, snapped me into my seat belt, told me to put my head down, curl up to steel myself against what was coming." His words catch on themselves, his nose visibly pinching. "Look, I don't know how we're here, why we were the ones who made it. But I do know that I owe my life to you—I would have been tossed ten miles from that plane if you hadn't strapped me in, had the clear sense to keep me calm."

I stare at him for a beat and replay his words, my concentration lagging. I decide that I'd heard him right—that I'd saved him, that I'd been someone's life vest, that in the horror of this situation, I'd come out of it a hero.

"You're welcome." I suck on the gash on my upper lip, trying to put the pieces back together. "How'd I do that? Keep you calm." A small rush swells inside of me, that yes, I was that woman, that go-to gal-about-town, that I *was the one who kept people calm*! Of course I was. *Of course I was.* I already knew myself, even when I didn't know anything else to know.

"Just talking to me, holding my hand. You told me to focus on something other than what was happening, so we started coming up with our favorite songs, our favorite lyrics . . . it was chaos, but . . ." He stops. "I mean, obviously, it was chaos, people scream- ing, lights flashing, smoke pouring in, and well, I don't know how you did it exactly, but you made me not lose my mind during it all."

"Who did I say?" I ask.

"Sorry?"

"My favorite band. Who did I say?"

"Oh." He angles his head to think. "I don't know, we were just naming names, throwing stuff out to keep going. To be honest, I can't even remember a lot of specifics."

"To be honest, I can't, either," I joke, unsure if I'm joking at all.

"If it matters," he says, "you're famous."

He flips over a *People* magazine in his lap. There we are: him— when he was ripe and alive, healthy, perfect, the kind you *do* do a double take on the street—with his arm linked around the waist of some svelte model-looking type emerging from a nightclub; me, in a navy cardigan and pearl stud earrings, looking very much like I've never stepped foot in a nightclub in the first place, looking nothing like the girl-about-town. *No, no, no. This can't be me. I am the hero, the go-to gal.*

"Survivor Stories!" the headline screams in bold print.

"Probably not the best shot." He shrugs, as if he's responsible for the way my mouth curls under like I've just bitten into a sour orange. "I kind of hate it—I think they pulled it from a website."

"I look like I've never had fun for a second in my life."

Anderson laughs, and I laugh, too, because, what the hell, I don't really get the joke, but why not?

"What?" he says. "No, I meant me. But regardless, I'm indebted. Truly. For the rest of my life, whatever you need, I've got your back." Somewhere in the base of my neck, a headache begins to spin up through me. I wince, and he detects it.

He starts to reach for the call button.

"So how badly are you banged up?" I say, stopping him, refusing to relent to the pain for now. Part of me is exhausted, but the other part of me is grateful for his easy company, that he's not hovering, close to a breakdown at any moment like my mother or my husband.

"Fractured some vertebrae," he says. "Any worse, and I'd have been in this thing for life." His arms flop around the wheelchair.

"So, technically, we're lucky."

"Technically," he says. "Though rehab for the foreseeable future may be construed as less than that. I was supposed to be on a set, but now, it's Des Moines until fall."

"A set?" The wires connect from the news report. The moments of short-term cognitive clarity are unpredictable, coming and going at random. "Ah, yes. That's right—you're an actor?"

"I am," he says.

"Like, big-time actor or a guy who says he's an actor and actually waits tables?"

He laughs. "I was the worst waiter you'd ever seen, but yeah, I bussed my fair share for a few years. But now"—he clears his throat, suddenly ever-so-slightly self-conscious—"I guess I've earned my keep. Successfully retired my tip jar." He shrugs. "A big TV show, some film stuff." He smiles with his perfect teeth, and I can see it then: the movie star.

"Did I recognize you on the plane?"

"Maybe." He shrugs. "We didn't talk about it, and then, you know, I passed out." I try to imagine it: the sour-faced me from that *People* cover chatting him up in first class. I can't conjure it up, so I replace it with the fabulous me chatting him up in first class. *Yes, that seems better.*

I sigh. "I suppose I'll be here for a while, too," I say, "though I don't think I have anywhere as glamorous as a movie set to be."

"Don't sell yourself short—you were on your way to meet with some new hot artist." He shakes his head. "Again, can't remember her name: Harmony, Faith something, maybe? Something hippie like that."

My mother had hinted at something similar—the art gallery. I

rattle it around in my brain: it seems reasonable enough. Not repel-
lent, not a terrible fit, not something that the fabulous me couldn't
be doing to take the world on by storm.

"I promised you I'd come in and buy something the next time
I was in New York," Anderson says.

"A genuine promise or a promise by way of flirting?" I ask, and
he bows his head faux bashfully and smiles. He's an easy read
already. I smile in return. "I'm married."

He shrugs. "It sounded complicated."

Complicated? I'm sorry, I don't remember!

"Besides," I say, "aren't you, like, twenty-two?"

"Twenty-eight. I play young." He exhales. "Listen, you look
tired. Let me get out of your hair. I just wanted to come by and
thank you as soon as I could."

My eyes do feel heavy, so I let him go with the promise that he'll
come back tomorrow. The nurse returns to wheel him back to his
own recovery, but not before he places the *People* magazine next to
me, next to the photo album filled with disparate faces of strangers, and I'm left to wonder, just before I slip into slumber, how my
life can be so well documented when I can't recall one single second, one tiny sliver of an iota of the life that came before.

By my fourth day of consciousness and a week and a half since
my plane split in two, I have submitted myself to every test
possible—the MRI, the CAT scan, the interviews with the hospital
shrink, an oxygen test, an I'm-not-sure-what-the-hell-that-was-for
test, the how-many-presidents-can-you-name test (zero, but Peter

kindly reminded the psychologist that I'd never been one for history), and we are no closer to assessing the cause behind my memory loss.

Physically, I am also an anomaly, an equation with no solution. The neck brace came off today, and my left wrist is fractured and splinted, and a few of my upper ribs are bruised, such that a sharp jolt of pain greets me when I try to shift too quickly, but for the most part—the welts on my face and the scabs from the surface wounds aside—I am remarkably in one piece. Other than my brain, of course. Other than that, I'm nearly perfect.

My mother has placed crystals by my bed—*healing crystals,* she says, as if she is wiser than the men armed with their degrees in modern medicine—and she has paraded an endless slide show of pictures in front of me. Still, nothing from my thirty-two years of experience has returned to my cerebral landscape. I ask about my father—*where is he?*—and am told only that we lost him when I was a teenager. That he was once a famous painter but now he is gone. My mom hushes me and says that she'll explain it all when I'm stronger, when I'm ready.

Samantha, my slightly anorexic—but not in a diagnosable way—college roommate whose brown roots have been left untouched too long and whose cheeks are in much need of a blush brush, arrived yesterday: I recognize her only from the photos, of her standing beside me at my wedding, and of us in sorority T-shirts after two too many shots of god knows what, grinning ridiculous grins as if our whole lives were in front of us. Invincible. That's how we looked. Untouchable. She sits beside me and tries not to cry but, like everyone else—Peter, my mom—mostly fails at the task, and so sniffles and gasps while trying to offer me a shoulder on which to lean.

My younger sister, Rory, who comes from a seemingly entirely different gene pool—with luminescent red hair, six extra inches, and eyes the color of ripe moss, shuffles in after Samantha. She is pretty in a way that makes my pupils pop, an immaculate blend of DNA that unites every once in a while to create something exquisite. She forces a smile and says that we run the art gallery together, and I forge a real smile back, at the idea of our fabulous selves tackling the world together, ascending the heights of New York City: the two of us, sisters. Strangers now, but sisters once. I bask in the idea of this, even without knowing her. Once I knew her. Once, way back when, when I had a life, and I'm comforted in the idea that we had a life together.

"It was my fault you went," she says, pulling me from the moment. Her face muscles quiver like they're too exhausted to function properly, and I can see her consciously trying to tame them, to abate the torrent of tears that will be inevitable. Her guilt clouds her perfect green eyes, darkening the glow of her obviously flawless skin. "I normally do the artist meetings, but Hugh had tickets to Springsteen before the holiday weekend, so I made you go." Hugh, she explains in a sidebar, is her boyfriend of two years, and is back at their hotel. He flew out here with her for support— at least until he has to be back at work on Monday. She confides that this is a precursor to their engagement. But then she catches herself, as if there's a rule against thinking happy thoughts in my company.

"It's no one's fault," I answer, though maybe it actually is. Maybe it *is* her fault, and I have a million reasons to be furious with her. Who knows? Not me.

Samantha stops in two nights in a row before pushing back to Hoboken, back to her eighty-hour-a-week job as a big-firm lawyer, and back to her husband and his hundred-hour-a-week job at an investment bank. "Sometimes, I wish we could just be twenty-one again," she says as she lays an old sorority shirt over my torso and snaps a picture with her iPhone, thrusting it close to me. The shirt reads GOLF NIGHT, and Sam explains that this was a mixer in which we went to our favorite fraternity and imbibed a different drink in each room.

"Like, a hole, a golf hole," she says. "You were always the most levelheaded, stayed the most sober, but still it was our favorite party of the year. We always tried to get you to do a drink in every room, but you held your ground: too mature for us even at twenty-one." She laughs, and even though I know she means this as a compliment, mostly it breaks my heart. I stare around at the hospital room and the gravity that life can bring and wonder why anyone would ever want to grow up too soon, take it all too seriously.

"How did we meet?" I say, suspecting I can get it right: that we stumbled into each other at an underground off-campus party, or that I was so dazzling in an art history seminar that she couldn't help but introduce herself, or that I was strolling around the campus and simply had *it,* the magnetic it that everyone was drawn to. But even before she tells me, even before I'm done telling myself these things, I know this can't be true. That the face on the cover of *People,* with the frown, with its matching commas that cratered into my chin, well, she wasn't *it. She may not have even know what it was in the first place.*

"Oh, funny story," Sam says. "We met the first week at school. In the breakfast line. Neither of us knew anyone else to sit with, and since we both reached for the Frosted Flakes vat, we chose each other."

"Not exactly something to write home about."

"No," she laughs. "But we milked *'they're great'* for the longest time after that." I look at her blankly, and she tries to smile. "Inside joke. Tony the Tiger. Better told another time."

Dutifully, every morning during this first week, Peter has come by to refill the vase on the windowsill with daisies.

"They're your favorite," he said the first time he arrived with a bouquet.

"Really?" I answered, because it seemed hard to believe that daisies could be anyone's favorite.

"Well," he conceded. "They weren't, but I gave them to you on our first date, and then they sort of became our thing. Like, *shouldn't I have known better?*" He laughed but it sounded more like a hiccup. "I probably should have known that you'd want something elegant, perfect, long-lasting. But you know, you being you, you just told me you loved them—didn't want to be rude to this imbecile who showed up with cheap flowers, and didn't tell me otherwise until a year later when you actually decided that you did love them." He shrugged. "They were the only flower I could afford when we first met."

"So what were my favorites? My real favorites?" I asked. I

pictured it, or tried to anyway. Him: half a decade younger, without the pallor of grief on his face, wooing me with daisies. Me: also half a decade younger, no awareness of what life would bring, liking him enough to allow him to woo me with said daisies. I smiled. It was cute, almost, if you didn't know what happens next. But even then, I reconsidered—it was still cute. His ineptitude with the flowers, and that I didn't want to embarrass him over this ineptitude. I must have really liked him, really been smitten. And now, even though he felt too tall for me, like I'd have to stand on my tippy tiptoes to kiss him, and too broad, too, like he might crush me if he rolled over on me one night while I was sleeping too heavily to notice, I softened in the re-created, subjective memory of it all.

My husband. I wasn't quite used to him, to the idea of him, but still, if my younger self loved him, I'd find a way to do the same.

He squinted his face to remember my favorite flowers. "What are they called? Oh. Hyacinths. Something about their fragrance. Reminded you of being a kid. I'll track some down and bring them tomorrow—maybe that will help."

"Maybe that will," I said, and we both looked at the other with a hopefulness that hyacinths might actually be the answer to this.

When everyone finally leaves me alone, I sleep and try to remember, but there's nothing there, nothing *to remember,* and after a while, it feels like I'm trying to use a limb that's not connected to me. What's that phenomenon? *A phantom. Yes, that's exactly what it is.* How can I flex my foot if it's not attached? How can I curl my fingers into my palm if my brain has no way to send the message?

Mostly, I zone out at Jamie Reardon—that reporter from the local news who now covers the story for the one national cable station the hospital receives. He reminds me of someone whom I can't recall, but the reminder is comfort enough. Like he could be my confidant, an old high school love, a brother. He looks sturdy, reliable, and though he's just a projection on the screen, I already feel like we are friends.

Sometimes, Anderson comes by, and we sit—strangers but not really strangers—and watch Jamie in silence as he transmits the details of the crash, of our recovery, to the world that gobbles them up. We confer over our mutual gratefulness to have survived, leaving the murkier details—the guilt, the families of those who didn't, the enormity of the questions like *Why us?*—untouched. To be alive is enough for now, and when it's not, Jamie Reardon fills in the quiet spaces that are too difficult to consider if we allowed for them anyway.

On day five back into the waking world, Dr. Macht, my mother, and Peter weave their way into my room. My mom instinctively reaches for the remote, zapping the white noise.

"Nell, we need to tell you something," the doctor says, with Peter shadowing his shoulder, looking like he might fall apart at any second. Without his baseball cap, he looks fifteen years older— the circles under his eyes the color of dark bruises, the pallor of his cheeks near-dead.

"I know that you can't remember this." Dr. Macht hesitates, but then puts on his best doctor voice and continues. "But it's important that you know that you were pregnant."

I feel my eyelashes flutter.

"Unfortunately, with all the damage your body sustained, that pregnancy is no longer viable." He hesitates. "Actually, you miscarried when you first came in. We needed to wait until you were stable to tell you."

Peter starts weeping behind him, and I wish, in a way, that I could, too. Wish that I could feel the loss of this as tangibly as he does. Something akin to a wad of emotion forms in my throat but it's easily swallowed.

"How far along was I?"

"Relatively early into the pregnancy—it appears well within the first trimester, maybe eight weeks or so. We have a call in to your insurance company to track down your New York obstetrician, maybe get some answers from her." He glances toward Peter. "I'll give you two some privacy to digest this."

He shuts the door and leaves Peter and me in a vacuum of silence, barring Peter's unsuccessful attempts to clamp down his emotion.

"I'm sorry," I say. "I know that this whole thing is hard on you. Were we trying for long?"

"No," he says quietly. "It was a surprise."

I nod and stare out the window. *Everything to me is a surprise.*

"I know that this sounds weird for me to tell you, and I don't mean it rudely, but it feels strange to be discussing this with you," I say. "Not that I'm not sure that we didn't have a great life together, it's just . . . you know . . . I don't remember where we lived or us having sex or trying for a baby. Any of that."

His face looks like he mistakenly swallowed vodka when he meant for water.

"I'll tell you what," he says, when he's pieced himself back together—I watch him, forcibly trying to do so, stitch himself back up so he doesn't totally come undone right here in my hospital room. He leans down to kiss my forehead, and I breathe deeply and try to recognize a familiar scent. "Get some rest. And when you're ready—tomorrow, the next day, the day after that—I'll sit down and tell you our story."

Our story, I think, after he goes, and I've flipped the volume back up on the television. *Yes, that sounds nice. Everyone, after all, has a story.*

3

There is good news and bad news on day seven. The bad news is that Anderson is being transferred to a rehab clinic.

When he comes to offer his good-byes, I ease out of bed, slowly, delicately, self-conscious in my hospital gown, and embrace him the best that we can—with my bruised ribs and his wheelchair-folded body. He smiles the smile that likely made him a star. It's magnetic, infectious, damn near hypnotizing. I've read his section of the *People* article, though, seen the clips on *Access Hollywood*. I know that he has spent the past few years bedding too many women for him to remember their names, being chastised for showing up drunk more than once on set. I know that he is immensely talented but that he is his own worst enemy: torpedoing a career that could be taken to a grander scale if he would only stop doing it in. I know all this, and so I both trust him and am wary. That smile. That goddamn smile is so absorbing that I want to hurl myself onto his wheelchair and bus to rehab with him, and yet, I suspect that I am just one of many women to feel this way.

And also, of course, there is Peter. And my marriage. And my life before this. I feel myself blushing at my idiocy, at the fantasy of escaping this life with Anderson, even though there's nothing— and yet everything—to escape from. Samantha wished that she was twenty-one again, but I don't have twenty-one to wish for. I only have something else—make-believe—to dream of.

"Give everyone else a chance," Anderson says kindly, though not particularly like he wants me to hurl myself on his wheelchair and run with him, though not particularly like he doesn't, either. More like confidants, which I suppose we've become. "Take it day by day. That's the only way to deal."

"You've been in therapy, haven't you?" I center myself, my thoughts, pulling back into the real world, into this, into the moment. "The shrink who comes by here every day keeps telling me the same thing."

"Years," he laughs. "More years of therapy than anyone has the right to. Started at sixteen—my parents forced me when they heard I was doing whippets every day after school."

"What screwed you up?" I am prolonging it now, his exit.

"Nothing screwed me up," he says. "That's the joke of it now. Nothing at all screwed me up—I had a perfectly decent child-hood, perfectly wonderful parents. My dad is a dentist. I don't know . . . I just *was*. Screwed up"—he pauses—"though now I need therapy for entirely different reasons. The nightmares, all of that."

"In some ways, maybe it's better that I don't remember."

"Catch-22," he says.

Neither of us knows quite how you say good-bye to the former stranger with whom you fell from the sky, so he hands me the new issue of *People*—we've been bumped from the headline to the corner cover story—and promises to e-mail or call as soon as he settles in.

I'm glancing through the Star Tracks section of the magazine, when Rory and Dr. Macht, in blue surgery scrubs and a white lab coat, wander in. They are armed with the good news of the day.

"Mom's on her way," Rory says, like I've asked a question. I smile at her because she has been so giving this past week, so available when I know she's had other things to attend to: her life back home, the gallery she's left to come take care of me. The old me didn't seem like someone who needed taking care of, but Rory does it well all the same.

"So there's good news," Dr. Macht says. "We've gone over your CAT scans, the MRIs, sent them to the best specialists out at UCLA, and it doesn't appear that there's anything permanent going on in your brain."

"So why can't I remember anything?"

"Could be a variety of things." He clears his throat. "It could be psychosomatic . . ."

"Wait, you think this is intentional?" I stutter. *Of all the things that have occurred to me lying here through the endless hours, intentional amnesia wasn't one of them.*

"No, no, nothing like that, not *intentional*. That wouldn't be the word to use. But sometimes when people undergo an extremely traumatic event, their brain shuts down for them. It's called dissociative amnesia—in reaction to the stress of what you've been through, the brain has blocked it out. Only yours took it too far—it blocked out too much. With dissociative amnesia, you can still remember all of the generalities of the way life works—you may remember world history references or what the Statue of Liberty is, for example, or"—he gestures to the television—"how a remote control works or that you flush the toilet upon using it. You just can't remember the way that *your* life has worked." He hedges, waiting for me to absorb this, to protest and say, *Well of course that's just utterly ridiculous! I'm not some sort of whacked-out head case!* But I don't. Don't say that. Because who knows? Just who the hell knows? Maybe I am. A quick glance at the photo on the cover of *People* tells me that I don't have any idea of who I really am, how the square pegs of my life refuse to fit into the round holes.

When I don't respond, he continues. "But, that said, we're just working on theories here. Amnesia—any form of it—is quite rare, and I happen to think it's more likely that there is indeed some damage, and with time, and with use, your memory should return. Maybe in bits and pieces."

"So my options are that I have actual brain damage or that my brain is damaging itself?" I say finally.

"What's the time frame?" Rory interrupts, and Dr. Macht opts for the less prickly of the two questions.

"Unclear. Could be anywhere from tomorrow to months from now. Your therapist," he says to me, "will come in and explain what you can do to nurture your memory back. Think of it as a muscle: you need to flex it to regain strength."

The overhead PA system pages him to the nurses' station, and he's off with a nod and a promise to check in later that evening before he goes back into surgery.

"This all feels a little preposterous," I say to Rory, using my good arm to rub the apex of my neck, "like someone is pulling the world's worst practical joke." I flop my hand down and hold up my palm. I'd noticed the scar there earlier today, running from my lifeline clear down my wrist.

"This," I say, thrusting my hand upward. "How'd I get this?"

"Childhood accident—a broken plate," Rory says, leaving it at that and easing into the chair beside the bed. She roots around in her bag, unveiling a mini box of doughnuts and two Snapple bottles, which clang against each other in her hand. A melody of iced tea. "I know it's junk," she says, "and that it can't really fix anything. But we always ate doughnuts and Snapple when we signed an artist or had something else to celebrate. The day I convinced you to open the gallery in the first place, we binged like we've never binged before." She pauses, awash in happy nostalgia. "Mom used to make doughnuts fresh for us when we were kids. Now we settle for Dunkin'."

"What are we celebrating?" I ask. "That one day—maybe in ten years, maybe never, according to the experts—I might not be committed to an asylum?"

"No, nothing specific." She unscrews the top of one of the Snapples. "But I thought it might be nice. Something your little sister can do for you. We're all . . . well, we're all feeling a little helpless." She hands me a jelly doughnut, which promptly explodes upon my first bite all over my gown. "Now you look like you're bleeding, too." She giggles.

"That's not so funny."

"No, you're right."

We snicker anyway. I lick the jelly off of my lips.

"Do you always have to watch this guy?" She nudges her head up toward the TV, toward Jamie Reardon. "It's on every time I'm in here. Sort of macabre, isn't it?"

"I like him." I shrug.

"He's just some talking head, a piranha circling the waters."

"No, he seems different," I say, like I have experience discerning between tabloid reporters and not, between different and not. But Anderson did, and he liked him, too. Something wholesome, welcoming about him. "I don't know, he feels like he'd be easy to talk to."

"Funny, he stopped me outside—there's an entire mass of reporters out there—and asked if you were up for an interview. I told him to stop being such a leech, feeding on catastrophe." She crosses her six-inches-longer-than-mine legs. "Please tell me you're not going to think about talking to him. That would just be so entirely out of character."

"I don't know," I say. "Who knows what my character is anyway?"

"Well, I do, for one. I've lived with you for twenty-seven years. And you were never one to seek publicity. I practically had to beg you to agree to help me promote the gallery, consider anything out of the straight and narrow. That you agreed to consider Hope Kingsley—the artist you were going out to see in San Francisco— was no small miracle. She was from the slush pile and, oh man, were you a bitch about the slush pile."

"The slush pile?"

"The commoners, as you said. The un-agented. In theory, you'd think *you* of all people would want to nurture untapped talent, but it was just the opposite."

This does not at all sound like the *fabulous me*!

"Why me of all people?"

"Because you had more talent in your left toe than just about anyone I know. Maybe other than Dad. But maybe even more than him. It made me crazy as a kid."

"Painting?" I ask, surprised.

"Music," she says, like I should have already known.

I chew on this, and then, apropos of nothing but because I no longer have a filter, I say, "Did you know that I was pregnant?"

"Oh god." Her lower lip starts to tremble.

"No, that's not what I meant. I wasn't blaming you. I meant, since I can't remember it, did you know that I was pregnant?"

She shakes her head, composing herself. "No. I'm surprised, actually." She considers it. "What does Peter say about it?"

"We haven't talked much about it yet. It feels weird—having a husband who I don't remember."

"You have a sister who you don't remember, either."

"True," I say. "But he's always darting around, sort of skulking in the corner. It just feels . . . different. He's seen me naked, seen my orgasm face, you know, stuff like that. I know that for all intents and purposes you and I don't know each other, either . . . but it feels like we do, it feels like we're family." I laugh. "Though maybe I shouldn't be talking about my orgasm face to you, either."

"Well, it's an adjustment period for all of us," she says, firming her jaw, closing the subject.

"I know." I exhale. "Maybe I'm the one who's being weird, not him."

She wipes her hands on her jeans and stands to go.

"Oh, I forgot, one more thing." She reaches into her bag and yanks out a stack of DVDs. "Here. Your favorite movies, TV shows, whatever, from when we were kids. I thought it might help." She fingers something else and pulls it out. "And this—here's an iPod, a music player. I put together all of the bands that I could remember that you loved, that meant something to you. I had Hugh search your closet for the box of mix tapes that you kept."

"Hugh?"

"My boyfriend?" she says, and I detect a flash of annoyance, that the detail has slipped my mind, when so many details have slipped my mind.

"Yes, *yes,* I'm sorry. I lose track of things."

"Well, I asked him to get the box from your apartment, and *he did,* and I made what I think is *The Best of Nell Slattery.* It's all on there, hundreds of songs—everything from, I don't know, your wedding song . . ."

"My wedding song? Which was?"

"Joe Cocker—'Have a Little Faith in Me,'" she says, like that means anything to me. "To the Beatles to the Smiths to, well, just listen to it. You'll get the idea." She pops the earbuds in my ears and hits a button. My sensory system feels like I'm going through a car wash—poured over and cleaned. The music, it's a balm, an anesthetic, and for a few seconds, it's as if none of this happened, and I'm already healed. Or didn't need to be healed in the first place.

"You're a pretty great sister," I say, popping out the headphones, a rush of gratitude warming me, though it could have been the sugar high.

"Sometimes." She smiles, though it's not necessarily a happy one. "Sometimes not."

The first season of *Friends* is as funny as I remember it, or more accurately, as funny as I probably remembered it, since I'm theoretically watching it for the first time. Rory has overloaded me with DVDs, and upon reading the description of each—*Good Will Hunting, Party of Five, Reality Bites, Saving Private Ryan, Pretty in Pink*—this seemed like the safest bet to ensure that I didn't beg the nurses to euthanize me in my sleep.

The six of them—the crew from *Friends* at their hangout of Central Perk—make life in New York seem glamorous, effortless almost, even though their dating lives are woeful, and their jobs relatively unfulfilling, and Ross has discovered that his lesbian ex-wife is having a baby, and he wants Rachel so badly that his whole face has evolved into a basset hound. But still, their apartments are huge and sparkling, and their clothes tight-fitting around their lithe bodies, and damn if it didn't make me crave my old life, even if I didn't know what that old life was. Maybe it was like *Friends*. Maybe an episode straight out of *Friends* in which Samantha and I hung out on faux-velvet couches at our local coffee joint, and Peter and Rory and her boyfriend, Hugh, filled in the crevices with off-the-cuff jokes and witty banter that made everyone around us green with envy. I could see that, even if I couldn't really see that. *Yes, that would be a nice life to return to.*

Remember, goddammit!

I hit pause on the DVD player and sweep some scattered photos off my nightstand. Rory has left the stack of photos along with the DVDs. In them, I'm on the cusp of adulthood, she's on the cusp of puberty. The date stamp reads 1994, and though she is eleven, and I am sixteen, she's already sprouted nearly taller than I. I'm dressed in some god-awful prom attire, while she wears a violet sundress with smocking across the chest that can't conceal her little breast buds that are poking through. Even at eleven, she's breathtaking— vacuuming up all of the beauty between us, your eyes inevitably drawn to her, not me. I'm in a red-and-white-polka-dotted concoction with a skirt comprising three taffeta tiers and a bustier that makes my own breasts look lopsided. My smile is reflected in the flash of the camera, thanks to upper and bottom braces, and my hair—evidently the victim of both a perm and an overdose of Sun-In—does my heart-shaped face no favors. I have a corsage around my wrist, and just in the edge of the corner, I can make out the shoulder of a man-boy in a tuxedo who must have been my date.

Upon closer inspection, my smile looks more like a wince, and I stare at my old self and wonder who I was at sixteen. Who that boy was. If we steamed up the windows to his mom's station wagon that night, if we got drunk on wine coolers at the after-party. *No, of course not. Everyone from Samantha to Rory has already well informed me that I was the straitlaced, buttoned-up one.*

I stop and rewrite this in my mind: that I broke curfew, that I unsnapped my bra and let him feel me up before we went skinny-dipping after one too many wine coolers, that I slipped home through a bedroom window so I didn't tip off my mom.

I feel my nose pinch, my cheeks spasm, my chest seize, and suddenly, really, for the first time, I am gutted at my loss. Sliced open. Fatally punctured with no hope of resuscitation. I'm overwhelmed with the loneliness of living the life of a skeleton—no meat, no flesh, nothing to fill in the holes, and the tears come quickly and furiously, my free hand wiping away what it can, but no match for the onslaught. I briefly consider the 152 people who didn't even have this opportunity: *Jesus! Get real! At least you're alive, living, breathing, here, and with the chance to try to remember!* But my brain can't linger on the vastness of that loss, so it's no use. There's a time for appreciating the moment, and this isn't it. Maybe eventually. Maybe I'll call Anderson, and eventually we'll find a way to answer the question: *Why us?* But now, it's only my pain, eviscerating and hollow all at once. I reach for the iPod in an attempt to soothe myself, the way a baby does a pacifier, but the music only makes it worse—piercing my wounds, penetrating me from all angles.

Alicia must hear my sobbing because soon she's wiping my cheeks dry, flushing my nose of snot.

"What can I get you, sweetheart?" she says.

"Nothing." I hiccup. "No one can get me anything."

She picks up the remote, flicks off the DVD, and the TV returns to the news channel I had on earlier.

She rubs my back until I've stopped crying, and then I reconsider.

"Could you get my sister on the phone?"

"Of course, dear." She reaches for the telephone and punches in the digits, then places the cradle under my shoulder.

"Rory, it's me," I say when she picks up. "Listen, who was I before?"

"What do you mean?" She sounds like I've woken her. "You were my older sister. We worked together at the gallery. We've been over this."

"No, no, I remember *that*. I mean, like, who was I? Who did I go to prom with?"

"Oh god, um . . ." She pauses. "Oh, yeah, his name was Mitchell Loomis. Um, he was on the wrestling team."

"Was he my boyfriend? Like, did we make out at prom, go skinny-dipping, get drunk, go crazy?"

She laughs, even through her grogginess. "Of all the things you were, Nellie, crazy was never one of them." She hesitates. "I don't really know what you did at prom, to be honest. I was in middle school. But if I had to bet, I'd bet that no, you probably weren't making out in a corner, much less going skinny-dipping." I sigh. *No, that can't be right! I was out all night in an open-aired convertible, braying at the moon.*

"So me, I mean, my life, it wasn't like *Friends*?" Flashy! Vibrant! Perfect hair! I can't let the idea go.

"Like *Friends* the sitcom?" She laughs. "Nell, nobody's life is like *Friends*. That's why we all watched it." I hear the sheets stirring beneath her.

"So what you're saying is that I was the rational one? Not a live-by-the-seat-of-my-pants type of girl?" I think of Anderson, of his infectious, mischievous energy, of how the space he occupied seemed bigger than oxygen, bigger than life. Of Monica and Rachel—*screw it if it's make-believe*—and their ever-present laugh track. *I* wanted a laugh track. I wanted the life that came with that fucking laugh track.

"Not so much, but that's what we loved about you," Rory says. "You were the one we could count on. There's a reason you went to law school, you know."

"I went to law school?"

"You didn't know?"

"Rory"—I sigh—"please. Don't make me repeat myself. When I doubt, I don't know. *I don't know.* Okay?"

"Jesus, *okay.*"

Both of us linger, the friction passing through the line, then evaporating.

"So, wait, I was a *lawyer*?" That doesn't feel right at all.

"No, you only went for a year and a half. Then you quit and Mom found you a job with one of her friends who was a director for *One Life to Live.*"

"The soap opera?" I'd seen it on during endless looping hours of my day.

"Yes, the soap opera!" Exasperation on her end. *Like you have any right to be exasperated!* "You were good at it, what can I say?" She sighs. "Eventually, you ran the office there—you know, paper-work and contracts and managing the staff and whatnot. Which is why I knew you could do the same thing at the gallery. And which is why you finally agreed. That and because Dad always told you that you had the eye, could have been great."

"Great like him?" I sit up taller, intently staring out the window. Maybe this was my entree, my opening to the fabulous me. *Yes, yes! I could have been great!*

"Great like him," she affirms. "Though you never quite were." And just like that, I sink back into the pillow. "Not that I mean that rudely," she says. "I just mean, you know, he was never quite satisfied. Music was always your thing anyway. I don't know why he wouldn't just let that be." She snips herself, like maybe she's revealed too much.

I gaze at the ceiling and make myself a vow: in this life, in this new life, I'll have that greatness, that laugh track that the fabulous me deserved. A hundred and fifty-two people died. I didn't. Maybe this is my chance, my rewind button, my fast-forward button. Both. Whichever. Either way, this is my chance to do things differently.

"I don't want to be that person," I say, "the one who could have been great."

"Okay," she says. I'm pretty sure I can hear her peeing in the background. "But it's who you are."

"I want the laugh track."

"You've lost me," she says.

"I want the excitement, I want some fun," I say. "I want to be, well, extraordinary."

"I think you've given us enough excitement for a while," she says. The toilet flushes.

I glance up at the television. There he is.

"I need a favor."

"Shoot."

"Tomorrow, on your way in, stop Jamie Reardon and tell him

that I'll talk to him. Go out there and tell him that I'll tell him my story."

"That's nuts," she says. "You're fragile! You're not ready for that."

"The thing is, Rory, I'm not ready for anything."

4

Jamie Reardon looks exactly like he does on TV: perfectly gelled blond hair, perfectly robin's-egg-blue eyes. His teeth are alabaster, his smile more impish than you'd expect for a news reporter. He has a smattering of freckles across his nose that makeup must cover up on camera, and he's lankier than I envisioned: the blazers that he sports on air make him look like a man, but when he shows up in my hospital room, he's more of an overgrown boy. A farm boy, a replica of the type you'd think would be born and bred in Iowa.

Two days after I have vowed that I will take this second chance by the reins and steer the new me someplace better, after I have issued my decree to Rory—go out there and tell him that I'll talk to him—here he is. Dr. Macht ushers him in and tells me he can think of better ideas than this. That I shouldn't be wasting my energy granting press access, but I wave my arm at him because he doesn't get it: that this is my chance to start being something great, that this is the first step toward fulfillment. Isn't this my second chance? Who wouldn't try to shake things up if they plummeted to the ground and discovered that their life wasn't much of a life at all, and that a clean slate might be theirs for the taking? Maybe someone, but not me. Not the new me, anyway.

Rory staged a halfhearted intervention this morning—she showed up with my mother trailing behind her, who was muttering about privacy and exploitation and how I really didn't know what I was doing. But I'd already decided. *Who cared what Jamie Reardon unearthed,* I said to my mom and Rory. *Why did it matter? There wasn't anything to hide from, to run from, right? This was the time to do the opposite of what I'd done before. Shouldn't I be doing that?* I pointed to the cover of *People. Shouldn't I be running as far from that person as possible?* They stuttered, and my mother said that I was being crazy, that I was close to perfect before, which we both knew wasn't true at all, and then Alicia came in to take my blood pressure, and that was that.

It's only once we're left alone and Jamie has taken out his digital recorder, plopped himself on the side of my bed like an old confidant, and cracked his knuckles, ready to go, that I realize I don't have much of a story to tell. I feel myself blanch with the embarrassment of being so unprepared. I suspect that the old me wouldn't have approved of such unpreparedness at all.

"I really didn't think this through," I say. "I, well, you probably know that I can't remember anything. I don't know how much I can help you."

"Don't worry," he says. "Let's just talk. I won't even record it."

"Okay." I will myself to relax. "I'm very well versed in the first season of *Friends,* in Jamie Reardon's reporting on cable TV, and on sleeping sixteen hours a day. And this." I hold up the iPod on my lap. "The wider selection of musical hits from the past two decades. Any of those subjects are fair game."

"So what you're saying is you're either rapidly becoming a pop culture expert or you're about to lose your mind to boredom?"

"In a nutshell, yes." I laugh.

"So you're talking to me simply because you have nothing better to do?"

He's good at this, I can see. Even as a local reporter. He's smooth, comforting, intentionally easy to be around, like we've been friends since forever.

"No, it's not just that." I consider it. "I don't know, this is going to sound weird, but I feel like everything I've learned about myself so far hasn't resonated, is . . . indigestible." I search for how to better articulate it. "Like, have you ever thought that you're in a rut, even without realizing that you're in a rut in the first place?"

I'm suddenly self-conscious, like I'm in an overly-meta TV show that I can't quite reference. "That sounds ridiculous." I hiccup. "After all I've been through, I know. That after all of that, I need to shake things up, try something new. This is what the new me should be doing: trying something the old me never would have done."

"It doesn't sound ridiculous to me at all," he says, and looks at me with such openness that I believe him. He's a professional but I'm buying it all the same. "Well, whatever your reason"—he clears his throat—"do know that I'm indebted to you for this."

"For being blown up at thirty thousand feet and surviving?"

"No"—he shakes his sandy hair—"for talking to me." He tilts his head like a rooster and eyes me. "You're pretty cavalier for what you've gone through."

"I'm sure I wouldn't be if I could remember any of it. I'm sure I'd be horrified, in therapy for life." I think of Anderson, who told me that he wakes each night, despite medication, in soaking sweats from the nightmares. "Come to think of it," I say, "I might be anyway."

"Well, I have to thank you regardless. This story—you really—you're changing my life, too. I've been trying to get out of Iowa since I was eighteen. This might do it."

"So I'm nothing more than leverage for you?"

His eyes noticeably widen and he rights himself upward.

"I'm kidding, Jamie. I'm kidding." *Who is he? Why is he so familiar? Why am I acting like we've known each other our lives through?*

"You're nothing like I expected you to be," he says. "Not from what I've researched."

Finally! Someone who frigging gets it! I think, but instead say, "What have you researched? You probably know more than I do."

"Eleanor Slattery. Thirty-two. Named for the Beatles song 'Eleanor Rigby' but goes by Nell. Grew up in Bedford, New York. Sister of Rory Slattery—older by five years. Daughter of Francis Slattery, one of the geniuses behind the pop art movement of the sixties. Friend of Andy Warhol. Total recluse whom no one has heard from in years."

"I thought my dad was dead." I hear my heart beat.

"Dead?" He laughs, missing the innuendo of the moment. "No, not unless no one has reported it. Very much alive."

I swallow, absorbing this. My mother told me that he was gone, but maybe I misinterpreted. Yes, maybe it was that. She simply meant gone—vanished. I'd assumed gone—dead. I chew the cuticle of my good hand, the one with the scar.

"Go on."

"Well, underground or not, he was brilliant. May still be brilliant. That's how you and your sister started your gallery: sold some prime pieces of his, established a reputation in the art world, and made your connections with old collectors in your very first show. You guys opened about six years ago—Rory was basically straight out of college at UVM."

"And what do you mean, can you elaborate on . . . recluse?"

"Like . . . recluse," he says, bewildered that he's the one to fill me in on this gaping branch in my family tree. "Like, fell off the map when you were a teenager—thirteenish, I believe. J. D. Salinger–like." He pauses. "Wait, that probably doesn't help you."

"No, it doesn't really," I answer.

I think of that big-haired, braced-teeth teenager in her polka-dotted prom dress, and the pity in my core nearly slices my guts open. That she—that I—had to deal with such nuclear emotional fallout of my father abandoning us right when I may have needed him the most, to come into my own. But I offer none of this to Jamie. It's too much too soon to share with him, despite how much I want to, how much I want him to solve everything, put the bow on the package for me.

I say, "Don't you need notes for this or something?"

"Not really." His cheeks turn pink now. "Like I said, this is the big story for me. I'm pretty well versed on it."

"Okay, continue." I clamp down on the open-ended questions that this news has brought, too interested, like a masochist, in what else Jamie might unspool.

"Graduated third in your class in high school. Rumor had it that you were your father's musical equivalent, but opted to focus on tennis in high school instead."

"What does that mean?" I interrupt.

"That his thing was painting, your thing was music, but that it all blended together in your genes." He hesitates, the reporter in him alarmed that he may have overlooked a fact. "I don't know much about that angle, to be honest."

I nod. "Keep going."

"Earned a tennis scholarship to Lehigh but went to school in Binghamton. Dropped out of NYU law. Married Peter Horner five years ago, started your gallery with your sister shortly before that. Now recently separated from Peter Horner. Boarded plane that crashed in Iowa, and that's where we're at."

Recently separated from Peter Horner? What?

"Wait, what? I'm separated from Peter?" I sit up, trying to get closer to him, as if that might clarify what he just said.

"Oh, shit. You didn't know?" His already pink cheeks burn red, and yes, there it is, I trust him—he's human in his mistakes, human in his empathy—a good reporter but still amateur enough to lower his guard. "Oh my god, you didn't know? Oh god, oh god, oh god, oh god. I didn't know that you didn't know." He stands and starts pacing. "Shit. I thought you'd have known this! How can you not have known this?" He inhales and stares and reminds me of what I imagine he looked like at eight. "Please don't have a heart attack."

"You mean a literal heart attack, don't you?" I say, and his head bounces. "No, Jamie, I'm not going to have a heart attack." *But I might fucking maim my family for not telling me! First my dad, then this? What else? Who else? What else is tucked in darkened corners that they know I can't get to in my present state?*

"Shit, shit, shit. I shouldn't have said anything—Dr. Macht was very clear about not upsetting you, that you're not ready for jarring conversations or emotional news." He sits back on the edge of the bed. "Christ, I'm sorry."

I chew the inside of my lip, assessing how pissed off I am, how devastated I am by the realization of my broken marriage. The answer: not so much. Probably not as much as if I remembered why I should be devastated in the first place.

"Why did we separate?" I ask simply.

"I'm not sure I should tell you," he says.

"Look, Jamie, I like you. I have no idea why, but I like you. I trust you. Evidently, you're the only one around here who is willing to tell me the facts of my life, facts that I cannot *goddamn* remember. So please. Level with me."

He exhales, then runs his palms over and down his cheeks.

"I have significant doubts about this."

I eye him, mulling how I can best deconstruct the situation to my advantage. It comes naturally, the idea, the manipulation to get him on my side for good. Like an old sweatshirt, too long tucked into the back of my closet. I slide it on and *oh, yes, that feels just about right.*

"Jamie, do you want to be part of Operation Free Nell Slattery?" I'd heard a similar such phrase on the news. It had a nice ring to it. Inspiring, I think.

"I'm sorry?"

"Do you want to be part of Operation Free Nell Slattery—you know, like, free me from the hospital?" *Free me from this void of blackness.*

"I do," he says, taking it too seriously.

"Relax," I say aloud. "You're not selling me your soul. Besides, I thought journalists didn't have souls to begin with."

Ha ha, we say together.

"I have a soul," he assures me. "That's why I didn't want to upset you in the first place." *You do.* I nod. *He does,* I think. Which is exactly why I went to him to begin with. My gut instinct. I might not be armed with much, but at least I can listen to that. How it's imploring me to start over, be different, tell him my story. All of the above.

"You're not upsetting me, you're educating me. Telling me things that for reasons unknown, no one else is." He bobs his head. He gets it. He's a journalist after all—wise enough to know how both the medium and the message can change things. "Look. You know as well as I that there's a wall of reporters out there, waiting to talk to me, to get some information. I hear them call the nurses' station, I see them jockeying next to you when you go live. But I chose you. I *choose* you. So let's do this: you tell me what I need to know, what I *want* to know, and I promise you exclusive access."

"Exclusive access?"

"Yes, to me, to my story, to my family. You can use me for all you need to get, as you said, the hell out of Iowa. I just want you to keep me on the straight and narrow, be sure that I'm getting the whole truth and nothing but it."

He swallows, and I can tell that I have him, that he's taken the bait. *He wants this, more than he wants to be kind to me. It's human nature after all. Self-preservation.*

"So tell me," I say. "If we have a deal, if you're going to be part of Operation Free Nell Slattery, explain to me why Peter and I separated. Just tell me quickly, like pulling off the Band-Aid."

He watches me for a beat, gauging my strength and my sincerity, and deems them both to be hearty. Then he says, "Okay, we have a deal." He goes still for a moment, a newscaster once more. "He was cheating on you."

"Huh," I say, and stare at my cuticles—they're tattered, the nail beds fraying, white crescent moons butting up from the skin. I check my internal pulse. I should feel sicker over this, I know that I should feel sicker over this. *Get mad, goddammit! Get so god-damned pissed off that you think you'll never speak to that asshole again!* "With whom?"

"Some woman he works with," he says, his head moving almost undetectably. "I didn't want to exploit it, so I didn't dig too deeply—that's why you never heard it on the air. I just knew that he'd moved out, that you kicked him out, actually. Four months ago or so."

"But I was eight weeks pregnant."

"I don't know the intimate details just yet." He stutters, human again. "I mean, if you want me to, I can ask some questions, I just . . . well, there's a line that I didn't want to cross. It didn't seem fair, after what you'd been through."

My eyes purge themselves with a quick rash of tears, not for Peter, but for Jamie's kindness. Or maybe they are for Peter, maybe this is my true visceral reaction, but I just can't remember how I should be reacting in the first place. Jamie freezes, uncertain what to do next, so I run my hands over my cheeks and push away the lump of emotion that's boring down on my chest.

"You're too moral to be a journalist," I say after a few minutes have passed, almost half-smiling.

"It's nothing like that." He half smiles in return. "Trust me. But they're tearing through Anderson's past—old girlfriends emerging to give sound bites, one-night stands who are cashing in on their fifteen minutes, neighbors who can't get to the *Enquirer* fast enough—it didn't seem right to do it to you, who didn't ask for any of this. I just wanted—despite my journalistic instincts—to let this one go for now." He clears his throat. "The affair, the pregnancy, that is. The rest of it, obviously, I've been covering."

I lean back and stare out the window into the cloudless Iowa summer sky. The sun will sink lower soon enough, turning the fields into open black space, ushering another day out, another day in—one after the next, all the same for me: a void, a crater.

"In everything you've read about me, everything you've seen, do you think I was happy?" I say, finally.

"Oh, gosh, Nell, I'm not the person to ask that." He averts his eyes. "Surely, there's someone better to ask."

I close my eyes as a way of answering. Because the thing is, the thing that we both already know, is that it is now all too clear that there's not.

When I wake again, the sky is dark, my room silent, and my body feels exhausted in a way that it hasn't for a few days.

"Nell." Peter is sitting in the corner.

"Why didn't you tell me?" I say. I shut my eyes and wish he'd vanish like a real apparition might. "You should have told me." My voice bounces around the room, cutting through the solitude. *Of course you should have told me! If not you, then Rory. If not Rory, then my mother! How many layers do I have to unpeel to get to the core of my life?* But I don't say this, don't act on my indignation. I'm not sure whom I can trust now, why I should trust them, even when they tell me otherwise.

"I know. I know I should have." His own voice cracks, and instead of pity, I feel revulsion. That after everything I'm dealing with, now I have to bear his pain, his selfishness, too. "They told me not to. They didn't want to stress you. We were given instructions not to do anything upsetting. So . . ." His hands flop by his sides. "So I didn't."

A barely quantifiable excuse.

"Fine," I say. "I know now."

"I'm sorry," he answers and starts to sob. "I mean, I told you that a thousand times before, but . . . you can't remember. But I am. So sorry."

"I'm too tired for this. If this is what I can't remember, then that's fine. Who wants to remember how her husband slept with someone else?"

"Let me tell you what happened," he pleads. "Maybe it will help."

"Help me or you?" I want to press the call button and get him the hell out of here.

"Both of us," he says. "Maybe it can help both of us." He sputters. "More than anything in the world, I need you to let me fix us." He adjusts his baseball cap, clutching it in his hand for a beat too long before replacing it. His unwashed hair is matted to his forehead, the grief of these past two weeks erasing any hint of healthfulness in his cheeks. I imagine what the *fabulous me,* the one who would never have needed to pledge herself to a second chance, might have seen in him: even through the scrim, I can see how he is good-looking, how maybe I should be appreciative that he is here, penitent, open, begging for a reprieve.

"Before . . . was I letting you fix us?" I'm hovering over the murky divide that separates numbness and anger.

"Kind of. I mean, I was doing everything I could . . ." His voice cracks again, and I want to slug him right across the chin.

"Well, you know that I have no recollection of that."

"I know." He nods, a pitiful concession that he is powerless here.

Aren't we all powerless here? I want to scream at him. *Why the hell does it matter what you want so badly, anyway? What about what I want? Like how I want to remember my prom date, remember that last picture of my father at my eighth-grade graduation.*

"And this baby? What of that?"

He breaks here, and as his shoulders start to shake, his meaty torso trembling, I stare up at the ceiling and wait for his contrition to pass. Finally, he sutures himself up.

"I didn't know," he says, meeting my eyes. "Okay? I didn't know. Didn't know about the baby. You never told me." He mats his damp face with the back of his hand. "But it, the baby, was mine. We . . . we had reconciled." His voice shakes here but he presses on. "So knowing now—knowing what I lost for the both of us—I will do anything, *anything,* for a second chance."

"Why should I give you that?" I say, listening to the steady hum of the medical machinery, wishing it could drown out all this other noise.

"Because I want to fill in the blank spaces, remind you of how you loved me, how we loved each other. I think I can do that. I want to remind you of your memories of us, of who we were." He clears his throat, almost back together now. "Of who we are."

I don't say that I've already employed Jamie to do this. I want to say this, but somewhere tucked very, very deep inside of me, a surprising voice urges me not to. That the heartbreak has been enough for now and that maybe he knows this without my saying so. That I can still be furious and disgusted, and yet also let it go, if only for this hour. The new me. Softened, with her slightly rose-tinted glasses.

"Please," he says, sensing my hesitation. "Nell. I'll do anything."

I sigh and notice the clock in the corner. It's only 8:35 p.m. Jamie won't be on TV until morning and Anderson has gone to rehab and I need the nurse to reload the next *Friends* DVD anyway and

I've listened to my iPod so many times today that the battery is depleted beyond a quick recharge. So what else do I have to do with my time?

I close my eyes and envision picking up my distrust, my rage, and setting it aside, like a tumor carved out by a surgeon.

"Fine," I say. "Tell me. Tell me our story. Though I can't make any promises that it will help."

5

"Have a Little Faith in Me"
—Joe Cocker

*P*eter chews his bottom lip. You can tell that he wants to pick the best place to start because he has so much riding on this. That if he inadvertently chooses the wrong place to begin, she'll never concede, never look at him the way she once did, never, of course—and this is all that mattered—take him back.

She stares at him expectantly, but only for a few moments. Then she flicks her eyes away and rolls her jaw around, as if she's reconsidering, but then she finds her way back toward him, breathing and waiting and breathing.

He flicks off his baseball cap, runs his fingers through his hair that the low-pressure hotel shower did no favors to, and inhales. And then he begins.

"I should start at our wedding," he says, unintentionally nodding, like he's reassuring himself even more so than he's reassuring her. He knows how much he has to lose here. He knows that he can't return to that shitty one-bedroom apartment that he rented when she kicked him out. The type that you lease just out of college and erect a plaster wall in the living room to create an extra bedroom for your just-as-broke roommate. Where the residents are a decade younger and stumble in from walks of shame while he's already heading out to work in the morning, reminding him of his lost youth and, well, of how the rest of him has been pretty lost, too. "Let's start at our wedding because, well, really, I know it's cliché and all, but it was the best day of my life"—he clears his throat—"of our lives."

Was it really the best day of hers? He doesn't know. But there are enough land mines to avoid in the stories of their life together, and this one seems safe, a round, comforting place to get a toehold.

"I saw the pictures," she says, and he hesitates again, unsure if she's simply making conversation or if she's trying to make this harder on him.

"I know, I know." His head bobbles up and down. "But they can't convey how great it was, how seriously magical it was."

"Magical?" she says, and stifles a laugh.

His ears burn when she laughs at him, though he's used to it all the same. She was never the kindest of wives, not the type who rubbed his feet nightly on the couch, not the type who relied on him day in and day out, leaning on his shoulder when the chips crumbled. No, she was the mother ship and he was her wake—though she didn't look over her shoulder too often to ensure that he hadn't drowned while swimming behind her. At first, it had worked well, this configuration: his friends told him how lucky he was, that his wife let him have endless guys' nights, that she wasn't clingy and begging him for a baby when he wasn't yet ready. And sure, he loved his guys' nights and was *as appreciative as any new husband would be that his days hadn't been totally upended because they swapped vows. But, let's face it, he told himself about a year ago in the mirror while shaving, "You are a guy who likes to be needed, and she, well, she didn't really need anyone," so their banter grew less funny and more acerbic, and one thing led to another and, eventually, that led to Ginger, his coworker.*

"Say what you want, mock me if you must," he says today in the hospital, holding his ground, trying to forget all about Ginger. Ginger! *The massive fucking mind-blowing mistake of Ginger.* "Our wedding was magical."

He pauses, and she smiles, and he can tell that she's not being cruel now, not mocking him like maybe she would have before, so he smiles back. She seems different, he thinks—happier, less angry despite the circumstances. Then he worries that he's pushing his luck, jinxing himself. Like your wife surviving a plane crash isn't lucky enough and that hoping it's somehow changed her for the better is just too much, pushing the Vegas odds too far in the wrong direction.

"We got married in Saint Lucia in April. April twenty-third. Your mom tried to talk us out of it—she wanted us to do it in her backyard or even at your dad's old studio in Vermont, but you fought her on it. You were very, very sure of Saint Lucia."

"Why Saint Lucia?"

He shrugs. "I suppose it was anywhere your mother, well, I don't know, and your dad—reminders of him or whatever—were not. And hell, I didn't care where we got married. But you cared—you cared about that, and you cared about our music. So I just shut up and did what I was told."

"Joe Cocker," she says, because her sister had told her.

"Joe Cocker," he says back, then sings a line, embarrassed at himself but desperate all the same. " 'Give these loving arms a try, baby, and have a little faith in me.' " He veers slightly off-key, but it's not a half-bad rendition. Not her perfect-pitch level, but still, not awful.

She stares at him for a beat, and he steels against it, ready for the mockery. But instead, she squints and says, "Just put a tux on you and you'll be there," like this is an inside joke of theirs, which it was, even though she can't remember.

"Yep. Exactly! That's more or less what I said." Peter grins now, genuinely, less nervously, and she can see, for one of the first times, how he is handsome beyond the generically handsome way that he already is. In the tiny folds around his eyes, in the dimple that craters into his left cheek. He is almost large enough to be oafish, but bent over in his chair, he looks more compact, less imposing, and she can see that way back when, maybe in high school, his size would have made him the lead tackle on the football team rather than just the biggest guy at a cocktail party, which he probably is these days.

"It was a small wedding—we invited only fifty or so, and about thirty made their way down. But you wanted it private and not a big to-do, and again, your mom wanted two hundred, but this was all the hotel could accommodate, so you won that argument in the end."

"Up on the cliff," she says. "There's a picture here somewhere of the wedding—we got married up on a cliff?"

"Yes, yes," he says, a wave of momentum building in his voice. "It had rained about an hour earlier and you were devastated—sitting in your room getting ready with Rory and Samantha and your mom and sobbing because it turns out that the weather was the one aspect you couldn't control—but then it cleared up right before we started." He

smiles now, lost in the vision of what he's trying to re-create for her.
"And you—and this is the part that I'll never forget. You surprised me
with your guitar. For the first time in forever, you played, much less
played for me. I still—to this day—don't know how you got that
guitar down to Saint Lucia without my noticing." He floats his eyes
down to meet hers. "I don't know. It was just, like, out of a movie or
something. The clouds rolled out, and the sun came through, and you
were making music for me again, and it felt like God was watching
down on us."

"But he wasn't," she says, the conversation flailing instantly from
where he intended. She thinks she might cry for a beat but then real-
izes that her sadness has already passed. She wants to consider the
wedding, the simple white gown she saw in the photos and how
euphoric she looked. But without the background to their love and
their history, she feels like he's reading her a story about someone
else's life. There was something for a moment—in the melody when
he sang, in the lyrics—that maybe resonated, but like everything else,
that's gone now, a flicker that has been extinguished.

Peter's sucked back into the reality of the moment. He narrows his
eyes at her as he intuits her meaning and shrugs.

"You're here, aren't you? Doesn't that mean something?"

"Who knows what it means?"

"I think it means that we're supposed to be together. To do great
things."

Easy for you to say, she thinks.

"That cliff, you don't think it's a metaphor?"

"A metaphor?" he apes. "Like, for us?"

"Yes, like for us," she says. "Our marriage. Your cheating."

He sighs and rubs his nose, his wedding band tarnished but still catching the dim hint of the overhead lights. Indira, Nell's mother, had told him yesterday, when they were refilling their sour coffee in the hospital cafeteria, that she, too, thought Nell seemed different since the crash, that—despite the physical damage—she somehow seemed more buoyant, less controlling than she used to be. Indira had patted his right shoulder and said, "Hang in there," like he had any choice in the matter. "She'll come around. I'll talk to her," she'd said, though Peter didn't add that Indira talking to Nell, in just about any context, was often among the worst ideas. He didn't have many options here, so he'd gulped down a bitter swallow of coffee and nodded his okay.

As if intuiting his thoughts, Nell gives him an out now, skips the conversation about cliffs and affairs and how their relationship may well have plunged off the side of the mountain and shattered into tiny, untraceable splinters.

"Forget the wedding, forget the great things about it," she says. "Tell me one thing in your life that you've already done that's a great thing." She thinks of her promise to herself, to find her own greatness.

He stumbles, the question catching him off guard.

"A great thing? Jesus . . ." He shifts his watch around his left wrist, something to do, a way to buy himself some time.

"Okay, I'll make it easier," she offers. "Let's start with something basic: What do you do in real life? Would you consider that a great thing?"

He hesitates because before, before she would have judged him for this. Judged him because she was the one with the gift, the ear, the *aptitude. Even though she abandoned it and only played for him, or with him, in their finest—and rarest—of moments anymore. When they first met, it was all the time. It was their thing—guitar or piano late into the evening, the music the thread that bound them together. So she knows or she knew. Knew that he would never have what she did.*

He inhales and says: "I write music. Commercial jingles." He reaches for the remote, feeling his fingers shaking, and flips on the TV. A truck commercial with a country music riff is playing on that cable station she always has on. "Like that." He gestures toward it. "That's the type of thing I write." Then he flicks the TV right back off.

"That's not really a great thing," she says, and he holds his breath. Then she laughs, and he can tell that she's joking, not because she's mocking him but because, well, it's decidedly not a great thing.

"No." He laughs, too. "It's not. But it pays okay. And I like it. For now." He doesn't bring up Ginger. That she sits in the office two doors down from him and that they produce nearly 80 percent of their music together. He doesn't mention that Rory had been the one to tell Nell of the indiscretion—she had heard from a friend of a friend—and that this only added to the pile of their—both Rory's and Peter's—problems with Nell. He doesn't say that the last time he and Nell spoke of his work— four months ago—she threatened him with a meat mallet in their kitchen and then kicked him out of the apartment for good. Their one drunken interlude nine weeks back—he assumed she was still on the pill, but perhaps she'd given that up, too—notwithstanding. Even though he has now realized that of course he wasn't in fucking love with Ginger! Of course he never should have looked twice (or three times) when she leaned low (then lower) in that scoop-neck top over the

mixing board. Jesus Christ! Of course he'd give his left nut to have a take-back.

No, he doesn't bring any of that up.

"Still, though, it's not the stuff on which dreams are built," Nell says. "Commercial jingles. Who knew there was such a job?"

"No, it's true. My legacy will hopefully be something greater than having written the jingle for Pizza Hut," he concedes.

"So you don't have your one great thing, then?"

He pauses, wondering how far he can push this, push her, push their bond. He feels her equivocating, trying not to like him but trying to like him all the same, giving him a little rope, whereas in the past, she would have simply knotted it into a noose and cavalierly tied it over his neck. Maybe Indira was right: maybe she's returned to him a little changed, like her reset button was jiggered in the crash.

He decides to go for it. She doesn't remember all the carnage, after all. Doesn't remember the things they've said to each other, how Ginger ruined them. Well, if he were being totally honest, really, how he ruined them—though for a long time, and even still now, part of him thinks that Nell shares some of the blame, too. If she did remember— if she could remember—he'd never have gone for it because she'd never have gone for it, either.

She wasn't even speaking with him when the crash occurred. He got the phone call from Rory about the accident—she was fleeing Giants Stadium and he could barely make her out over the crowd— oh god, pack some things and meet her at the airport, she said. He didn't even comprehend quite what she meant. And then all of a sudden, he got it: bam—his wife, who, by the way, hates him down to his core, is dead. Only it turns out she's not dead. He finds this out six hours later, and swears, upon hearing this undead news, that there is nothing he won't do to remedy his marriage.

So this is why he pushes it now. This is what he's been through. This is what he's learned.

"Maybe you can be my something great," he says, hoping she won't make fun of his sincerity. Before all of this, she had no time for senti-mentality, even when he was wooing her, but now, perhaps she will. "Maybe I've been working up to this, and now you, fixing you, helping you, proving to you that I am a better man, maybe that's my something great."

She hesitates for a beat, then another, and he knows that this can fall either way. He watches the clock in the hallway through the glass window, the second hand looping a full circle once and then again. Finally, he sighs, thinking she has fallen back to sleep, so he pushes himself from the chair, its legs squeaking in reply. His hand is on the metal knob of the door when she opens her eyes, and as if he can hear this, he turns and meets them.

"Stay," she says. "For now."

He nods.

Yes, he thinks, forever.

6

You would think that after a month, I'd be itching to leave the hospital. That when Dr. Macht and Alicia come in, shake me from my state of half-dreaming, with *The Best of Nell Slattery* as the sound track to those dreams, and tell me that I can head home, albeit with a rigorous rehab schedule and biweekly shrink appointments, I would leap out of bed—my nearly resealed ribs notwithstanding—and tackle them with euphoria. But when they do tell me this—that I'm ready to return to my old life, mostly—I want to reply, *What old life?*

Earlier in the week, Peter returned to New York for work obligations, and truth be told, though I am trying, *trying,* to let us be something great—to honor that promise I made to myself—I'm relieved to have the space to breathe, to sort it all through. My mother, too, has been muddying the waters, urging me to give this second chance an honest go, a buzz in my ear that can't be swatted away.

Shortly after Peter confessed his one-night stand, my mom swooped by and convinced the doctors to let me take a spin outside. In hindsight, of course, she also knew that this would indebt me to her—the first person to offer me a literal breath of fresh air after two weeks of sterilized, recirculated hospital oxygen. And she must have known that she was thus bound to earn her way into my good graces. She's cunning, my mother. Even without knowing her well, I know this. But she wheeled me outside, delicately, like a china vase, and I inhaled the lung-expanding sunshine while she talked to me about forgiveness. About how you never regret doing it and how it can be the greatest gift you'll ever give yourself—*Take the other party out of it entirely and do it for yourself,* she said. About how things aren't always black and white, even though my earlier incarnation almost always thought that they were. *There is gray, you know,* she said. About how vulnerability was never my strong suit but now, she thinks, it might be. I confessed to her about my vow to seize this second chance, and she in turn embraced me and said, "There is life in you yet, a new life, a new course." I nodded and felt the heat of the late July air burn my cheeks, and I felt good enough, forgiving enough, to want to dance on the sun. *Okay,* I nodded to her in agreement. *Forgiveness. Yes. I will try. That's what the new me might want anyway.* My mother rubbed my forearm and smiled in a way that reminded me of someone who had taken too much morphine, and told me that she knew it, she knew that I had it in me now.

Still, though, I'm relieved that Peter has gone back to New York all the same, not because I don't want to rebuild, or that I don't think I can trust him again, but because working toward this forgiveness that my mother impugns is exhausting. It requires tangible effort. And I'm already exhausted enough.

Not that Peter knows this. Before he flew back on Monday, I was breeziness and happy anecdotes (from him, not me, as I still have no anecdotes of my own to speak of) and the occasional kiss, which still felt like a first-date kiss—all hesitation and question marks. He brought me chocolate bars and vanilla pudding, which he said were my favorites before, and which now taste good, mediocre good, and the fabulous me wonders if maybe I might enjoy something more exotic, more *me,* but I thank him and don't say anything else.

While I ate, he told me of our first date—a setup, and not a good one at that—stilted conversation, no common ground. But then he got up to put a song on the jukebox, and that he chose "Sister Christian" made me smile and tell him of my sick, deep crush for the lead singer of Night Ranger in the seventh grade. And then we both loosened ourselves up and ordered another beer, and when he walked me home, he kissed me, and—extra beer or not—I kissed him back.

"You guys had that," Samantha said over the phone the other night, "that music thing. Every once in a while in college, we'd karaoke and we'd all see how good you were—*perfect pitch,* you said, but mostly, you were over it. But with him, you found it again."

"What do you mean, over it?" I fingered the iPod on my lap, where it almost always sat—plugged into my ear—when I wasn't being tested, rehabbed, prodded.

"I don't know," she said. "You didn't talk about it. Only that you once loved it, were great at it, but then . . . I guess you just lost interest." I heard her pause to bite into her lo mein, still at her office, stuck waiting for a client to file some paperwork. "Like I said, to be honest, I don't know all of the details."

"Funny, isn't it? How people only know what we want them to know?" I said.

I think of Peter, of the confession he made after the first-date story: "In the interest of full disclosure, I want you to hear it from me, all of it," he had said. That one evening, I was staying late at the gallery to put up a show and we'd been fighting, though about what, he couldn't remember, only that we were fighting badly and often. And that he and Ginger had just wrapped an H and R Block commercial (*they have music in H and R Block commercials?* I'd asked), and that they went to the bar in their building to celebrate. And that when closing time came—armed with either too much alcohol or, in his case, too much vitriol at his wife—they'd become that coworker cliché by retreating to their mixing studio and doing it on the floor. But that was it, he said.

How well do I know you, Peter?

"I knew you plenty well," Sam said, and pulled me back to the conversation.

"Still though." I shrugged, though she couldn't see me.

"Well, also, you liked that Peter was reliable," she offered.

"Ironic since he wasn't," I said back.

"True enough," she agreed. "The easy reads are never what they appear. Though you are. You were."

"I'm not sure if that's a compliment," I said.

"I'm your best friend. Of course it's a compliment," she said.

"So if it wasn't music, what was it, then?" I asked. "What made me happy? What did I do in my downtime?"

She hesitated, and I wondered if it was because she was still chewing or if it was because she didn't yet know the answer.

"Work, I guess."

"Work, you guess?"

"Well, I mean, the truth of the matter is, now that I'm really thinking about it, most of the time when we catch up, we're . . . well, we're bitching about something."

"Like what?" I asked. The face from the cover of *People* certainly looked like she had plenty to bitch about.

"Oh, my mother-in-law, your mother. My sleep schedule, my work schedule. Your sister. Things like that." She exhaled. "I never really thought about it until now—how little of our time we spend discussing the things that actually make us happy."

"What would I say about my sister?" I said, ignoring her prophecy on happiness. "What could I possibly complain about with Rory?"

Sam laughed. "Oh god, see, and I don't mean this to come out wrong, but in some ways, it's probably better that you don't remember. Clean slate and all. But you guys—you were always getting into it. You know, sister stuff. Competitive stuff. Driving each other crazy with gallery disagreements, nitpicky things. You were meticulous, she was less worried about the details. You were reserved, she was a show-off. Yin and yang, oil and water."

"I don't see that at all," I said.

"Well, that's the good thing about those clean slates," she said, right before her brief came in and she had to run. "You don't see what you just wiped away."

Shortly after Dr. Macht informs me that he has granted me freedom to fly back to my sister, to my husband, and to discover why I once made music for him, Jamie pops his head through the door frame.

"News," he says. "I have news."

"Me, too," I say. "I also have news."

"You're going home. I already know." He grins, a little too self-importantly.

"Of course you do." I close my eyes.

"It's part of the job."

I hear him sliding a chair next to the bed, and I open my eyes to find him already seated.

"So you already know mine. What's yours?"

"*American Profiles,*" he says.

"*American Profiles?*" I say.

"Yes, *American Profiles.*" He emphasizes both words like that will answer my question. "That show on Thursday nights?" I shake my head, still unknowing. "Well, they 'profile' all these amazing stories, amazing people. I think they might be interested."

"Interested?"

"In us, in a story!" He claps his hands for emphasis. "I've been pitching it like crazy, and I think today they bit."

I busy myself wrapping the headphone wire around the iPod and consider it. My instinct—despite my initial zeal for Operation

Free Nell Slattery, a zeal that has since waned, as these cockeyed ideas often do—is to burrow under the covers until the public loses interest. But the new me, the *fabulous me,* the one that conceived of OFNS in the first place, and the one I committed to as a penance for surviving the crash, implores my instincts to rethink this, to see it as an opportunity—for what, I'm not even yet sure. Maybe just to live on a grander scale, to fly down life's zip line instead of standing beneath it, craning my head to see what was coasting by. Besides, Jamie is a means to an end—he's out there, uncovering details, angling for information—and my new instinct, my new gut is telling me to trust him, telling me that there's something here to believe in. Just last week, we did an hour-long interview that his station stretched over three nights, and viewers marveled at my voided memory and told us as much in e-mails.

What I wouldn't do to erase the memory of my lousy ex-husbands (three of 'em) and son-of-a-bitch boss, Clara from Iowa City wrote in.

My heart goes out to this poor girl. What a loss—I have asked my church group to pray for her this Sunday, Eugenia from neighboring Wichita, which now received the show via satellite, told us.

"Before you answer, I have these." Jamie reaches into his bag and thrusts a pack of postcards in my hand.

I finger through the lot of them. They're semi-abstract paintings—if you look hard enough you can see the shape of a woman's breast or the ampleness in her butt cheek or the curve of her chin in almost all of them. They are in glaring, blinding colors—cherry red the shade of fresh blood, vibrant blue so vivid you couldn't find it in nature, a yellow that forces me to squint.

"My dad's, I take it?" I ask. "I thought he did pop art?"

"This was his early work. And it wasn't easy to find. Rory blew me off when I asked about getting some prints and your mom flaked on me twice. I finally called a friend of a former colleague who's an assistant art professor at Columbia. These were from some of your dad's old shows." He pauses. "Anything look familiar?"

"I'll give you two guesses." I pause and cock my head, turning one of the images vertically. "Still, though, I can tell he was amazing."

"Rory told me—curtly, I should add—that you were his apprentice." He shakes his head. "No, maybe she said muse."

"I could have been. I wouldn't know." I look again at the photos. "But these aren't of me. Not if he left when I was thirteen."

"No." Jamie reaches for a postcard and examines it. "These predate you."

"My mom, maybe?" I suggest helpfully.

"Maybe," he says, handing it back, refocusing. "But that's not the point. The point is *American Profiles*."

"Well, you're not making your point about it." I pause, examining the scattered postcards, of the archaeology that Jamie has uncovered when no one else has. "So what exactly is your point about *American Profiles*?"

"I think they're going to make us an offer: you, me, Anderson—none of their regular anchors—a four-part series tracking your recovery, your transition back into the real world. I'm still negotiating it."

"Shouldn't people be sick of us by now?" I say this, and yet I know they are not. I still hear the calls to the nurses' station, can still see the media trucks parked on the street outside my window.

There have been no other national catastrophes since the crash and until there is—a bomb threat, a sports star scandal—I'm still it.

"If I've learned anything in my job, it's that people get stuck on stories that resonate. I mean, you were just some up-and-coming thirty-something woman whose life was wiped out, which to a lot of them seems like a blessing, not a curse—a second chance but also an unwanted chance. And they read about you and think, 'What if that were me? What then?' You are them, they are you. That's what they're thinking every time they see you."

"I get it, I know." I do get it and I do know. *I want the laugh track!* "Anderson will never agree. He wants anonymity now, not more hype."

In fact, Anderson had just been released from his rehab center early last week, his body healing at an unexpectedly remarkable pace, and had flown back to New York to regroup, to see if he could pick up the shards where his life left off. His sister and mother came down from Boston to help him acclimate.

He called two nights ago, after getting settled. I was watching *Fatal Attraction,* an ill-advised selection, to be sure, but a pop-culture classic all the same, and Rory had told me we used to watch the boiled-bunny scene over and over again, partially to terrorize ourselves, partially because we knew it was coming and would start giggling five minutes prior.

When the cell phone vibrated, I was taking the movie a little too personally, letting it hit a little too close to my core, and all of those initial doubts about Peter were firing at full throttle—despite my mother's plea for forgiveness, despite Peter's own. I stared at Glenn

Close and her savage eyes and wild, curly hair and wondered if that wasn't Ginger, wasn't Ginger exactly. And then I wondered if Michael Douglas could go back and do it over—before she boiled his bunny, before he realized the damage he had wrought on his wife and family—if he had really learned his lesson. Not because Glenn nearly kills them, but because he never should have done it in the first place. There's a difference there, you know. But that's the part we'll never know.

Ginger! Glenn!

Even though I'd promised Peter I'd put it out of my head, that it didn't matter, I couldn't put it out of my head entirely. There was nothing else to fill it: no history to fall back on, no soft space to catch me when I was free-falling through my doubts. So when Anderson called, it was a relief—to plug that space with something else.

"I wish you wouldn't trust this guy Jamie too much," he said. "My sister showed me those spots he did with you that ran last week. The three-parter. They're up on YouTube."

I considered it. "Trust is a moving target right now. And besides, didn't you once tell me that you have to control the press, not let them control you?"

"Ah." He laughed. "Now the student is the master. Like the Jet Li movies I used to watch when I got stoned."

Hollywood, I thought, a snap of a reminder of how different our worlds are.

Today, in the hospital room, Jamie drops his head an inch, an acknowledgment that Anderson is no longer a feasible get. The master has checked out of the competition.

"I told *American Profiles* as much. But I convinced them to take a serious look at just you."

"Why?"

"Why take a look at just you? Or why would I do that?"

"Why to both."

"The answer to both questions is the same," he says. "When I pitched them, they told me that one of their producers has an in. Might have old information on your dad. To up the ante of the story, keep things going in case the audience is ready to move on."

"What kind of information?" A wave of adrenaline couched as a question.

"Unclear," Jamie says. "They didn't want to play their hand until they were sure." He hesitates. "The thing is, Nell, you asked me to find out what I can. So I am. I mean, without Anderson, this story could be dead or at least deadish. Dying. But if there's a chance to find your dad . . ." He trails off because he doesn't have to finish the thought out loud.

I consider it: it seems like an easy swap, a no-brainer.

"So this is what happens when I send an Iowa farm boy out to solve the great mysteries of my life."

"This is indeed," he says.

"The chance to maybe get the answers to everything."

"And who," he says, "wouldn't bet the house on chances like that?"

7

"Sweet Child o' Mine"
—Guns N' Roses

*T*wo days before I am set to head home to my husband, to my old—but new!—life, my mother and Rory converge to ensure that I am okay returning home with Peter, to Peter.

"It's your choice," my mother says, all the while intimating her obvious preference. That moving forward mattered here, that *forgiveness* mattered here. "You are, of course, welcome to move back into my house." She wraps her palm over mine.

"I'd take her up on that," Rory says.

"Peter has assured me that he is more than capable," my mother says, her words running over Rory's.

"I'm sure he assured you of many things," Rory retorts, the two of them behaving as if I'm not sitting there listening to their bickering.

"Whatever you'd like, dear," my mother says, ignoring Rory. "Though certainly, your therapy will be easier to attend in New

York, and there's the whole issue of immersing yourself in your old world, which Dr. Macht says may help your memory."

Rory *pshaw*s at this until she realizes she's done so out loud, and then halfheartedly apologizes. "I wasn't disrespecting Dr. Macht."

"You're still stuck on Peter," I say.

"Some things are worth sticking to."

"Exactly!" my mom interjects, either misinterpreting or opting to misinterpret. "Her husband. Her marriage. Let her try to make it stick." She pauses. "And," she tuts, "there's this whole concept of your vision of your makeover. I know that this is integral to that. We all—you, Peter, everyone—deserve a second chance. Darling, don't forget that I'm sixty-five and still reinventing myself!"

I listen to her, and while the old me might have rolled her eyes and internally retched, the new me tries to take heed. To do the opposite of what I'd have done before. And also, because, at the very least, I trust Dr. Macht. So I tell them that I'm choosing to make my marriage stick. I choose Peter, despite Rory's misgivings, despite the small but pervasive voice that clangs in my ear, telling me otherwise. My mom tightens her grip on my hand and assures me that I won't be sorry. Rory chews her gum and says nothing.

And now, the day is here. Time, after all, marches on, with or without my memory, ushering my old life forward with it. Peter flies in to helm my entourage in taking me home.

"You'll be in excellent hands in New York," Dr. Macht assures me, hours before my departure. "Besides, you must be itching to get back to it."

"I am," I concede, though in fact, I am *not*. What is there to get back to? Rory and I have agreed that I'll start back at the gallery—tentatively, a bit of time here and there—when I have the energy, and Peter has offered to sleep on the couch while we work toward forgiveness. He said it exactly like that, and I knew that my mother had gotten to him, too.

My mom is bustling about, tittering and tattering—reminding me of a Road Runner cartoon I'd seen early one morning when I couldn't sleep, and I wish she'd just *be quiet.* But I bite my lip and try to be grateful, try to remember that there are many things to be annoyed with, but my annoying mother caring too much probably isn't one of them. She begins to hum to herself while puttering around the room, oblivious to the melody, until I instinctually join her. Then she pops her head up and says, "Oh!" and then melts a bit and embraces me and says, "We used to do that all the time when you were growing up."

Despite her whirlwind, however, there isn't much to pack, but there are instructions to be dictated, charts and forms to transfer, a long list of good-byes and thank-yous to be said, and I say them all genuinely, with mixed emotions. My grief at leaving the calm and predictability of the hospital is a lump in my throat that I try actively to swallow.

The airline has arranged for a private flight, which is sort of cushy and enjoyable, even if the last time I was cloud-bound, I found myself falling from the sky, but since I don't recall this, it's all kind of placid, inoffensive. There is an overly kind flight attendant who keeps misting up every time she refills my water glass, and the copilot personally comes out to introduce himself, and my mom clutches my wrist a little too tightly at the warning Dr. Macht had issued—that the flight might elicit some post-traumatic symptoms, that a few slips of memory might find their way in. But when I lean my seat back and close my eyes, my earphones and accompanying music drowning out the engine noise, there is nothing. I try to envision that conversation with Anderson on the doomed plane—him imbibing a few too many vodka tonics, me telling him the story of the way my marriage had gone to shit—but still nothing. It's only when we hit a pocket of angry air, with Guns N' Roses screaming in my eardrums from my iPod—*"She's got a smile that it seems to me, reminds me of childhood memories"*—that something rises up in me.

Fear. Terror. Not a memory of the downed flight, but something almost as alive. Something else, from way back when, though what it is or what it was, I can't nail down. It sparks up through my neck, my goose bumps alert like pinpricks, then down to my bowels, and for a good minute, I think I'm going to puke. I slam the headphones down, lower my head toward my lap, my ribs barking, and breathe.

Breathe.

Peter, alarmed, tosses aside his *Sports Illustrated* and peppers me to ensure that I'm okay, but I'm too busy mentally searching for something concrete, a sliver of a recollection, to answer. Finally, the turbulence passes and so, too, does the horror, the accompanying nausea.

"Did you remember?" he asks.

"Almost," I say, because it feels like I almost did. "An emotional memory, maybe. My subconscious."

"That's a start," he says, squeezing my hand. I right myself and squeeze it back. He is sturdy, this one. Not perfect. *Ginger!* But sturdy all the same. A port in this treacherous storm. So maybe my mother was right: that to find your way back to something worth keeping, you have to bob and weave, throw your fists up, and fight. I can do that: throw my fists up, even if my initial instincts—*he's too meaty, the betrayal too large*—told me otherwise.

Anderson greets us at touchdown, and a security officer stewards us through the intestines of the airport—the back hallways, the poorly lit corridors, toward the exit. I'm begrudgingly in a wheelchair, accepting Dr. Macht's advice not to push myself, to be kind to my body, to trust what it can do for me *when* it's ready to do it for me.

"There's more press here for you than there were for me," Anderson says, a sly smile awash his still movie-star-handsome face, his recovery complete in the few weeks since I've seen him. "I'd be jealous if I weren't trying hard not to care." He laughs. "My ego is the one thing that hasn't been dented in all of this." I laugh, too, and we agree that it is so good to see each other, like a homecoming of sorts.

We've already put a plan in place: that Peter will go out and make a statement on my behalf. The flight has exhausted me, and besides, I've promised Jamie his *American Profiles* exclusive. The security guard steers Peter left, and we break off like a wishbone toward the right. Anderson presses the doors open to the outside, and my mom wheels me into the blinding sun high in the New York sky. The early August humidity swaddles me—a warm embrace when I've spent too much of the past four weeks indoors in a hospital with its reminder that death is never too far away—and I inhale deeply, gloriously. Unexpected relief when I'd been dreading this unknown and what it could bring. *Yes, it was wise to listen to my mother, to swim past the stream I would have chosen and let her guide me to something new.*

I glance over my shoulder at her now, in her turquoise muumuu and loose gold earrings, and then at Anderson whose face has mostly healed and doesn't betray a single scar of what we've been through. He is skinnier now, though, his cheekbones like knives.

I'm home, I think, and *I might actually be okay.*

Of course—and I can only know this later, know this with hindsight that time can bring—therein lies the problem with forgetting everything: you don't remember that trouble is always just around the bend.

8

"Running on Empty"
—Jackson Browne

O ur apartment is nothing like the one I'd seen on *Friends*. I know it's ridiculous, but I can't help but be just a little disappointed. There are no vaulted ceilings, no quirky knickknacks, no sweeping balcony or expansive living room in which to host gathered pals for board game night.

"Well, here we are," Peter says, my suitcase landing with a thud beside him. "I hope it's, er, what you were expecting. You had a say in most of it."

"It's good, it's great," I answer, shuffling into the (tiny!) living room that wouldn't even make up one quarter of Monica and Rachel's. I leave the wheelchair in the hallway—I don't, even symbolically, want to bring it over the threshold. That promise of the *new me*!

"I, um, decorated this?"

"Mostly." He goes into the kitchen, which isn't much of a

kitchen, more of an abutting space off the living room with a few sad-looking appliances. I can see him through the pass-through in the wall. He's nervous—I don't know him well anymore, but I can tell that much. He fidgets around the kitchen, opening the refrigerator, closing it, opening a cabinet, closing that, too, finally settling on a giant plastic container of mixed nuts left out on the counter. He pushes them through the open-aired square toward me.

"Hungry?"

I shake my head and circle the space, the rubber of my sneakers squeaking along the wood flooring.

"It's strange. This place doesn't much feel like me. Like, this rug?" I run my toe back and forth over the worn, though beautiful, Oriental pattern atop the wood. "This rug doesn't feel like me at all."

"Your mom gave that to us. It was from one of your dad's studios back in the day."

Upon hearing this, I ease myself down, slowly, running my fingers over the tapestry, like maybe I'll intuit something, hear—*what?*—the guidance of my father telling me who I am? What happened to him? Why he is no longer family? I've asked my mother twice for an explanation of not only why he left but why she intimated that he died ("You misunderstood, dear! I only said that he was gone!"), but I can see how much it pains her to discuss it, and *besides,* she says, *it is only one dark cloud in our history— there are so many brighter ones. Let's leave it for another time.* So I do. Jamie's lead at *American Profiles,* though, is making calls, and he assures me every time I ask—which is often—that we'll know more soon.

I stand as sharply as my body allows—it's weary from a month of mostly nonuse, and my hip emits an angry crack. "Ow, shit!"

Peter is next to me like lightning. "Here, sit, *sit.*" He guides me to a faded, plush golden couch that seems better suited for a Victorian old-age home.

"Erg, I'm okay. I just forgot for a second."

He grins. "Well, for more than just a second."

It takes me a moment to realize what he means.

"Touché." I smile.

"Well, that's a good thing, that you were able to forget about it."

We fall silent.

"This is weird," I say finally.

He laughs so violently, tiny shards of cashews spray onto the gilded sofa.

"I'm sorry!" He bats a hand in front of his face. "I'm nervous . . . I don't know why."

"Me, too," I say, even though I'm not so much, but it seems to put him at ease. He has told me that he knows I am risking everything by taking a chance on him again, and I have thanked him for this acknowledgment, for realizing that there is work, *tangible work,* to be done on both our parts. That, even with my amnesia, I can't just pretend to forget. Or remember.

"That painting right there." I point to the one over the mantel, an abstract that is big and boisterous with red and gold concentric circles, and also sad and bleak with stark shards of black cutting through, evoking how the sun might look on its last day, right before it exploded and decimated the earth and its population. "My dad's?"

"It was your favorite. The only one we have."

"Just one?"

"Just that one," he says.

"Huh," I say finally, turning away. I look around and notice that the white walls are either bare or covered in black-and-white photographs. A bulletin board next to the kitchen pass-through is pocked with Post-its, small pieces of itemized papers, receipts, but it's an organized chaos, meticulous almost. Where's the bright blue wall from *Friends*? Where's the joy? Where's the color? Where is the sectional that we all sink into after a shitty day at the office and nurse our cheap wine on?

I slide onto the couch, running my fingers over the faded fabric. "Please tell me this couch was also a hand-me-down from my mom."

He laughs. "No, this couch was all you. I hated it. But you saw it at the flea market and insisted."

"It's sort of awful." I push myself to stand, and he steadies me, both of us staring down at the monstrosity. "I can't believe I insisted."

"We'd just moved in together, and you were trying on your sea legs. I don't know. You wanted 'funky-chic,' or something like that. I think it was a direct reaction to some fight you and Rory were in."

"About what?"

"God, I don't know, but the general nature of your fights seemed to be about your finding her irresponsible and her finding you tightly wound. So you got annoyed with her, tried to prove her wrong, and we ended up with this." He raises his eyebrows.

"And that?" I gesture toward a faded black piano in the corner next to the television. "Yours for work, I assume?"

"Ours, actually. Well, technically yours." He clears his throat. "I bought it for you as a wedding present. Hoped you'd play more, again. With me. Alone. Both."

"And did I?"

The phone rings, surprising us, before he can answer. He steps into the kitchen and pulls it from the receiver.

"Yes, yes, no, yes. Can you call back tomorrow? We just got home." He presses off and tosses it on the counter. "Media. They keep calling."

I sigh and fall back—gently—on the sofa cushions.

"What can I get you? Should I run out and grab some food? Some groceries? A bowl of cereal?" He waves a hand. "I'm sorry, I didn't have a chance to stock up when I was home—I was either at work or asleep, and then I was right back to Iowa."

"No worries, though a soda or something might be nice." I hear him open the refrigerator, then the hiss of the liter opening, and then the cracking of the ice as he pours it atop. I push myself upward toward the piano, lifting the lid, delicately pressing one key, then another, my fingers sliding up naturally into a scale, like they already know what they're doing. I close the fallboard and turn toward him.

He places the soda on the coffee table and carefully arranges himself on the couch. A beat passes between us, neither one of us sure what to say next. I wonder if I should ask again about Ginger but decide that the new me wouldn't need further reassurances. That she would flip her (gorgeous) hair and laugh into the wind with confidence that when Peter told her—as he did a few nights earlier when he called the hospital from work—that he really and truly ended it (which gave the new me slight pause because the old me was certain that he had ended it months ago), and find a way to put it out of her mind entirely. That forgiveness, as my mom had said, will weave into me over time, and what I needed now was that time, not regurgitation.

"Why don't I go get some Chinese food?" Peter says. He stands abruptly when neither of us finds a way to break the silence. "I'll let you settle in, feel at home without me hovering."

"I don't feel like you're hovering."

"Still, though, let's get some food." He jerks toward his wallet on the pass-through counter. "I know what you like. Don't worry."

"Okay," I say, though I'm not at all hungry. I wonder if I still like what I used to like but say nothing.

He bolts away, exiting quickly, like a dog startled, scampering from a room. I watch the door close behind him, and my relief puffs up like a cloud. I stand and sniff around the apartment again, running my fingers over the mantel, stepping back and assessing the bookshelf, flipping on the stereo in the TV cabinet to keep me company.

I hobble into the bedroom. One nightstand—his, I assume—is barren but for a glass lamp. The other holds a collection of picture frames, a stack of *New Yorker* magazines with a thin film of dust. The walls are a cool but welcoming yellow, the only accessory an enormous mural-size mirror hanging over the bureau opposite the bed. I catch a glimpse of myself in the corner of it: fragile, that's what Rory had called me weeks back, and that's exactly how I appear. Tiny. Like a dehydrated prune. That's what I remind myself of. Old and dried-up fruit. My limbs look breakable, my muscles are flimsy, my hair is a ratty mess with roots that betray the deep brunette of my childhood, a fact I know strictly from photo albums.

I slip onto the comforter, then slide onto my back and gaze up at the ceiling, adjusting an angora pillow under my neck. It's less comfortable than I thought it would be. It's itchy against my skin, so I tug it away and toss it on the floor. The speakers from the living room filter a song through the open door, and I hum along to Jackson Browne, a song I recognize from my iPod, from *The Best of Nell Slattery.* I can feel the harmony reverberate in my chest, behind my eyes, in my heart.

I exhale and push onto my elbows, but then something hits me—a sliver of *something, something ethereal but honest*—of a warm evening, of grass tickling my legs, of a little girl giggling beside me, and of a wide expanse of stars up above.

Think, goddammit, Nell! Think!

I press my brain into places I'm not sure it can go. I flex it, I stretch it, I squint, and I try to squeeze out something more.

The girl, yes, it is Rory. She's wearing short pajamas with green stars on them and is drinking lemonade. There is a white house in the background, with a porch that looks like it belongs in Georgia—a swing and two loungers and a lantern by the door. It feels like there is jazz in the air, but maybe I'm just making that up. Maybe not jazz, but something else that makes my body feel electric. Maybe Jackson Browne, but maybe that's just from the radio. It smells like honeysuckle, like summer, and I call out to Rory—"Rory," I say, "come on! Stop wiggling around. Come sit beside me or else we'll miss it."

"I'm coming," she responds. "Stop being such a turd. Geez, I'm coming."

Then, just as quickly as it comes, it's gone. I try to find more, more than that small snippet. I lie in my bed and I clench my jaw and press myself like a sponge, hoping that if I force it, another morsel will drip out.

There's nothing more. I hear the front door slam, and Peter yells, "Chinese!" and I sit up too quickly so that my head spins with dizzy stars, and then I yell back, "Peter, get me the phone! I need to call Rory! I've remembered."

Neither Rory nor my mother can verify my account of a childhood summer evening.

I tell this to my newly assigned shrink, Liv, two afternoons later, when she makes a house call.

"Hmmm, maybe," Rory had said when I reached her at Hugh's apartment. They were planning to move in together, and from what I could tell in the few days since I've been home, they more or less already cohabitated. "It sounds familiar, but I might have been too young to remember."

"Perhaps, dear," my mom said when she arrived later the same evening I had the flash, with her own boyfriend, Tate, in tow—a published poet who took to wearing a scarf around his neck despite the swampy late-summer air—and whom I immediately disliked on sight. He kissed me hello and rubbed my back like we were old friends, and who knows, maybe we were, but all the same, he gave me the willies. "That certainly *could* have happened," my mom said. "But our house doesn't have a porch like the one you seem to remember. And I've never been a fan of jazz. Still though, darling, feel *proud* of yourself. You are working toward something here! Give yourself a pat on the back for that!"

Liv interrupts me here. "This is interesting, that this is the first thing you tell me. That this is how your mom still speaks to you."

"Well, this is how she does," I say. "And I should also add that this feels like her baseline—like this is the sort of thing she says often. Or said often. 'Be *proud* of yourself, darling!' God, we couldn't be more different."

Liv smiles and twists her long dirty-blond hair into a bun at the nape of her neck, securing it with an elastic from her wrist. She is young, my age maybe, give or take a few years, and easy to talk to, whether or not this is part of her job requirement. She makes a note in her file while I spin her name into a made-up melody—*Liv, Liv, how do I live? Livie, Livie, what you gonna give me?*

She sets her pen down. "It's nice to see, even though we've just met, that you still have humor despite what has happened. Joy is important."

"I don't know that I would characterize myself as joyful."

"So how would you characterize yourself, then?"

I recline in my armchair and consider it.

"Well, I don't know. But joyful isn't the first thing that comes to mind." I think of my question to Samantha from weeks ago—*what made me happy?* Who knew? Who knows?

"So how about we make it a goal?" she says. "To figure out how you would define yourself. Who you are now."

"You mean, who I was before."

"No," she says simply. "Well, yes. That's part of the goal, too." She unscrews the top of her water bottle and sips. "But they may not necessarily be the same. That's important to know. Scary, too. But important."

"But the stuff from before—I mean, my life. Will I remember that? Get that back, regardless of who I am now?" The idea of my brain being a whitewash forever is too terrifying to digest.

"Well, not to sound like your mother, but she's right that having a memory at all is a *wonderful* step," Liv says, placing the lid back on her water bottle, setting it on the floor by the leg of the couch. "It's a breakthrough. It's your brain trying to reconnect the wires."

"But it might have connected wires that aren't even there. Neither she nor Rory remembers anything like that!"

"Could be," she says, "though I doubt it. You said it felt real, like a déjà vu. You shouldn't second-guess yourself if it was that tangible. Perhaps it was pulling together pieces from disparate memories, but it was *something*. Don't underestimate that."

"I would say, given my life right now, that I don't underestimate much."

The phone rings, interrupting us, and the machine clicks on. Another reporter leaves a message.

"Sorry for that," I say. "We get a call every few hours. I don't know what part of 'no comment' they don't get. Remind me the next time I'm in a plane crash and lose my memory to unlist my number."

She laughs, then chews her pen for a moment. "So some logistics. We'll do this twice a week. Sometimes you'll feel like talking, sometimes you won't. Sometimes we'll use different methods: guided meditation, free association . . . we'll see what works and what doesn't. Which is something for you to think about, too—what's drawing out these ephemeral feelings? What work can you do on your own?" She smiles. "But you won't be on your own. Even if you feel like you are, I'll be here to help."

"I wouldn't mind a little help."

"But I don't want to give you the impression that this is going to be easy."

"I've never had that impression," I say. "Nothing about this gives me that impression at all."

9

A full week after I've landed back in New York, Rory opens the gallery—which has been booming thanks to public curiosity—for a reunion, a welcome-back party. I don't bother asking welcome back to what, though the thought has certainly crossed my mind. WELCOME BACK TO ... NOTHING! No, that banner wouldn't be celebratory enough at all. I dot concealer under my eyes, flush my eyelids with a hint of brownish shadow that I've found in the vanity, and spike my lashes with mascara. I stare into the mirror and imagine it—the gallery, the pulse of the crowd, the huddle of troops who are rushing to rally for me. Maybe this is where the fabulous me was hidden. Maybe this was my element, the thing I did best, maybe this is where I cast off the dourness of that *People* photo and flitted about the art world, my deals, my acumen, as a spotlight. *Yes*, I think, *this is where I'll finally uncover her, glimpse the road map to the new Nell, the hint of who I could have been all along.*

I flatten my hair with my palms and wonder if it doesn't feel four inches too long for me. Why I wore it so plainly—straight, middle part—when something else might have brought out the softness of my jaw, illuminated my heart-shaped face. I push the wrinkles out of my gray sleeveless dress—my closet is a study in the palette of neutral—and exhale.

Peter hires a town car, and my mother, wearing a perfume that reminds me of patchouli, and Tate, wearing a blazer and oxford with one button too many undone, accompany us down there. Truthfully, I'm relieved for the company, even if it means I have to watch Tate damply kiss my mother, and then see her wipe her scarlet lipstick stain off his mouth. They're like teenagers, these two, straight out of a sitcom. *They have the laugh track, dammit!*

But I tolerate their company all the same. The simple truth is that with the chaos dying down and more quiet space to fill, Peter and I have run out of things to talk about, and these two help soak up the still air. Of course there are discussions to be had, but mostly Peter and I shuffle around each other and turn the TV louder when things shift from silent to awkward. Last night, after he got home from the gym, he pulled me to the piano bench and asked if I might want to play—for him, with him—and even though I rolled my fingers over the keys, and the muscles found their natural curl, the instinct of rhythm pulsing through them, I shook my head and declined. Then I pushed the bench back, the feet squeaking against the floor, and climbed into the shower. Where I stayed until the mirrors steamed up—chiding myself for doing so—*this is not what a seize-life-by-the-balls girl would do!*—but unable to find the strength to go back out to him all the same.

Time. Forgiveness. My mother had implored. I was trying to pay respect to both. Perhaps our wedding song was no coincidence: have a little faith. Indeed.

The gallery is on Twentieth Street in Chelsea, and the sun is only beginning to tuck itself behind the downtown skyscrapers when we pull up. We're running late thanks to traffic on the West Side Highway, so there's already a herd of faces there to greet me, all unfamiliar yet familiar from my photo albums. That is to be expected. What's not is the bottleneck of camera crews parked on the sidewalk.

Anderson pushes through them and opens the town car door. He pulls me out, and we braid our now-healed limbs around each other.

"The girl who saved my life!" he says, burying his chin in my shoulder.

God, it is good to see him, though it's only been a few days. A safe space in this tornado.

"Come on, don't mind them," he says, when we break from our embrace and he notices my saucer eyes. I know I should be used to this—that I've made magazine covers and that three-parter with Jamie back on the local news in Iowa, and with the interest from *American Profiles,* and Rory had even told me about the TV crews camped out at the gallery—but mostly, I've been folded inside a hospital room and now my apartment, so this loss of anonymity is startling. I feel like the empress who has been stripped of her clothes.

Of all of us embroiled in the debacle, however, Anderson knows how to handle this particular aspect.

"She's not doing press," he says to them all, guiding me by the elbow.

"Is it true your memory is returning?" shouts a woman who is holding a digital recorder.

"How would you know that?" I spin my neck too quickly toward her and a vertebra flares up. *How could someone possibly know that?*

"Our sources are reporting that your memory is back," she says, smiling now, like she's doing me a favor.

"Hang on," Anderson says to me, just as I'm thinking, *Your sources? Who is out there citing themselves as a source? Like my life is a covert op that can be clandestinely reported on?* Anderson turns back to the reporter while I'm in mid-thought, stepping two inches too close to the microphone. "Listen, Paige, back off. *Back off.* She's not required to verify anything with you. So leave her alone."

He double-steps back to me, and I tilt my head and assess the oddities of the situation: the paparazzi, the party, and that Anderson, B-list newly turned A-list actor, is jumping to my defense in the midst of both.

"Nice to see you again, Anderson!" she shouts back.

"You know her?" I ask once he's beside me.

"We have a history," he says, offering nothing more, so I leave it be.

"Should I be concerned that I have 'sources' now?" I say.

"They save those for the most important people." He smiles.

"Ha ha." I smile in return.

"No, I've just been through this before—I mean, even *before* before. I figure if I can help the girl who saved my life . . ." He holds the door open and I squeeze my way inside. We both fall silent, surveying the landscape, a moment of peace before we're swallowed up.

"Stay close," I say finally. "Who knows who half these ghosts are and what they'll conjure up."

He grasps my elbow. "Don't worry," he says. "I'm not going any-where."

At first, this party seems like an ingenious idea. The new me agrees. The techno music is on just the right level—loud enough to give the energy a needed pulse, quiet enough so that I can still hear everyone's cheers of encouragement, reintroductions, and the occasional awkward pause because they really don't make a greet-ing card for your friend who defied death and lost—nearly literally—her mind.

Still though, it feels good, welcoming, almost *heartwarming,* to be here. Rory hands me a club soda after a gaggle of college friends wander off. I'd recognized their faces from my pictures: pressed together, holding spilling plastic cups of beer, in some fraternity basement—*Golf Night!*—our cheeks glistening with sweat, our bra straps askew under our tank tops. Tonight, they hug me and rub my back, and everyone takes out their phones to schedule a girls' night, which is something we evidently used to do whenever we were all in the same place at the same time, which, Samantha tells me, wasn't too often.

"Life got so busy," she says, like this is something to feel guilty about. "You were always here, at the gallery; I'm usually in London or Hong Kong for work; the moms could never find a sitter." I think she's about to start crying. *Jesus, please don't start crying! What I would really like is if people could stop crying around me!* But she glues herself together. "Let's not do that again? Okay?" She reaches for my hand. "Let's be better about it this time."

So we pull out our phones and promise to be better about it this time. I already suspect that we won't be. Old patterns, old dogs, new tricks. All of that. Until I catch myself slipping back into the former me. *No, no, no. Things will be different, things must be different.*

"I know I can't remember everyone," I say to Rory when she brings me the club soda. "But it's nice to know I was this loved, that these people can all be my parachute."

"Oh my god, have you been watching *Oprah*? Because you'd never have said that before," she says. If one can manage to simultaneously roll her eyes *and* make them bulge with surprise, Rory does so.

"Well, before, I could remember everyone."

"No, but the part about being loved. The parachute." She shakes her head, taking the high road, setting aside her default response of sarcastic derision. "Anyway, it's nice to know, nice to hear." She hugs me, and the scent in her hair reminds me of that memory: the one in my dream that was really a dream about nothing. Honeysuckle. She smells like honeysuckle. But it's a splinter, a fleeting spark of imagination I conjured up from somewhere deep inside.

No matter what Liv says. No one can verify it, and if no one can verify your memory, who knows if it ever really happened?

We're interrupted by Jamie, who tugs me away by the arm into a corner near a skinny cylindrical sculpture that reminds me of a penis but that Rory assures me sells for nearly twenty grand. Behind it, Anderson is talking two inches too close to three women, all stark lines and black eyeliner and towering heels, whom I know somehow from the art world.

"*American Profiles,*" Jamie says, his skin flush clear down his neck. "They said yes!" He is glowing, beaming. If he were any more excited, he'd be levitating. "I just got the news. And their connection—he came through. At least partially."

"My dad? You found him?" I have to lean up against the wall to steady myself.

"No, not quite. It's not that easy." He glances toward the crowd. "But the producer—she made a call. To your dad's best friend. He's here tonight. Or will be."

"He's coming here tonight?" My nerves flare.

"I thought this is what you wanted. She scrambled to make it happen."

"No, no"—I wave a hand—"it is. I just . . . didn't expect it. There are so many questions to be asked."

"I know," he starts, but then sees someone in the crowd beckoning. "I'll circle back, don't worry. I just want to grab this writer while I have her. Keep an eye out for him." He's sucked back into well-wishers, armed with their chardonnay and cheese cubes and cold purple grapes.

I stand there, frozen, keeping that eye out, until I see him. Well, until he sees me, really, since I wouldn't spot him in the first place, and moves through the crowd toward me. He is older, likely my father's age, but still handsome, with wavy, boyishly blond hair and wrinkles around his eyes that he's grown into. He clutches me in too close a grasp for a man I'd never met, and after two claustrophobic seconds, I push my hands against his shoulders and politely wedge some air between us.

"I'm sorry," I say. "I don't remember you." It comes out rudely, and I'm unsure if I'm embarrassed at my brusqueness or not. Would this sort of thing embarrass me? Being so trite, so forthcoming. The old me, probably not. No, that brusqueness was actually my defining characteristic.

He's not offended, and instead, smiles widely.

"You're still your father's girl, I see. Blunt to the end. He'd admire that."

"I'm glad," I respond because it seems like the right thing to say.

"I'm Jasper Aarons," he says. "Your dad's oldest friend in the world." He laughs. "And if you look at me, I really might be the *oldest* friend in the world."

"Ah. I was told you might be here," I say. "*American Profiles.*" I spot my mom over Jasper's left shoulder eyeing us carefully, looking like she's trying not to stare but staring all the same. He turns and catches her glimpses and offers a sort of sophisticated half-wave, but she startles at him and scampers away.

"*American Profiles* or not, it's an honor. A privilege," he says, glancing back at me.

I nod because now, this seems like the right thing for him to say.

"I have a lot of questions," I stutter.

"And I'm happy to do my best to answer them."

"How did I know you . . . before? From when I was a child?"

"You wouldn't remember. I haven't seen you in many, many years." He stops and tries to pin it down. "Maybe since that summer that he left. *Jesus*." He pales. "Could it have been that long?" He catches himself for a moment, lost in a place he doesn't share. "Well, however long it's been, when Nancy called—she's a dear, very old friend who is now at *American Profiles*—well, I wanted to come down here tonight and tell you how much you meant to him. He'd be devastated to know that you couldn't remember him, remember your childhood spent with him, so . . . even though I promised him I'd watch out for you, and I guess I failed at that, I wanted to come down and make sure that you knew."

He adjusts his glasses, and I notice his green eyes, and I imagine how stunning he must have been thirty years ago. He's an artist, I can sense that from his worn hands and his earthy demeanor, and I can already see my father and him lighting up the world. A twinge of envy pinches my insides, at their brazenness, at their glory.

"Thank you, I mean, obviously I really don't know much," I say, then consider the specifics of what he's said. "So you knew that he was leaving? Leaving . . . us? You're the first one who's been willing to speak frankly about it."

He clears his throat. "I wouldn't say that I knew . . . explicitly. But on a more fleeting level, I suppose I did. He . . . struggled.

That's probably the best way of putting it. He struggled for a long time to conform himself to the straight and narrow. . . ."

"The straight and narrow?" I interrupt. "Like, living within the law or living with my mother, being married?"

"The latter." He smiles, and I try to force one, too, but don't find much funny in this. "It just broke him. *Conventional society,* he used to say. Some men aren't cut out for it, and then the fame"—he flops a hand—"so I knew that it was perhaps too much for him, and when he hinted that he might be, well, *leaving,* I didn't press him for more because I wasn't sure if he meant this earth or just his current life."

"So you think he could have killed himself?" My throat feels like it's closing in on itself, the visceral emotional reaction that comes from stored memories, even if I can't tap into them.

His shoulders bob, and he starts to reply, but my mom bumps into me at this exact moment and spills red wine clear down the side of my pale gray dress.

"Oh, Jesus!" she and I say together. Jasper grasps her arm but she jolts it away, purposefully ignoring him.

"Hello, Indira," he says. "It's so nice to see you."

She looks up as if she hadn't noticed him before and makes an enormous show of her false surprise.

"Oh, Jasper! Jasper Aarons, I didn't recognize you! It's been so long!"

No one involved in the charade believes it, so Jasper winks to break the tension, then grabs some cocktail napkins from a waiter. I dab at the spreading stain, but am forced to excuse myself before I look like a gunshot victim at my own welcome-back party.

"Listen, he'd want you to move on with your life, to be happy," Jasper says to me before I retreat to the back office to salvage my outfit, "to know that he loved you more than anything. I know you can't remember, but try not to forget *that*."

I replay his words a few minutes later, after I've found a bottle of club soda behind the bar and am blotting my dress with paper towels. I'm huddled in my old office, back behind the hive of activity out front. The chair squeaks when I sit down—*welcome back!*—and then I survey the furnishings from my former life. The desk is cast iron—spare but both antique and modern at once. There are stacks of papers neatly piled on the left corner, contracts, I'm sure, and a tumbling pile of mail scattered next to the printer. I can tell this is the slush pile—solicitations from aspiring artists who for some reason think that Rory and I can change their destinies, offer them open space on our walls, and alter their futures in doing so.

I flip through the desk calendar parked in front of the computer. Six weeks ago, there it is: *San Francisco. Hope Kingsley.*

The following week, I've scribbled, *9-week ultrasound.*

My chest seizes in grief, grief I wasn't even aware I was carrying around until I see it. Here. Confirmed. This lost child is like an apparition, something that I never had, never held, can't even fucking remember, but still, when I allow it to, it haunts me. Just because I can't remember it, like everything really, doesn't mean that it can't cause me pain. Because here, faced with proof, I'm eviscerated. I want to reach into those dark corners of my brain and pull out answers: *What was I going to do? What we were going to do? Become that cliché and hope that a baby can repair our relationship? Become a single mom? Not have it at all?*

Peter, in vague terms, has implied that we were working it out, that I was aiming toward forgiveness. But a niggling part of me wonders how much of this is true. Now, with my mind washed clean and without the memory at the outrage of his betrayal, maybe I can—can forgive him. But back then? Really? Was I capable of such a thing? Of forgiveness in the grandest of scales? I sigh, wondering how much it matters what I was going to do before. I flip the calendar a few weeks back and forth to see what else there is, what other bread crumbs I've left myself to follow.

Mostly, it's empty, but there. There it is: something. Something small, and who knows if it's anything. *Probably a dead end.* But I commit it to memory anyway. *Tina Marquis. 11 a.m.* Fifteen letters that mean nothing to me.

Peter pops his head through the door, breaking me free.

"Hey, you okay?"

I pat my dress. It's still damp and looks like a ruby reddish gray mosaic, but it's presentable enough. The stain almost looks intentional.

"I'm okay," I say. I stand and reach for his outstretched arm, and then I shuffle back toward the beckoning crowd.

Three hours later, the guests have scattered themselves out the front door and into the warm New York City night, and I am too tired to move. Really. So tired that I don't know how I'm going to make it home. Peter will take me, but I am oh-my-god-I-can't-even-walk-to-the-town-car tired.

"This was too much for her," my mom hisses at Rory, like I'm not perfectly present and can't hear her perfectly well.

"You're the one who told me to do it in the first place!" Rory replies, and I wish they would both shut the hell up and let me go to sleep right there on the bench underneath *Still Life with Purple Chair* by Antonio Molinero, an artist Rory discovered last year in Barcelona. The lights of the stark gallery are burning my pupils: too much white, too much brightness, all contrast and glare in here. It is hip, it is fabulous, and I can't take one second more of it. If I had an ounce of energy left, I'd use it for the new me to chastise the old me at being so quick to abandon her promises. As it is, I lie back, resting my head on a faux-glass bench, and accidentally knock over a wayward plastic wineglass.

"I'm here, you know. Right in front of you. So you can stop talking about me like I'm not," I bleat.

"Yes, of course you are, dear. We're only trying to sort out what's best for you," my mom says, kneeling to mop up the spill.

"Who died and made you my keeper?" I answer, until I realize that 152 people died. And then we all just shut up. Finally, I say, "Can someone please just take me home?"

"Yes, we should go," Peter says, until Rory gives him a stare that could wither a flower. I've seen how she eyes him now—distrustful, distasteful, but when I ask her about it, she usually just hiccups and says, "He has a lot to prove," which is true, so I let it rest.

"You can stay and help clean," Rory says. "Anderson can take her home."

"Don't be ridiculous. I'm taking her," Peter says.

"Don't be ridiculous my ass," Rory says back. "Half of the drunks here were your friends, and I'm not cleaning up their mess by myself."

"I'm helping," my mom says, still on her knees. "And Tate's here, too. And Hugh." Rory rolls her eyes, and Hugh, as if on cue for his boyfriend-of-the-year award, strolls from the back office with a box of garbage bags, ready to man up. If he didn't love my sister so much, he'd make me sick.

"Great, then the five of us should get it done in no time," Rory tuts, retreating to the office, extinguishing the argument.

Peter starts to disagree but I see him reassess and opt not to push it—it being what? His luck, Rory's nerves? Instead, he plucks his keys from his jeans pocket and stuffs them in Anderson's hand.

"Thank you, Ror, it was fun," I say, righting myself from the bench, kissing her cheek.

"Did it . . . help? Jog anything?"

I shake my head no. "But it was fun all the same."

"I'll be home right after you," Peter says, pecking my forehead.

"No hurry." I'm already dreaming of my bed, of swaddling myself in the down comforter and tumbling to sleep. Besides, Peter is still banished to the couch, so it's not like I'll notice that he's gone.

"I drank too much," Anderson confesses once the town car has pulled away and we're coasting up the West Side Highway. "I shouldn't be drinking with my meds."

"I've told you as much," I say, trying not to sound judgmental, though judgmental might be the old me's natural setting, my auto-tune. But I get it. I do. If I were brave enough to wash this all with a pill or a few drinks on top of a pill, I might, too.

"Thanks again for coming. I know you have fancy places to be."

"Nowhere fancy to be at all. New York in August?" He laughs. "All the cool kids have left anyway."

"But you're a cool kid."

"Less cool than you'd think. Or trying to be anyway."

"How's that going?" I've read Page Six. I know that he was out at some underground club two nights ago, know that he went home with a Victoria's Secret model, that the lead gossip story the next day read "Crash and Yearn!"

The town car cruises over a bump and Anderson winces, giving him an out. "You're still in pain?" I ask.

"Not that much," he says. "Well, psychological. The night-mares. They don't stop, not with therapy, not with a girl, not with anything. I'm trying to wean myself, you know, off the meds, but then my brain goes into overdrive. Night sweats, heart palpitations . . . My therapist says it might take a year to stop thinking about it, and even then, it might come back in fits and starts."

"That will be weird, too, though, right? I can't even imagine what we thought about before we thought about this."

"I can," he says. "I thought about landing my next job, push-ing my career to the next level, breaking up or hooking up with whomever I was with . . . I don't know, ridiculous stuff. But still, I'd give my balls to be able to just think about all of that."

I reach over and squeeze his hand.

"You're still doing well with the breaking up–hooking up stuff."

He accepts the jab. "Medicinal balm."

"In addition to the meds."

"In addition to the meds," he says, then smiles. "Can't hurt."

"Old habits die hard."

"Something like that."

"Did I tell you," I say, letting go of his fingers, "that I remembered something?" His eyes pop but he burps into his hand as his way of saying no. "It was almost like a dream, but it wasn't. Even though I don't really remember it, and even though my mom and sister tell me otherwise, it happened, I know it. Or so my therapist says."

"That's my new favorite line," he says. " 'So my therapist says.' Mine's the only one I trust anymore."

"Well, there's me." I rest my head on his shoulder.

"Well, there's you. That's true. The girl who saved my life. But you're as fucked up as I am."

We both laugh, and I straighten myself up.

"But anyway," I say, "I did, I did see something. I just don't know what it means yet."

"Our brains are strange beasts."

"That's helpful."

"Sorry," he says. "Too actorly. Ugh, what a stereotype I've turned into. I'm trying not to be, though—not to be such a stereotype."

"Stumbling around drunk isn't exactly breaking the cliché."

"I know." He hangs his head. "My shrink says the same thing." He catches himself. "There it is again." We both go quiet. "Oh, so here's some good news," he says finally. "All of this excitement has significantly upped my Hollywood stock."

"Ha ha."

"I've been offered a Spielberg film. We start shooting in North Carolina just after Thanksgiving, if I accept."

"If you accept? You can't say no to that."

He shrugs. "Like I said, I'm reprioritizing."

"Don't abandon your life because of this one terrible thing that happened to us, Anderson. I thought the whole point of the two of us surviving was that we got our second chance, our chance to live the lives we were meant to be living."

I consider the promise I made to the new me. *Isn't that it? Isn't that the entire purpose?*

"That's it exactly!" he says, clapping his hands together. "What if this isn't the life I'm meant to be living? I mean, this acting thing is so flimsy—it's me dressing up in costumes and saying someone else's words!"

"But don't you love it?"

"Sometimes," he says. "Sometimes it just seems like life."

The car stops abruptly at a light, and we both—too tensely— grab the other's wrist. When we finally let go, I'm certain he can feel the imprint of my grasp, as I can his. Holding him, just like I had outside the gallery, feels solid, like I'm finally sinking into something that won't ebb out beneath me. He says that I'm the girl who saved his life, but what if he's the one person to understand me, the one person to save mine? I shake my head and shrug this off. No, there's also Peter.

"Aftershocks," he says once we've started moving again. "Even with the therapy and medication, there are always the aftershocks."

10

"Every Breath You Take"
—The Police

Jamie, Peter, and I decamp to my mother's house in Bedford for the weekend. Jamie, because we're forging ahead with *American Profiles* and this is our initial background research. They'd announced the exclusive just yesterday; Page Six had covered it this morning with the headline "Whoa, Nelly!" I actually laughed when Anderson called to tell me. Peter, because, well, we can use a weekend away, even if that means enduring my mother and Tate.

My mom is right about both my so-called memory and the house: there's no wraparound porch, no lanterns at the entry. Still, though, there is a sweeping expanse of lawn, and it seems entirely feasible that while parts of my recollection were indeed conjured up, parts of it could certainly be plausible. The late summer night on the grass with my sister. Well, why not?

Jamie is staying in the guesthouse behind the main house, while

I'm in my childhood room and Peter is in Rory's. My mom twirls around like a holistic whirlybird: she knows better than to be swirling around in a fit of nervous energy, but she can't help herself. *Just calm the fuck down!* I want to yell at her, like she shouldn't know about energy transference and Zen postures and *blah, blah, blah*—how she's making the rest of us tense—but I clamp down and shut it. Maybe there is something to be learned from her kindness, her generous spirit, even if that same spirit irritates the hell out of me. I tell myself to force a smile whenever I feel like snapping. Eventually, she turns on the living room stereo and seems to decompress, almost visibly, at the lilt of the classical music. I stand in the door frame and watch her, until she catches me and says, "I'm sorry. I know that I'm a nut. This helps."

She walks over to me and kisses the top of my head. "You got that from me, you know. People said that you got it from your dad, your love of music, but it was from me. He couldn't sing to save his life.

"You'll have to forgive the guesthouse," she says to Jamie, after we've made our way out back, as he drops his duffel onto the creaking farmhouse floors. "I had it cleaned but it's still a little musty, I'm afraid. It hasn't been used for guests in years. But with all the company we're having this weekend, it's the only way to make it work."

Rory and Hugh are taking the train up this afternoon, and since Peter and I aren't currently sharing beds, the two of them were now deposed to the extra bedroom on the third floor. The house itself is huge—too big for my mom alone—but she'd long ago tossed out the ancillary family rooms and bedrooms to make way for her yoga room, her sewing room, her "quiet" room where Tate could write poetry and nary a word could be spoken, though sometimes, she whispered, as she gave me a tour, "we like to make love in here without any sound."

My old room, much like my apartment with Peter, is nothing like I would have pictured for myself. Where are the teenage heart-throb posters? Where are the old record albums and drawers full of letters to camp friends? Instead, there is a collection of tennis trophies on a bureau, a ceiling-high bookshelf stuffed with fraying guitar sheet music and old high school textbooks—physics, biology, French, European art—a barren white desk, and a wicker rocking chair adorned with faded flowery pillows better suited for an old- age home. If you were to look around here—a detective in search of whom I would grow up to be—there'd be no signs: my teenage self is a generic whiteboard, a canvas with no color. I feel a pang of sadness for her, for me.

I ease down onto the bed and breathe through the ache in my ribs. Seven weeks now after the crash, my pain has mostly dissipated. It pops up now and again when I've stretched myself too thin—a reminder that I'm not who I used to be: I'm less strong, more breakable. Though it could be worse—it could be like Anderson's: ever-present, constant, unwilling to be tamed.

Peter knocks on the door.

"Going to jump in the pool. Want to join?"

"In a minute," I answer.

I lie back on the bed, with its Holly Hobbit–esque comforter that feels too childish for the woman I grew into in this room, and listen to the noises of the house, hoping they will bring something back. A floor below, in the kitchen, I can hear my mother working the blender, making god knows what—a spinach smoothie? a tofu shake?—and out the open window, a lawn mower in the distance. Then, a splash as Peter catapults himself into the pool. I close my eyes. What did I used to hear when I was drifting off to sleep at night? Nothing comes, so I try to envision it anyway. My parents— while my dad was still around—playing Dylan or the Smiths in the living room, or in later years, my sister's thumping hip-hop from her closed door across the hall. Crickets on the lawn? Neighbors pulling into their driveways? A ringing phone from a boy on whom I had a crush?

All of that seems right but none of it is confirmation of anything, so I thrust myself to my elbows and make my way toward the pool.

Outside, Jamie is dipping his feet in, while Peter is moored on a raft. They've uncovered an old beat box from Rory's room, the radio making conversation between them. "It's eighties weekend!" the DJ says. "Call in and share your favorite hit from the decade."

The late August air is surprisingly devoid of humidity—just one of those crystalline days that you wish could go on forever—filling your lungs and your being with a type of unmatched lightness. I squint at the two of them, my farm-boy journalist and my repentant husband, staring for a beat until Peter notices me and offers me a wave.

"Hey." Jamie jumps to his feet. "Before you sit, come here for a sec."

He steers me toward the guesthouse, holding my waist steady with a comforting familiarity.

"Are you okay in here? Is everything settled and cleaned up?" I ask.

"Yes, perfect," he answers. "I'm glad you invited me. I can't imagine a better place to start."

The guesthouse used to be my father's studio, as evidenced by the occasional paint spatter that my mother had never quite erased, and the ceiling mural of jewel-toned waves that—my mom explained to Jamie—my father concocted during a particularly bad spate of insomnia. A queen-size bed is pushed against the back wall, a set of drawers with an old TV atop it sits to the side, and a faded rug, so much like the one found in my apartment, conceals the rest of the scars of my father's work. Every few feet, you encounter a giant splotch of oil paint or acrylic that hadn't come up. Though my mom redid the main house, she didn't have it in her, I suppose, to gut this one, too.

The scent inside is familiar—part paint, part paint thinner, part coffee, part lemon cleaner—and it hits me with both purpose and electricity—that still after all of these years, it can smell like what? *What is that smell? Who is that smell?* Jamie unhinges a window, and I can hear Peter on his raft, singing freely along to the Police on the radio.

The floor spins for a moment, and I lose my way. *"Every smile you fake, every claim you stake, I'll be watching you."*

"You okay?" Jamie asks.

"The smell in here . . . and with the music . . . it's just . . ." I inhale and try to imagine. *Yes, that's it.* "It's exactly like my father." I fall still and wait for something else to come.

"You remember something?"

I shake my head. "Only that this reminds me of him." I don't say that the pulse in my neck feels like it might detonate inside of me, and that something about this smell is both exhilarating and ter-rifying. I make a mental note to raise it with Liv. *That's my new favorite line.* Anderson had said, *Or so my therapist says.*

Jamie steps over to a closet on the right side of the bed. "And what about this?" The door creaks as he opens it, a small tuft of grime kicking up. No one has sniffed around here in years.

I shuffle closer and peer inside. Even in the half-darkness, I can make out canvases leaning atop one another like dominoes.

"Are these my dad's?"

"Yours," he says. "I went to hang up my shirts and here they were." He kneels down. "Look, you signed the bottom."

I can't comfortably squat to join him, so he lifts the front paint-ing and raises it to me.

"I've never seen my own stuff." I wrinkle my brow. "Not great, but not bad. Not my father by a long shot."

"Who says you have to be your father? I mean, I'm no expert or anything, but for a kid—look, it's dated—you weren't more than thirteen. I'd say this is pretty good."

He's right: the way I'd blended the colors, the flare I placed on the horizon, the shadow of the far-off rolling hills, and the jagged lines to create an illusion of pine trees. You can tell that I've been taught by the best, even in the cliché of the landscape.

Jamie starts to place it back on the floor when we both—together, at once—notice the painting behind it.

I'm breathless, stunned, feel my chest closing in.

"Jesus Christ," we say simultaneously. He tugs it up, closer.

"It's the house I remembered!"

I feel like I'm hovering outside myself, having an out-of-body experience. But it's there—put down on the canvas years back. The white wooden front, the enormous porch with a picture-perfect bench, the lanterns aglow, the green landscape behind it.

"It's exactly like what you described," he confirms, and then his face morphs into a wide grin. "This is something, this is really *something!*"

"But my mom. She didn't remember it. Said *I* couldn't have remembered it."

"Well, that's one of the first rules of journalism," he says, as we both step closer, peering at the painting once again. "Unreliable narrators: you can never trust someone else when it's your story to tell."

11

*I*ndira is fussing around in the kitchen, slicing up tomatoes from the farmers' market and laying them out on a platter with mozzarella and basil, when she hears Nell's footsteps on the back porch and then the screen door slamming and then her daughter—looking so much like the put-upon teenager she used to be—in front of her. Jamie trails behind her, resting a canvas against the dining table, and then exits quietly, lingering on the porch to overhear, but not place himself in the line of fire directly.

"Well, hello to you," Indira says, trying to maintain the air of composure, but the knife rattling down on the tile counter betrays her. She wipes her hands slowly on a dish towel, the only slow movement she's made since the company arrived, and Nell, if she were of clear mind, would see that she's buying some time. But Nell is too angry to see this.

"What's this?" Indira says finally, her hands still slightly sticky *from the residue of the tomatoes. She steps closer to the painting, though she knows perfectly well what it depicts. "Is this one of yours?"*

"Yes, Mother, it's one of mine," Nell manages. There is a watermelon-colored splotch across her chest—a rush of angry blood, just above the V-neck of her T-shirt. "It's one of fucking mine, and I'm pretty sure it's exactly the memory I had, the one I told to you, and of which you denied its existence."

Indira slides out a chair and sits, and for the first time since the hospital room back in Iowa, looks—just for a fleeing moment— defeated, exhausted, frayed around all the edges. She can feel Nell bearing down on her, but after that flicker of self-doubt, she straightens her spine and tries not to buckle.

It's not like she hasn't seen this behavior before, not like she hasn't beaten it back with a figurative stick for the better half of Nell's teenage years after Francis left and Nell embraced stoicism, meticulousness, and such tightly controlled anger that you'd never know she was angry in the first place. But let's not forget about the anger. The endless hours beating the tennis ball against the backboard, her headphones blaring so loudly, you could hear them the next court over. Her abandonment of making her own music, which she had reveled in since she was no more than three, and her abandonment, also, of making her own art, which her father had pushed for her since about that age, too. Yes, Indira had seen all of this before, and she eyes Nell now, and sniffs her nose higher. She won't cave—she knows her daughter too well, even though she thought that after the crash, well, maybe she was different. That if Nell were to forget all of the scars and the sins, maybe that would change everything, change her.

"Sit down," Indira says, pointing to a chair.

"I don't want to fucking sit down," Nell says.

"Nell, darling, please calm down. And the language. There's no need for that language."

Nell chews on her bottom lip, debating whether to listen to her mother or indulge her own rage.

"Well, if I'm being honest," Indira continues, when Nell still refuses a seat, "I'd completely forgotten about that painting. And furthermore"—her voice elevates just a tinge here, and if Nell remembered her mom as she should, she'd know that this was her tell, her giveaway—"I didn't even remember that house when you told me your dream."

"It wasn't a dream, Mother. It was a memory," Nell barks. "And given my circumstances, that's a pretty big goddamn distinction."

"Please stop talking to me that way. I hate it when you're angry— this is the you of your past! We moved beyond that. You told me! You told yourself: the new you!" But Nell's face is metal, unrelenting, and Indira realizes this distinction is of no consequence to her right now. That there have been moments that were, but this isn't one of them. "I really didn't remember, and when I finally did, it was only a day or so ago, and I was thinking of your best interest in not bringing it up."

Nell snorts at this, and Indira sips her tea and mentally counts to ten. Of course she isn't telling her the full truth, though it's not just in Nell's best interest—it's in all of their best interest. Of course she remembered going down to that piece of shit house and retrieving the kids in a flurry of panic. Of course she hadn't forgotten Nell's choice, and how it was always about Francis and not about her—her own goddamn mother!

Indira says none of this, and instead offers: "Has your therapist suggested yoga for you? I very much think it could help."

"Shut up, Mother, and tell me about the house!"

Indira stares at her for a second, debating. Nell is slipping back—here's the proof—already being tucked behind old habits. The anger! The distrust! Telling her the truth would push her farther down the rabbit hole, and Indira's been there, tried to rescue her before. When she woke up that morning to Francis's note that he was leaving—this time for good—she considered telling the girls that he had died suddenly but instead sat them on the couch and prepared a plate of shortbread and 7-Up, and bore witness to the axis in Nell's world grinding to a halt. In the months, many, many months that followed, she tried to introduce her to meditation and suggested family therapy, but there was no budging on her end. There wasn't space for forgiveness of her father's faults or of the fact that he couldn't control himself, that his brain and his wiring and his chemistry forced him to choose a more solitary path. No, Nell just zipped herself up, and soon enough she was defined by her hard edges, her backbone made of steel. Nell was his muse, and he was her life. There was no forgiving that.

Finally, Indira blinks and inhales. She will tell her, she thinks, in bits and pieces, dribble out enough to inform her, not enough to snap that rigid backbone upright all over again. But before she can say anything, the front door squeaks open and Rory and Hugh shout, "Hello!"

"What are we interrupting?" Rory says, her enormous black sunglasses perched atop her head, her legs skinny and lean in denim cutoffs. Indira feels a wave of pity for Nell, at her younger sister's beauty and how, though she was smarter and certainly pretty in her own way, she would never live up to it. And never live up to her father's

projected expectations, either. Is it any wonder she grew so far removed?

"Mom is telling me about the house."

"The house? Oh, that's a good idea," Rory says, moving to the fridge to get a beer while Hugh juts his head in for a quick hello, then hauls their bags upstairs. "There's probably a lot here that might help with your memory."

"Not this house," Nell says. "I found this painting."

Rory pops the top of her bottle and swigs, moving toward the table and eyeing the canvas. "I've never seen this." She steps back and assesses. "It's not bad. I mean, I wouldn't buy it for the gallery or anything, but still, it's not total shit."

"Rory!" Indira snaps. "Please."

"What? It's true. And by the way, you're welcome for saving you from Peter the other night."

"What are you talking about?" Nell says, and Indira feels herself relax, thinking she might just dodge the bullet. *Yes, let's talk about anything other than this goddamn house.*

"The other night. At the gallery. I made him stay so you wouldn't have to spend more time with him."

"I don't mind spending time with him," Nell says, to which Rory rolls her eyes.

"Just trying to, you know, do you a favor," she says.

"Rory," Indira says in her most meditative of voices, "you really need to stop holding this grudge. If your sister doesn't, then you shouldn't, either. He is a man who made a mistake and who has apologized for that mistake. We're all human, and we all have our desires and temptations."

"We're not talking about Dad here," Rory says, gulping her beer deeply now. She's heard this before. She flicks her hand, already tired of the conversation, and heads up to find Hugh.

"Want to explain that?" Nell says after the footsteps up the stairs have subsided.

Not really, Indira thinks, then wonders which she'd rather talk about less: the house or Francis and his complications in that very house. She rises to get more tea while Nell eyes her, waiting, looking just like she used to as a toddler, always waiting for someone—usually Francis—to tell her what to do.

Indira pours the tea slowly into the mug, watching the steam rise, wishing—just like Peter had a few weeks back—that Nell would never have to remember any of it. Would it all just be so much easier if she couldn't remember any of it?

But she knows that isn't possible, so she puts out a morsel, hoping it will satisfy her for the time being.

"That house you remembered," she says, turning back to her daughter. "I wasn't there with you in it. Rory was—just for a week—you were there for the summer. You were thirteen the last time you went."

"The last time? There were others?"

Indira exhales and nods. "A few others. I can't recall exactly—two, three." Four, she thinks, knowing full well how many.

"And that last one? Why was it the last?"

"That was the summer your father left us."

Nell furrows her brow, absorbing this. "Jamie told me that he left in the fall."

"Does it matter?" Indira says.

"Yes," Nell answers. "Yes, of course it matters."

Indira knows that it matters, too, but still she hedges. "It was all very complicated. That time. That time in our marriage. He left and came back, left and came back. Finally, he just left."

Indira doesn't tell her of that last summer, when Nell had been given the choice—stay with Indira and Rory—go to day camp and spend lazy evenings in the pool or chasing butterflies or pressing out lemonade—or join him on the farm down there. Her farm. Heather's farm. And Nell made her choice, clear as glass.

She doesn't share now that Nell didn't even hesitate when Indira sat her down in June with a double scoop of ice cream and explained that Daddy would be moving out, and she longed for her to stay behind, but that he longed for her to go with him. Not even an iota of hesitation. Indira doesn't talk about his demons, how he tried to remove himself when those combustible bouts hit, but that depression was a tricky beast—as were the beasts he fed his depression with whenever it got bad: cocaine, booze, opiates. She doesn't say that she thought the kids were oblivious to it until everything crystallized later, as it regrettably does sometimes with parenting. That the kids, of course, weren't oblivious at all. Nor does she speak of the strange mix of pride and shame she felt—still feels—for enduring it, for sticking with him until he opted to no longer stick with her. That the broken lamps, the shattered plates, the wineglasses against the wall—that maybe part of Indira still thinks that this was simply passion, even though a very needling part of her knows that this is among the worst of the untruths she tells herself. But Francis created his best work at his lowest moments, and the immature seed in Indira still *can't free herself from the satisfaction this knowledge brings her. That she was there for the war, and that from that war came something beautiful.*

"So, anyway, with all due respect, Mom," Nell says, snapping Indira to, "I don't give a shit about your marriage. I want to know about the house."

Indira tries not to look relieved at this, because there are too many things that she doesn't want to explain, to dredge up, things that she thinks neither of the girls can possibly remember—though before her accident, yes, maybe Nell knew. Definitely Nell knew, though the two of them, mother and daughter, had both spent a decade pretending that Nell didn't know anything at all.

Indira sips her tea as calmly as possible, hoping that her quivering fingers don't betray her.

"Yes, the house." *That's an easier question to answer.* "The house is in Charlottesville. Virginia." *She clarifies because she can never remember just what Nell has retained: facts, states, statistics, or if that's all gone, too.*

"Why there?"

Indira clears her throat and wonders how much of a nonanswer she can provide while still providing enough of one. "That's where your father lived. That's where he lived the other half of his life. That's where he lived his life without us."

12

"Eleanor Rigby"
—The Beatles

S o, today, we're going to do some free association," Liv says from the armchair in my living room.

"Okay." I shrug.

"I don't want you to think about anything before you speak. I want to tap directly into that emotional wall, see what comes over it—or under it—before your brain kicks in."

"Emotional wall? Explain the metaphor, please."

"I'm sorry." She waves her fingers, and I notice that her light pink polish is chipped. That if you don't look closely, she's immaculate—sleek pants, fitted cashmere sweater—but she's more than that, too: the chipped polish and the dog hair on her shins make her likable, human. "It's a term I use to describe the dams we build around ourselves. Our safe havens. Though sometimes these havens do more harm than good. Sometimes, they block us from getting to the really good stuff. The real emotional core."

"Gotcha."

"So just . . . the first thing that comes to mind, just spit it out."

"That's generally how I work these days, anyway," I say, and she smiles, so I smile, and I feel the knot in the crevasse of my right shoulder blade untangle ever so slightly. It's been there, wedged in, for the forty-eight hours since we returned from my mother's.

"In some ways, perhaps that's gratifying—the living-in-the-moment experience," Liv says.

"Well, I'm trying to be different, intentionally or not."

"How so?"

"Less buttoned-up, I guess. More . . . open. More fabulous."

"Fabulous?"

"I know it sounds silly. I feel this pressure to take this chance and do things differently. I . . . well, I have this image of myself—like . . . Rachel from *Friends*." I immediately regret saying it, chiding my immaturity. *I want the laugh track!*

"Rachel from *Friends*." She grins. If she's laughing at me, she doesn't give it away. "How so?"

"Just . . . carefree. Without the problems that my dysfunctional family has wrought. Well, really, without all of my problems, period." *The clothes! The apartment! The love life!* I want that, I need that. I promised myself back in the hospital.

"That doesn't seem unreasonable," she says, "though I wonder if you find it strange—that a difficult tragedy might actually be an improvement to where you were before." I eye her. I can see now how she might trick me into thinking she's my friend when, really, there's no doubt that she's my therapist. Dr. Macht picked wisely, it seems, in assigning the two of us to each other.

"It's not the change that is the most difficult," I say. "The change is actually the best part about it. It's the constant surprises. Like these paintings I found of mine. Or the playlist—*The Best of Nell Slattery.*"

"*The Best of Nell Slattery?*"

"My sister made a playlist, filled with all the bands of my old life. I guess I took music pretty seriously for a while there." I reach for the iPod on the coffee table, scrolling through its files. "Did you know that I was named for a Beatles song?" I flick my chin toward her notes. "Is that in there? That my father insisted on naming me for a Beatles song that's about the loneliest woman in the world?"

"No, that's not in my file." Her eyes are kind when she says this.

I answer her by pressing play, the living room echoing with Paul McCartney.

"*Eleanor Rigby died in a church and was buried along with her name. Nobody came.*"

I hit stop. Enough to make my point.

"My sister put the song on there, on the playlist. And I listen to it, and I just think, What sort of parent would do this to a child? Like, what's the weight of that inheritance?" I smile, despite myself. "My mom swears that this isn't entirely true—that yes, he loved the song, but mostly, he loved the name, but still. Even the idea, even the instinct to maybe pay an homage to this woman—Eleanor Rigby—well, no wonder I didn't love my life."

"So you didn't love your life?"

I set the iPod back down. "No, that's probably too strong a statement. I don't even know if I loved my life. But all signs are pointing toward no. Toward the fact that I was moving through it, not"—I pause, considering—"not embracing it, I guess."

"And, to bring this back to the state of constant surprise, this discovery has unsettled you?"

"The discovery about the song that named me or the discovery about my sad-sack life?"

"Whichever." She flips up the palm of her hand.

"Well, mostly it makes me wonder what else he's done. What other surprises there are, that's all. Like, if I can't understand where I came from, how can I anticipate what else there is?"

"The weight of your inheritance," she says, writing something down. "The famous father, the expectations of you."

"All of that," I say, watching her scribble.

"And how does this make you feel? Angry, resentful, sad?"

I suck on the inside of my cheek and stare out the living room window. There's a siren whirling from somewhere down below that I only just now notice. The sky is overcast, ominous-looking, a warning that summer won't last forever, and a helicopter cuts through the clouds, there for a moment, then out of sight.

"I guess mostly it makes me feel lost. Though that's not particularly revelatory. Take someone's memory away and really, what's left? I'm sure there is space for anger or sadness or whatever, but who knows what I really feel?" I inhale. "You know, it's strange for me to be talking to you. Because we're really more or less strangers, although you've read my file. You know a lot about me."

"I know about as much about you as you know about you," she says. "Which is to say, what can be written down in a file."

"Not the important stuff," I offer.

"No, not the important stuff," she agrees.

"I would maybe feel a little bit more at ease if I knew something about you, too."

She smiles. "That's not really how this works, Nell."

"One thing," I say. "One thing so it won't feel so obvious that I'm sitting here talking to a shrink. That I might be talking to an old friend, someone who has known me forever." I gesture to her pants. "You have a dog."

She hesitates for a moment. "I do. A yellow Lab."

"Tell me one thing you like to do with your dog. That's it. One thing so I can picture it and think of you as a person, and that will be that."

She inhales, debating it. "Fine, fair enough. On the weekends, I like to take him early to the dog run, the one over here by the museum. I sit and read the paper, and we don't leave until I've read every last section. We both love it."

I envision it: her in a dog run in my neighborhood that I can't remember but is there all the same. I can see her in a tank top and shorts, folding over her crinkling paper, her dog at her feet. Like any friend of mine might do, not a hospital-issued therapist who is here to help me prove that the wires of my mind haven't permanently misfired.

"Thank you," I offer.

She nods. "So . . . do you want to talk more about your weekend or just go ahead with the free association?"

"How about if I start with a combination of them both, if I throw some free association words out to *you* about the weekend. For starters: *awkward*—that one was from when I opened the door on Peter, naked, just getting out of the shower; *infuriating*—that one was from when I realized that my mom knew about the house I remembered and didn't admit it; *reverential*—that one was from when I sat in the dining room and stared at my father's portrait of my mother that still hangs over the buffet and realized just how goddamn good he was. And that part was also *heartbreaking*—that I can't remember him, and . . . well also, there was *creepy*—that my mom has her own portrait, drawn by her ex-husband, in her dining room."

Liv smiles sympathetically. "And maybe a little indulgent."

"My mother is nothing if not indulgent. Not at all like me."

"Not at all like you?"

"What's the opposite of *indulgent*?" I ask, searching for the word, my eyes floating up to the ceiling.

"*Austere*?" she suggests.

I let it sink in, see if it sticks, resonates.

"You think I was austere?" I say, really more to myself than to her.

"I didn't know you then. I only know what you've told me. You've mentioned this in one of our early sessions—how different you and your mother are."

I shake my head. I don't remember saying this, though I may very well have.

"It's a strange thing to focus on, don't you think?" I ask. "That of the many things I could gravitate toward—of my failing marriage, of my miscarriage, of how lost I feel because of the amnesia—that I told you about my mom?"

"I won't quote Freud here, but a lot of who we are is defined by our families," Liv says. "Until we choose it not to be. *If* we can choose it not to be."

"So you think it's a choice, their influence, the way I intuitively react to my mom?"

"I think that everything that's within our control is a choice," she says.

"And what of the things that aren't?" I don't need to add in: *like my brain, like my memory.* "How do we choose when we can't control them?" I sulk for a moment and stare at the clock on the cable box.

"That's not my question to answer," she says after a beat. "That's yours."

The last word that Liv had asked me to explore in our free association exercise, to throw whatever thoughts against the wall, was *love,* and for reasons that I still can't explain several hours later when Peter has come through the door, I answered, "Beige." And then I started laughing—cackling really, because "beige," in the context of love, makes absolutely no sense. Until Liv let the air hover between us, silence clinging to the walls in the living room, and suddenly it made too much sense, and then gobsmacked me like a tsunami of depression that "beige" is how I would describe love.

Once I started to cry, really, really purging my guts out bawling, Liv interjected, offering me a tissue and asking what about my answer had made me so very sad.

I couldn't finger it exactly, what it was. The Beatles were still stuck in my head, and I couldn't shake those lyrics, the melody running through me like my own blood. So I told her that I had a sense of emotional memory, as silly as that sounded. She assured me that it didn't sound silly at all, but all the same, I felt self-conscious about how pretentious I sounded until she urged me to continue. That she wouldn't judge me. I thought of her in the dog run and that maybe we would have been friends in another life, so I told her.

I told her about how when I think of Peter, and then, when I really focused and thought about my dad, what struck me most was the general ambivalence that rises up within me. That I can't remember a single anecdote about my father, and yet still, in my core, there is this beigeness. *For lack of a better word,* I said, and she nodded because she got it. *Like something has been cut out, like I'm not allowed to feel anything, so I choose to feel indifference.*

"I'd like to feel red," I said, and her forehead wrinkled. "What I mean is, I'd like for my first association with love—whether with my husband or with my father—to be passionate, fulfilled. That should be part of my promise to be this new self."

"Love ebbs and flows," she said. "There can't be hot without being cold."

"I know that. Of course, I mean, I know that."

"But marriages do survive affairs," she counseled. "It's a question of forgiveness from one party and repentance from the other."

"But that's just it," I said. "The forgiveness part is both easy and hard—I can't remember what he did, other than what he's told me. And yet, I also have no history on which to rely to give me the faith to keep going."

"So how about you stop analyzing it?" She shifted in the armchair.

"Stop analyzing it? I'm an analyzer: that's what everyone says. I can't stop. That's what I do."

"But you've admitted you want to *be* different, so why not try a different tactic?"

"Like . . . just . . . what? Living it?"

"Well, why not?" She shrugged, though I knew this wasn't a casual suggestion. "Why not—for one week—just try to live day to day and see how you feel about that, see if it jars anything for you, and see if, for lack of a better word, as you said, it helps distill this beigeness."

"It seems too easy."

"It won't be the cure," she promised. "But for this particular aspect of your recovery, it may be helpful to tap into your emotional well, to see if we can get past the wall of ambivalence."

"Like that might then trigger something else?"

"Like, in the spirit of living in the moment, that might at least give you a different answer when I ask you about love next week."

"Small steps," I said.

"Small steps," she said. "Let's learn to walk before we can run."

13

By Friday, I have lived in enough moments that my brain has almost stopped its endless flurry of splintering feedback. Liv prescribed a sleeping pill that has helped smooth those sharp edges, and for four nights I have fallen deeply into slumber, unable to remember my dreams the next morning. I'm well rested in a way that I haven't been since the accident. I press back my irritation when my mother sends me a yoga mat and homemade gluten-free cookies via FedEx, manage a mostly cheery response when Samantha hesitantly shares the news of a friend's impending baby shower, abort a malignant thought when Peter's text-message alert goes off while he's standing in the kitchen—the idea of *Ginger* fleeing as quickly as it comes. By Labor Day weekend—nearly a month since I've been back home—I'm surprised at how easily I have taken to it: shoving it all aside and simply *being,* how it might actually be a choice: to embrace a different color in the spectrum of the rainbow.

Liv and my doctors at Mount Sinai Hospital have given me the go-ahead for sex.

"Anatomically," Dr. Hewitt, head of my new team tells me, "you're A-OK." Like she's a pediatrician, and I've beaten a case of the sniffles. "If you'd like to engage with your husband, you won't do yourself any harm."

"Psychologically," Liv said before she left on Tuesday, "it might be a positive step in the right direction for you guys to reconnect—though only if that feels right. There's no rush."

Tonight, with the long holiday weekend stretched out in front of us, Peter drops his messenger bag by the door, kisses me hello on the couch, then moves to the fridge where he is, no doubt, cracking open a beer. He has told me that in the Labor Days past, we'd retreat to the Hamptons—a gallery client would almost inevitably offer up a room in their weekend house. But this year, we're trapped, stuck, as I'm not ready for a trek, even if that trek is to a well-appointed six-bedroom with a view of the Atlantic. Peter doesn't seem to mind that we're one of the last few remaining in the city, and tries to make our three-day respite, three days of forced togetherness, sound like fun, an adventure. "We can go through all of our CDs and make, like, our own personal concert," he said last night. "Turn off the lights. Turn the living room into a Pink Floyd laser show." I didn't get the reference but I appreciated the effort all the same.

"Hey, come join me on the couch," I say to Peter tonight,

pausing my iPod, slipping it onto the coffee table. I've been sitting here for I don't know how long, lost in the music, living in the moment. And though this new tactic requires that I just *be*—just inhale and exhale and let life wash over me—the music, well, the music makes me itch, makes me once again try to wind my brain into the past, straddling the space between the past and memory. Discover the moments when I first heard these lyrics, first absorbed the melodies, and thought that something about them might change my life. That when Peter and I trucked out to Jones Beach to see the Counting Crows on a sticky July night for our fourth date, the night, he's told me, he decided he was in love with me because I knew every word to "A Murder of One," well, maybe I was already in love with him back. Maybe I was so heady in love with him that he was all I thought about—work and art and my dad and all the rest of it be damned. It was easy to imagine these things, after all, when who knows if they could have been true.

Peter grabs a handful of Cookie Crisp cereal from the open box on the counter, pops a few pieces in his mouth, and sinks down next to me on the gilded, hideous sofa, still chewing. He plops the beer on top of a magazine on the coffee table.

"What's up?" he says. "How was your day?"

"Boring. Went by too slowly. Went by too quickly. All of the above. Same story, different day. Next week, once I've been cleared to get out of here, really, like get out of here—back to the living world, my first stop is a new wardrobe. Second stop—new couch."

"I already know what's wrong with the couch. But what's wrong with your wardrobe?"

"Too boring, too beige." It's all goddamn neutrals is what it is. Where is the *red* that the fabulous me should be wearing?

"And you'll go back to the gallery soon," he says, eating the last of the cereal. "That will break up the monotony."

I nod, hopeful that he is right, doubtful that he is right all the same. But I resolve to *live in the moment!* and so I smile at him, stifling the urge to say that it's not just the *monotony, idiot! It's the void that is the blank space and the monotony is just the effect, not the cause!* No, I set that aside, and evaporate it from my mind, and there it goes, gone.

Here on the couch, Peter still feels too big for me, just like he did the first time I saw him in the hospital room, but I've grown used to his meatiness now. Now, his oversize hands and biceps shaped like barrels, well, now they're starting to provide comfort, a sign of safety. He's my shelter in my storm, my near-literal shelter. If I tucked myself under him, yes—I've almost convinced myself—I might be able to survive all of this, weather whatever comes next on the horizon.

I take one of his hulklike palms and press it against my cheek. He stops chewing, surprised, assessing the situation, and wipes his free hand, unconsciously, on his jeans.

"Tell me something wonderful about us," I say. I ask this of him every once in a while, use him to recount the past, and then I'll roll it around in my brain and dish it back to Jamie, who sometimes aims the camera on me, sometimes just listens. Sometimes, I'll add in tiny details upon regurgitation, slivers of information that come to me without warning, but most of the time I'm simply an echo of that which was fed to me. Though Rory has changed her mind thanks to the publicity bump for the gallery, my mom remains stalwartly against *American Profiles,* but she doesn't get it—she doesn't see that it's cathartic for me to put this stuff down on record. If I don't, what else might get lost or might evaporate with no warning at all, like it did the first time around? And she doesn't know, of course, that Jamie is going to get me the answers that she refuses to. Besides, I stopped listening to my mom after I found the painting of the white house, the one we both remembered but the one that she pretended not to. *His house for the other half of his life.* Now, I'm living in the moment by ignoring her.

"What do you want to hear?" Peter says, keeping his palm in place. He seems nervous now, senses that this might lead somewhere different than the prior conversations have.

"Anything," I say, then lean back against the velvet and gingerly swing my legs up into his lap. "Tell me anything wonderful about who we used to be."

He hesitates, waiting to home in on the perfect answer to my loaded invitation.

"Two months after we started dating, we—on a whim—flew to Paris for the weekend," he says, his face morphing into a smile. "I'd never been. You insisted on taking me, showing me the town."

"Why haven't you told me this before?" I ask, then close my eyes to see if I could recall any of it. The Eiffel Tower, the Seine, the sidewalk cafés with their fresh brie and their gluttonous, lingering lunches.

"To be honest, I just remembered. It was early on, and"—he shrugs—"I don't know. You forget things." I nod because you sure as hell do, and he continues.

"Anyway, I was nervous to fly there—there was a terrorism scare going on, so we splurged and went first class. Oh my god, we drank so much wine on the plane—and got these little toiletry sets that I think might still be stuffed in the bathroom cabinet—and by the time we got there, we were both hungover. But happy and on a high while hungover all the same—the good sort of drunk, you know? So we go there, and you insisted on blowing our budget by staying at the George V."

"What's the George V?"

"The nicest hotel in the city—like, super, super nice."

"How'd we afford that?"

"Er, you have money. Your mom didn't tell you this? I told her to tell you."

I shake my head no. God knows what else my mom hasn't told me.

"Well, yeah, you have a trust your dad set up for you before he, um, left. You never, *ever* touch it—the only exception was when you started the gallery. But for this trip, you said it was worth it. That you never do anything for yourself, and you wanted to go all out." He shrugs. "You were so excited about it that I wasn't going to stop you. If I'd been paying, we would have been at some fifty-buck-a-night fleabag, so . . . yeah."

"So this place was decadent?" I try to picture it: maid service, six-hundred-thread-count sheets, late-night deliveries of chocolates and champagne. The new me very much approves.

"For some perspective, we were on the same floor as Hugh Grant." He laughs, so I do, too. We'd watched *Notting Hill* last weekend, so I at least get the reference. "You kept trying to pretend that you weren't stalking him, but you were totally stalking him, until we were in the same elevator with him, and you finally introduced yourself, and he was very polite and kind considering that we could see the hives that had broken out on your neck from nerves."

"I don't believe you," I say, though I'm smiling and I do kind of believe him.

"Don't believe it all you want," he says. "My hand is to God."

"I don't seem like the freak-out-upon-celebrity-sighting type."

"You were a big *Four Weddings and a Funeral* fan."

"I'll have to watch it," I say, distracted from the story for a moment, remembering just how little I indeed remember. "Okay, keep going."

"So we spent all three days trekking from one museum to the next—the Louvre, the D'Orsay, the Orange Museum."

"The Orange Museum?"

"That's what I called it—I don't speak French, so I did the best I could." He laughs. "And you just couldn't get enough of the city— the art, the architecture. And that's when you told me that you used to paint but that you stopped when you were thirteen, and when I asked if you'd ever start again, and, you said, 'Never.' That it was really your dad's thing anyway. And you seemed so vulnerable and regretful over it, that I didn't say another word." He stops now and blinks his lashes too quickly, and I can tell, because he's been an emotional Ping-Pong ball since the second I woke up from my coma, that he's teetering too close to the line again.

"Please don't cry," I say, hoping this is enough to stop him. "Please, just tell me more about Paris. It sounds like heaven."

"Yes, okay." I see him fighting against himself. "I'm sorry. Jesus, I'm such a fucking pansy these days."

"It's fine." *It's not fine! This is not living in the moment!*

"I just . . . oh god, this sounds so lame, but what the hell. It's just that Paris was when I decided that I had to marry you, that you looked so goddamn sad over your confession, and well, your dad, and I just wanted to protect you from everything that had already happened. Even though I don't think I even knew the bulk of what had happened, still, that's what I wanted. We were standing in Notre Dame, staring up at the stained-glass windows, and I know it sounds cheesy, like one of those asinine commercials that I'd score, but I looked at you, and the light was bouncing every which way, and I just thought: This is it. She is it. I'm with her until the day I die."

"Until you weren't," I say, and instantly regret it. Because now we are officially *not* living in the moment. Now we are dragging the whole mess of our shit into this moment with us.

"Until I wasn't," he concedes. "Like there are any other ways that I can say I'm sorry for that. If there were, I'd say them, too."

"No, don't. I'm sorry. I'm the one who shouldn't have said that. I was out of bounds."

I fall silent, and since there's nothing more to say about that, and the Paris story has run out of steam, I lean over and kiss him. Not because it's my first instinct but because maybe my doctors and therapists and—god help me—my mother, who e-mailed me three days ago to urge me to *share my body again with my husband,* are right: maybe it's time to reconnect, and the only way to find out is to jump in feet first. So I jump; I leap before I look, run before

I can walk, as Liv might say, though she's already implored me not to.

I kiss him hard, and he kisses me back, then pushes me away. I can still taste the Cookie Crisp and the Molson on his tongue.

"Are you sure?" he asks. "Are we past the other stuff? I mean, is it in the past?"

Everything is in the past! Everything and nothing and god knows what else all at once! I want to scream.

"I am. We should be. It is," I answer, though what I should really say is that *I might be, we'll try, who knows?* But I am wearing my guts on my sleeve now, and I can't stop the momentum of where Peter and I need to go. My mom was right. *It's only sex, dear!* she'd said in her e-mail, to which I hadn't replied.

He leans over and kisses me again slowly, softly, almost barely there, and I wonder if I'm kissing the way that I've always kissed, and if he's doing the same.

"I can't believe you initiated," he murmurs. "You never used to." He kisses me more forcefully now, and I try to keep up, but he's almost frantic, bearing down too hard. My lips feel puffy, my face braised from his two-day-old stubble.

"Slow down," I remind him. "Slow down or you'll hurt me."

He stops and checks himself, then smiles a smile both sad and joyful.

He starts to unbutton my top. "Never."

Our doorman buzzes two hours later. "Sending up your sister," he says, then clicks good-bye.

Peter is asleep in the bedroom and has been for the duration of our post-sex window. Afterward, he oohed and aahed over what we had managed to do to each other—despite my formerly fractured body, despite my formerly (and possibly still current) fractured trust in him, despite, well, *everything.* But afterward, I could tell it was a losing battle with his sinking eyelids, and soon enough, his breath grew patterned and his chest rose and fell, and I wobbled back to the couch and flipped on the TV. The sex itself was good, though again: no reference point. But it seemed good enough. I might not have remembered having slept with him before, but well, I seemed to remember *how* to sleep with him at least, and we laughed—both of us relieved—that I hadn't forgotten *everything.*

"What's with the bedhead?" Rory says as way of greeting when I swing open the door, and then lock it behind her. I shrug and look at the floor. "Oh no, you didn't!" she says.

"He's my husband. It's not like there's anything wrong with it!"

"I'm just . . . surprised. Knowing what you now know. I wouldn't have pegged you for this type of reaction." She stares at me for a bit, chewing on a thought she opts not to share. "You really are more like Mom than I realized." She steps into the kitchen and emerges with a Diet Coke.

"I wouldn't say that. Why would you say that? Ugh, god, please don't say that."

"Oh, she and Dad patched things up more times than I can remember. You got that gene, I guess, though I wouldn't have pegged you for it before all of this. You know your nickname in high school was Ice Queen."

"That's original," I say.

"Well, don't blame me," she answers. "I didn't give it to you. It started when you slipped on a patch of ice your sophomore year and broke your wrist. You went to a party anyway, ignoring the pain, until your arm swelled up like an elephant limb, and Aaron Sacks, the senior who had invited you there, drove you to the ER. Mom was stuck at home with me, and Aaron stayed with you all night, through the X-rays, the cast, all of that, and then—the way you told it from the way he told it—you refused to kiss him good night. The Ice Queen was born."

"I had standards." The new me tries not to betray her disappointment in the old me, that I couldn't have made out with him just a little. Just a fraction of a French kiss! Would that have killed the old me?

"Then explain this," she says, gesturing toward the bedroom. She pales. "Shit, that was too mean. No, you did have standards . . . I just . . . well, like I said, you were different before. This isn't what I was expecting, that's all. I guess I just didn't get the same gene."

The soda hisses as she opens it, and then, out of nowhere, she drops onto a dining chair, emitting some sort of animal sob, her shoulders heaving and shaking. It takes me a moment to realize that she's crying.

"Jesus, Rory, what? What's wrong? Is it Peter and me?"

She looks up at me, batting her hands in front of her face, her mascara gruesome under her eyes, her nose already pink and running amok.

"It's Hugh. We broke up."

"What? Why?" I help her—we help each other really—to the

couch. That goddamn unsightly disgusting gold couch. Despite my mess of a sister in front of me, I resolve to get to a furniture store like, this week. Like, yesterday. I cannot take another second of this monstrosity in my home. My former me's home.

"Oh, I don't know! No, I do know, but I don't really know!" She moans. "We've been fighting . . . I wanted to get married, he wasn't ready . . . I gave him . . . oh shit, Nell, I gave him an ultimatum. I mean, it's not like I'm getting any goddamn younger here! It's not like my ovaries are going to wait around forever!"

"You're only twenty-seven, Rory," I say kindly, trying to erase a mental image of my own ovaries, bruised, marred, expunged. I live in the moment and instead focus on the couch. Maybe I'll get something in a burnished red or a surprising shade of sea blue.

"Well, it's too late now!" She stands and starts pacing frantically, and I pull myself back to her, sensing her desperation. "It's too fucking late now! I gave him a time frame, and he blew past it, and now it's just too little, too late! I screamed at him, and he screamed at me, and we said things we shouldn't have said—he actually called me a demanding bitch and I might have called him a noncommittal prick, and now it's just all one giant effing mess!" She flings her hands in the air for extra drama and then flops back on the couch.

"People say things they shouldn't all the time," I say. "That's the easy fix, that's why we have apologies."

"No, it's more than that," she says quietly, her voice cracking. "I see how precious life can be. I see you, and that you almost died, and I see what's been taken away from you, and I just can't settle for his noncommittalness for one more second."

"Noncommittalness?"

"I probably just made that word up." She snorts, half grief, half gallows humor. "But like I said, I think I just don't have that gene . . . to settle." She shakes her head. "Not that you're settling. Jesus. I'm sorry. You know what I mean."

I don't, but it seems easier to ignore the comment than make something more of it than it needs to be. Rory doesn't know crap about forgiveness and isolation and despair, so why even bother?

"Things seemed perfect with you two last weekend."

"Don't judge what you can't see. Closed doors and all of that. If you could remember Mom and Dad, you'd know as much." She hesitates. "Actually, on second thought, maybe you wouldn't."

"Oh, Ror, you'll figure it out." I pull her head onto my shoulder and let her rest there, until the phone rings, jolting us both.

The nerves snap in my hip from moving too quickly and my earlier romp with Peter, a quick reminder that I'm not what I used to be.

"Erg, hello?" I manage when I pick up the phone from the pass-through on the third ring.

"I'm a block away," Anderson says. "I'm coming up."

I glance at Rory, who has flopped back on the couch, her arms thrust over her face.

"Now's not a good time."

"For me either," he says, and it's only then that I detect his drunkenness, his ever-so-slight slurring of words. *Formeeither.*

"And, you are *not* supposed to be drinking, mixing your meds!"

"Tell me about it, Mom," he says. "I'll be there in two." The line goes dead.

"I take it that wasn't my boyfriend calling to beg for my forgiveness?" Rory says.

Before I can answer, Peter pokes his head out of the bedroom door.

"Hey," he says sleepily, "what's with the commotion?"

"What's not with the commotion?" Rory says. "Hugh dumped me, Anderson is drunk, and you are very lucky to have gotten laid."

His eyes bulge, and I shrug, and we both realize there's no getting around it, so what the hell anyway. He moseys in and sits in the armchair opposite the sofa. He and Rory size each other up warily. The phone clangs again with my doorman's announcement of Anderson's arrival.

Anderson smells of bourbon when I kiss him hello, his cheeks pocked with sweat from the Labor Day heat wave.

"The paps followed me here," he says. "No one leave for a while. They're waiting outside." For a second, I remember how different we are, how far apart our worlds were before they literally collided.

"As if anyone here is in any condition to go anywhere," Rory mutters. "Besides, shouldn't you be in Saint Barts or the Hamptons, somewhere fancy, other than here?"

"I can't take the travel right now," he says from the kitchen. He leans into the sink and douses his face with water, staining the color of his faded green hipster tee.

"What distillery did you fall into?" I ask.

"Don't judge," he answers, then straightens himself and pours a glass of water.

"It's hard not to," I answer.

"Judging is her specialty," Rory says, still prostrate on the sofa, "at least when she wants it to be." Peter raises his eyebrows and washes his hands over his face.

"Shut up, Rory," I say. And just like that, we've unraveled.

She glances unobtrusively at Peter, then to me.

"You're right," she says, genuinely contrite. "That wasn't fair. Ignore me. I'm just a mess right now."

"That's beautiful," Anderson interjects.

"Oh, you shut up, too, and cut the sarcasm," I snap, startled at how quickly I can turn, how quickly my flip can switch. *I'm supposed to be living in the moment! What is wrong with all of you that you're all goddamn ruining it?*

"I wasn't being sarcastic—I was talking about the painting." He gestures to the sunburst—or whatever it's intended to be—over the mantel.

"It's my dad's," Rory and I say in unison.

"Jinx," she says, but no one has the energy to laugh.

I turn toward Anderson. "Oh, well, I'm sorry."

"Don't be." He shrugs.

I sink next to him on the couch and assess the sad lot of our situations. Eventually, Anderson starts breathing deeply next to me, and Peter retreats uninvited to the bedroom, and Rory, too, stretches out in the armchair, her feet propped up on the ottoman. I pull a blanket over Anderson, then her, and then lean back against the pass-through, staring at my father's brilliance, how I'd kept this magnificent, unavoidable reminder of him in my house, my home, the one place I could have exorcised him entirely. I stare at the reds and the golds and the biting black shards and absorb this contradiction, this realization that despite the many ways that my father scarred me, I never fully let myself heal.

What had Liv said? That everything within our control is a choice. I close my eyes and wonder which feels farther away: the time when I once had control or the time when I had a choice in the matter anyway.

14

Rory and I converge at the gallery on Monday morning, with a plan to go couch shopping afterward—my attempt to regain control, to have a choice in the matter over my old life, over my new life. Anderson, because he is bored and can't stand to be alone with everyone gone for the holiday weekend, joins us. "Besides," he said over the phone, "I'll sweet-talk the staff at Crate and Barrel and get you a discount. They do that for actors, you know." I sighed and wondered how someone could be both amiable and insufferable at the same time.

I've tried to go without sleeping pills for the weekend, anxious of becoming dependent, so rest has come in fits and starts, and last night was no exception: me, staring at my alarm clock at 2:32 a.m., and now my eyes feel like marshmallows. Too puffy to open properly. Anderson hands me an extra venti latte he thought to pick up for me.

"Ah, you read my mind," I say, feeling momentarily guilty for faulting his earlier display of narcissism.

He guzzles his own cup. "Insomnia. It's robbing us of our last shred of dignity. You look like a train wreck, I feel like a train wreck." But he smiles as he says this. We both know we could have lost much more by now.

"I could use your help over here," Rory says, her arms stacked with binders and free-floating papers.

Rory is doing no better than either of us, having spent the duration of the weekend fused to my couch or on the cusp of my bed or curled up against the radiator, hashing and rehashing her implosion with Hugh. I listened, I listened some more, and though I wanted to seize her by the shoulders and yell, *"Don't you get it, this isn't the end of the world!"* I instead brewed coffee and warmed up cold leftovers and tried to appease her when I could. Making that choice that Liv had imparted: choosing to be there for her, asserting control when I could. This, I could do.

Peter grew either bored or annoyed by Saturday evening, so offered a quick good-bye and headed out to . . . I don't even know where. Thinking about it now in the gallery, I'm not sure I even asked, and I'm not sure that he told me when I woke up on Sunday morning and found him asleep, still clothed and smelling like stale cigarettes, next to me. I trusted him. I had to trust him even if I didn't trust him. This was the bridge that we had to cross to get past beige.

Rory thuds the binders down on the desk, atop the desk calendar with its reminders of my obstetrician appointments, while Anderson slides up the spare office chair, the wheels squeaking on the tile floor. He nudges me into it.

"So this is what you did," she says, gesturing to the binders. "These are your files, how you kept everything in order."

"I was the paper pusher." *Oh god, was I really a paper pusher? Where is the sex? The glamour? The tiny smidge of excitement that I actually enjoyed any aspect of this job?*

"But a good paper pusher at that." Rory opens the top spiral. "Clients, all alphabetized—their last purchases, their likes and dislikes, their children's names, their jobs. It's all in here."

I flip through a few pages, amazed at how much about a person can be compartmentalized onto a single page. Just like my file, the one that tells Liv everything she needs to know about me. *Not everything,* I remind myself. *Not even close to everything.* I turn to the last page, then snap the cover closed, already uninterested. I sink back into the chair, scanning the room, my eyes surfing to the bookshelves against the wall. More binders. Only these are marked FRANCIS SLATTERY.

"Are those Dad's?" I flick my chin toward them.

Rory spins quickly, her fingers finding their way to her neck.

"What?" She laughs in a pitch too high to sound natural. "Oh, yes, *those.* Um, yes, those are Dad's."

"Of his work?"

She blinks an acknowledgment.

"Didn't Jamie ask you for these weeks ago? Back when he was researching?" I say. *Operation Free Nell Slattery. Yes, let's get back to that while we're thinking of it.*

She hesitates, wondering if she can slip through with the lie. "Okay, yes, he did. I'm sorry," she says, more irritated than sorry. "I just didn't want to drag all of this stuff back up again. And besides, I promised Mom."

You promised Mom? I start to say, until I think of my choice and my control over that choice, and I let it be. *Of course she promised Mom. Mom, who was asserting her own control over things, too.*

Anderson ignores us both, strides to the shelves, and pulls down the notebooks. He *thunks* one in front of me and it flops open, concealing the desk calendar entirely. I've been trying to pretend that it wasn't there, avoid eye contact like an ex-boyfriend at a cocktail party. *Nine-week doctor's appointment.* No, no, let's not think of such things right now. I try to refocus instead on OFNS, at what I might unearth.

"So what are we looking at here?" he says, peering more closely at the pages.

"Um, this one is of his stuff from the late eighties." Rory runs her finger over a laminated sheet. "Here, look, this one is of Mom. A sketch of that portrait in Mom's dining room," she says to me.

"Uh-uh," I manage, gazing at the image but not really focused. Truth be told, even with the calendar out of sight, I'm distracted— that ex-boyfriend is hovering by the bar, and I'm spending more energy avoiding him than enjoying the party. *Was I going to tell Peter? Was I going to keep it?* These are the questions, in the whole lot of this mess, that no one else can answer for me.

"She looks young here," Anderson says, "happy."

"She was—at least the former. The latter was always more complicated with her. With them," Rory offers, then shakes her head almost unconsciously. "Anyhoo, what's that saying? The apple doesn't fall far from the tree and all that."

Freud, I think, remembering Liv. How much are we defined by our parents? How much is it possible to break free of that?

"Rory, can I ask you something?" I can't stop thinking about that damn calendar, about that nine-week appointment. It's a pox on me, a blunt-force trauma. *What was I going to do?* "I know that you told me back in the hospital that you didn't know that I was pregnant . . . but . . . you didn't know anything? There were no signs? No indications about . . . my plans?"

Both of their faces wash with alarm, and Anderson reaches for my shoulder as if to steady me, even though I'm seated.

"You don't have to be overly concerned," I say. "I just, well, I'm just wondering."

"No, nothing," Rory says, her face drooping. "I *wish* I'd known. I never would have sent you out to San Francisco."

"Eight weeks pregnant didn't make me an invalid," I offer. "I would have gone anyway." I think about it. "Actually, I did go anyway."

"You told *me,*" Anderson offers.

He leans against the desk in his brown cords and graphic tee like this is the most natural thing in the world. Like he's delivering a line in one of his movies that will shift the tone of the scene entirely. And Rory and I, rightly so, play out the scene perfectly: double takes, popped eyes, then brows appropriately furrowed as if on cue.

"I did?" I say, just as Rory says, "She did?" and I can't tell if she's jealous or astonished. "I barely knew you."

"Like I told you back in the hospital, we talked most of the flight. I tried to get you a vodka tonic, and that's when you told me." He drifts off, his face scrunching. "I think, honestly, you didn't know what you were going to do. Or at least you didn't offer me specifics. Which, I know, isn't helpful, doesn't really answer questions."

"Did I sound excited about it?" I try to envision it, the idea of becoming a mother, even if it meant being a single mother. Yes, maybe.

"You know, I didn't press it. I was half-drunk, and, well, it didn't seem like the right thing to discuss with a stranger on a plane."

"Or maybe it's the perfect thing to discuss with a stranger on the plane. Maybe that's why I told you in the first place."

"Anyway," Rory says, too sharply, "do you want to look through these or not?" She grabs for her phone and checks her messages once again. From her expression, clearly, still nothing from Hugh.

"Jesus Christ, take it down a notch," I say, then assess her. "Are you okay? I mean, beyond . . . that?" I gesture to her phone.

"Okay, fine! Here's the truth: you didn't tell me you were pregnant because we weren't speaking." She sighs, runs her fingers through her greasy red hair, and sits atop the desk next to Anderson, a defeat. "I mean, we hadn't spoken for a week or so before you left. I should have called you and made up. And of course if I *knew* that you were pregnant or *knew* that you were going to nearly die in a plane crash, *of course* I would have called you and made up. But . . ."

"But what?" I say.

"But, well, you were just so *mean* during that last fight. You were mean and said terrible things, and to be fair, I said terrible things of my own, and I just couldn't forgive you like that, like snapping my fingers."

I exhale, closing my eyes, wishing it all didn't have to be, what? So difficult? Yes, why does it all have to be so difficult? So I make the choice—as Liv would say—to make it easier.

"I know that I should ask what I said, what we were fighting about, but . . . is it okay if I don't?" I look up at my little sister, and she's brokenhearted enough.

She angles herself and kisses the top of my head.

"It's more than okay if we don't." Her voice catches. "I'm sorry that I didn't know that you were pregnant. That you didn't tell me even before we weren't speaking. I should have, you should have. We should have made that space for each other. Sisters, you know? Always, before everything else."

I reach up and run my hands over her pale cheeks. "Sisters. Always. Before everything else. I know that I can't remember it, but I wish I'd told you, too."

The first of the *American Profiles* installments airs two and a half weeks later at nine o'clock. This one, Jamie explained when he called from his new office at the studio, will be mostly background—reacquainting viewers with who I was before the crash, piquing their interest so that they sign up for the months-long journey that we're asking them to take with us. We hadn't shot much new footage as a consequence, which was perfectly fine with me. What I was interested in—and I'd made this much clear to him—was unraveling my story, uncovering the pieces like an archaeologist who may have to brave the elements to dig up what really matters. Google had filled in enough of the obvious stuff: about the rise of my father into the art community, and later, about his spiral into the demons that he never quite tamed. But what I needed now were the intangibles, the things that Google—and Liv's file—can't quantify. *Who I was in the in-between spaces.*

We've all huddled at our apartment for the airing. I call it the housewarming party for my new couch, the one I'd bought Labor Day Monday, and had paid the premium for rush delivery a few days later. It is oversize and angular, and yes, per my cliché, it is red—too modern, too large for the space, but damn if I don't love it anyway. *It's something,* I told Peter when he got home and eyed it and gaped, but smartly said nothing more. *It's something for my new start.* So he nodded and kissed me hello, and then got himself a beer and sat down to break it in. The Salvation Army showed up and whisked the other one away, and I hoped, as I watched them stuff it out my front door, that maybe this could be symbolic: that they could truly usher out the old, wave in the new. I didn't have too much else to hope for, so this seemed reasonable.

Tonight, for my couch's housewarming party, Anderson shows up with an orchid, my mother and Tate arrive with brownies, Rory totes in three overflowing bags from her favorite Vietnamese restaurant, and Jamie comes strictly with sweaty palms.

Rory pops open the take-out containers, spreading them on the pass-through counter, and the apartment is filled with the tinkling of plates, the uncorking of wine bottles, the spread of conversation. Peter turns the TV on mute as we wait for the nine o'clock hour to draw near, and as I sink into my new lipstick-hued couch, I'm struck with the sense that despite everything, I'm almost sort of lucky. That maybe it's what my mother has opined: that if I didn't know better, I'm happy. Maybe *this* is living in the moment, the absorbing of the smaller joys that can then snowball into bigger ones. Because I *am* feeling grateful: For Jamie, who is helping me weave the mystery of my life back together. For my sister, who feels like my trusted ally, even if we weren't always so. For Anderson, who has his own set of issues to be sure—his inability to be alone, too much Hollywood speak, his love of all things alcoholic, but who isn't letting that detract from his loyalty toward my own set of issues. And even for Peter, who has proven he's willing to take whatever leaps I ask of him, even if I shouldn't have had to ask for those leaps in the first place. Even, god help me, for my mother and Tate, both of whom instinctively irritate me like sandpaper, but since I am learning to rewire those instincts—*choose it, control it!*—even, yes, for them.

Although Anderson has opted out of the segment, Jamie has found a way to weave him back in. He's there, in the background story, and I glance over to him, wondering if he's annoyed, but he catches my eye and bounces his shoulders, an acknowledgment that maybe we're in each other's background stories for life now, and that's that. They highlight various scenes from his movies, most of which I haven't seen, a few of which are vaguely familiar in a generic sort of way.

"Oh my god," Rory laughs, and it's good to hear her laugh. "I didn't realize you were in *Battleship Wars!*"

"It's a high point on my résumé," he shoots back, smiling.

"But Spielberg is calling now," I say.

As if on cue, the phone starts ringing, and Anderson catches my eye and winks.

"That must be him."

"Just leave it," I say to Peter, who has moved to pick it up. "Whoever it is, we can call back when this is over." The phone still rings often these days, even six weeks since I've been home—the media, the reporters—mostly at the gallery, but still, from time to time here, too.

Just before the commercial, Jamie reemerges on-screen, teasing my upcoming segment, his face stoic, his voice infused with just the right intonation of gravitas that the situation calls for.

"You're going to be a star someday," I say to him.

"You think?" he says, though I can tell he's pleased, like the thought itself is the greatest thing he can dream of.

The phone is now a constant bleat in the background: buzzing steadily at patterned intervals. I hear the machine click on and on and on—a few journalists calling for personal quotes, but mostly friends emerging from my past to wish me well. Jamie is fielding his texts, as are both Anderson and Peter, and I realize that though my life is anonymous to my own brain, I've never been more of an open book: the world is out there, gazing in, begging to sift through my open pores and see my guts.

A laundry detergent commercial wraps up the advertisements, and Peter pipes up to say, "Oh, my office wrote that one. Not bad, right?" He hums the melody, and my mom and Tate bob their heads in approval. Rory shoots me a look as if she has sucked on a rotten lime, and I know what she's thinking—*Ginger*—even though I am doing my best *not* to think of it. Because it is over, and your brain can tuck even the most serious of transgressions away if it wants to. I give her a look in return—*just shut up! Let it go!* And she rolls her eyes and does.

And then, the show is back and there I am. The makeup artist has bathed me in blush and dark eyeliner, and for a beat I don't recognize myself. Then I squint and shift closer and yes, there I am. Me. Different. Tweaked. Sexier? Yes, maybe sexier. Like if I actually want to pull off this new fabulous me, with my weight loss and my defined cheekbones and now perfectly tweezed eyebrows, I might just be a knockout, a title usually reserved for Rory. Peter's jaw unhinges and he glances toward me and winks.

"Gorgeous!" he says, totally oblivious to the undercurrent— *Ginger!*—that pulsed between Rory and me just seconds before.

"Every once in a while, miracles do happen," I say.

"You really do look good," Anderson says, and everyone murmurs their approval.

"Survive a plane crash, get a makeover. Seems like a fair trade," I say.

Jamie and I chat about the usual things: what I remember (a short segment), what I don't, what life has been like upon return. I share the few memories I've had—describing the house in Virginia and that summer evening in such acute detail that even my family sits rapt, my mother pushing the tears from her cheeks, Tate massaging her neck. I talk about the pregnancy, what I lost, though I don't share the great unknown question—*What was I going to do?*—and I try to watch Peter without letting him know that I'm watching, to see what he's thinking, how he reacts, what that might have meant for the future, as it was back then. Through it all, I don't cry, though I feared that I would. I speak strongly and valiantly, and toward the end, when Jamie asks, "So why do you think you survived?" I offer a shrug of my shoulders, a limp shaking of my head, and have no answers. Only that I am choosing to move forward each day, that I am trying to make this second chance worthwhile. *That's all I can do,* I tell him, and I hope that Liv is watching because I think she'd think my answer was the right one.

The phone is ringing and ringing, and Jamie goes to the tape, as images of my childhood—photos from junior high and tennis matches and that honeymoon in the Caribbean—are blended together as a montage of my life.

Finally, Peter throws an arm toward the cordless and says, "Can we please get that now? It's giving me a headache."

I push myself up from the couch and grab the phone from the base in the kitchen. The machine has twelve messages. I click the off button and rub my temples.

"Hello?" I say into the receiver.

"Nell?" says the voice. "I'm sorry to disturb you. It's Jasper. Jasper Aarons. We met at your gallery. I'm the old friend of your father's."

"Oh yes, of course," I say, already regretting answering. *Yes, I know that you're sorry for my losses and you're thrilled that I'm making a recovery!* All of these messages, the reporters aside, will echo much the same sentiments.

"Well, I just saw your *American Profiles* segment"—he clears his throat—"and I have something that I think you should see. I'd forgotten about it, to be honest, until tonight."

"What? A map to my dad's whereabouts?" I ask, trying to be funny but failing on every level.

"Not exactly," he answers. "Look, I'll take the train into the city tomorrow. Meet me for coffee. I'll explain then."

15

J asper Aarons meets me at a nondescript Starbucks two blocks from our building the next morning at ten. Peter has gone in to work, and as I shuffle down the sidewalk, my ribs still occasionally sore, it occurs to me that this is the first time I've gone anywhere on my own since I've been home. Like I'm a child who still needs a babysitter, a dog who needs its owner to be walked.

Outside, with Labor Day having come and gone, summer is fighting a dying battle against the fall air. The leaves are hanging perilously on the trees, knowing full well they're going to make the plunge, clinging on as if they stand a chance not to. The garbage smell that has wafted around us for the better part of August is dissipating, ushered out with the humidity, and in its place a briskness is filtering in, like something you'd smell from a bottle of Tide. All around me, New Yorkers hustle to their daily lives, oblivious to those faltering leaves, to the scent of autumn in the air, to the winds that are blowing in from the north that are threatening to change everything, even if for today they will not.

More than a few people do a double take when they pass me on the sidewalk: a cute twenty-something hipster nodding and smiling, a harried mom overly apologetic—*Oh my god, I am so, so sooooo sorry!*—when her toddler knocks into my right leg. I tug my hoodie tighter around my neck, protecting my last vestiges of anonymity, and sidle inside the Starbucks, the aroma of burned coffee beans overtaking me.

He is there before me, reading the Arts section of the *New York Times,* which seems entirely stereotypical and yet entirely logical at the same time. I hesitate before moving closer, wondering whether or not I'm ready. To trust him. To believe him. And even with these things, whether or not I want to hear what he says in the first place.

Yesterday, in our session, Liv and I continued with our free-association exercise. We'd been discussing Peter, and the progress he and I had made, and then she asked me to explore the word *trust,* to spit out my first instinct.

"Ask again later," I said in reply.

" 'Ask again later' is your first instinct?" she said. "Or 'ask again later' because you're being cynical and thus your first instinct about trust is actually cynicism."

"Both," I said.

"There's a reason they call it blind trust," she said.

I gazed at her and thought not of Peter but instead of my mom, and how even though she knew I needed her to support my memory of that house in Virginia, she didn't: she instead hedged her bets and protected her own self-interest until it became clear that the ruse was up.

"I think I'm impaired enough," I said. "Do I need to add blindness to my list, too? People are who they are. Nothing changes."

She half-smiled, her eyes crinkling into fans. "People can surprise you."

"Well, you got that right."

"No, you're intentionally misinterpreting me." She spun her hair into a bun. "You're right: mostly, people are who they are. But if you accept this about them, you can move forward and build from there—*then,* they can surprise you. People do evolve, people do grow. Some of us may not. But some of us may. Maybe you and Peter can change together, can learn to trust again together."

Today, I watch Jasper Aarons studying the Arts section with a certain air of what?: Royalty? Snobbery? Je ne sais quoi? And I am more certain than ever that people are who they are—that I can sum him up in this snapshot of a moment.

Jasper spies me over the edge of his headline, crumples the paper onto the ground in a haphazard, almost violent way— surprising me, proving that, in fact, maybe I can't read everything about him in this one moment—and flags me over. He moves back the free chair at our table, and then, once I've eased in and gotten comfortable, inches a latte and a scone toward me.

"I hope you don't mind," he says. "I took the liberty of getting you something."

"Not at all." I flake the crust off the top of the scone and slide it into my mouth, the butter, the currants, the sugar colliding atop my tongue.

"I'm sure you're curious why I called, why the urgency," he says.

"I guess," I say. I'm trying to study him, employ what Liv would call heightening my senses, homing in on clues other than the obvious.

"Well, at the behest of my producer friend, I watched your *American Profiles* interview, and when they showed the retrospective of some of Francis's work, I remembered something." He shakes his head. "Your dad, he left me something for you, and Jesus, I have been a lousy friend—a gigantic screwup who royally let him down by not watching out for you in the way that I promised—but honestly, I sincerely forgot about this." He reaches into his bag, strung across the back of his chair, and pulls out a notebook, which he nudges toward me. "Your dad wanted you to have this. He told me before he, well, before he left, that when you were old enough, you were to have it." His hand flits. "Like I said, time got the best of me."

"What did you spend all those years doing?" I ask, like that has anything to do with anything. But I'm looking closer, picking things apart the way a medical examiner might, poring over the corpses left behind in my old life.

"Painting. Marriage. Rehab. Divorce. Repeat. Occasionally repeat again," he says, smiling but not smiling all the same.

"I'm sorry to hear that. Demons can be a hard thing."

"Your dad knew that better than anyone."

"I'm sorry?"

"No, it's nothing," he says. "Only that we artists are tortured souls, so to speak. Painting tells our story, attempts to exorcise those demons. Your dad did it better than any of us."

"Exorcised his demons?"

"No," he laughs softly. "I meant paint, but I guess you could take it any way you wanted to."

"My mom's already told me that they had their share of problems," I say. "But we all have our baggage." *A husband who cheated, a brain that's gone haywire. Yes, I have a few boatloads of my own.* I open the front cover of the notebook. "What's in here? Sketches?"

"The best I can tell. To be honest, I knew he wanted me to get that to you, so I set it aside and didn't really examine it too, too much, and then, well, I fell down the rabbit hole, and I never took the time to sort through it. Knew it was private."

"It's his diary?"

"Not really a diary, no. It's sketches, but maybe also a diary, if that makes sense. I remember—back when you were younger—you were quite a little painter yourself, so maybe it will make sense. Your dad thought you were quite good."

"Not as good as he was. Besides, if left to my own devices, I'd probably have chosen music."

"Easy to say that now, with hindsight," he says.

I don't correct him to say that, in fact, I have no hindsight at all.

He stops for a beat, watching the barista make change behind the counter. "You know, your dad wasn't always the best communicator. Get a little vodka in him, and then, yes, he could pour his fucking heart out, but mostly, he spoke via his work. That's what made him so damn magnificent."

"So this is him speaking to me?" I gesture toward the notebook, with its faded gray cover, its fraying corners, its yellowed sheets. I chew on the scone and mull it over.

"Look, Nell, you asked on the phone if I had a map. Well, this is him giving you one—of where he's been, what he wanted for you," he says, his green eyes meeting mine. I'm once again reminded—thrown back to that time when he and my dad must have inhaled this whole goddamn town. Jesus, they must have been glorious, lighting it on fire.

"And in all these years, you never heard from him? You were his best friend."

"And you were his daughter." He sips from his cup, which I'm sure is black, no sugar, no milk. "And yet, you didn't hear anything from him, either." He swallows and sighs, and now he looks so very tired, rumpled, like a messy-haired shar-pei. "Look, I wish that things had been done differently. God knows that I have my own list of regrets, and yes, I wish I'd stopped him or at least forced him to reconsider, but your dad was who he was. Once you're in that deep to your own skin, really, is there any turning back?"

The barista calls out an order for a double-tall skim latte, and Jasper and I fall silent at the truth of his words. That people don't change, and that after a certain point, there's no point in hoping.

16

*P*eter is working late, so Jamie and Samantha, who slips out of work for an hour before having to return, join me for pizza slices at the corner Ray's, while I flip through the notebook, trying to make sense of the images. I'd called Anderson, too, but he wasn't picking up, and I figured he was tipsy, asleep, or potentially on the other line with his agent.

"Maybe you should call your mom and ask," Sam says, blotting the grease from the corners of her mouth with a napkin.

"If she knew about this, she'd have told me." *Really? How can you be so sure?*

"People do strange things in strange circumstances," Jamie offers, like he's reading my mind.

"Meaning what?" Sam counters.

"Just that in my experience, I've seen an awful lot of people try to play the odds in their favor rather than show their full hands.

The kids mourning their parents who don't disclose that they're anxiously awaiting their inheritance, the husband who doesn't report his car accident until he's gotten his mistress safely away from the scene. That sort of thing. Everyone has their secrets."

Sam raises her eyebrows and turns her attention to her BlackBerry.

"So you think my mom isn't telling me everything?" *Of course she isn't telling you everything.*

Jamie pops part of the crust into his mouth by way of an answer, and I concede my agreement with a long sip of Diet Coke.

"You're very smart, you know."

"Ha, not so much!" he says. "But years with nothing to do on my parents' farm except sitting around observing—figuring out the story, the beginning, the middle, the end: I guess I got good at it. My mom always told me I'd be a good novelist because of my love of the story."

"And my story? Have you figured it out?"

"That's trickier because the only person who knows the truth and nothing but it can't remember it in the first place."

"She's not the only person who knows the truth," Sam interjects, back from typing a reply to her boss. "We're here. Her friends, family, we're trying, too."

"You're right, of course, Sam." I rest my head on her shoulder as my way of thanking her. I know that she's needed at the office, I know that she rarely has a spare thirty minutes to see her husband, work out at the gym. She doesn't have to be here, grubbing on slices that have been sitting under a warmer for the better part of an hour. "But still, Jamie, thank you, too—I know that you didn't have to, didn't have to push for your producer connection, help link me to Jasper."

His own e-mail vibrates, and he holds up a finger to say *hold on,* and then starts typing, greasy fingers and all, with fervor. I fold my chin into my palm, staring down at the images in the notebook. Sam leans over to take a peek, too.

There are abstracts, exaggerated notions of what appears to be fields, sun, sky, stars, what? They should be telling me a story; I can see that somewhere there's a line threaded between them, leading me from one to the next, but nothing is linear, none of it jumps out at me as making any sense.

I used to be good at this—I was the one with the eye, but now, with nothing to reason with, it's fled me entirely.

"This, right here, what does that say to you?" I ask Sam. "Quick, without thinking, the first thing that comes to mind. Free associate." I point at one of the pictures—like fragments of broken glass pieced back together again—and push the notebook toward her.

"I don't know . . . art was never my forte." She hesitates, squinting, taking another bite of the pizza. "Maybe a farm? A silo?"

"A silo?"

"Yes, those buildings they have on farms? I grew up in Chicago, so maybe I'm not articulating it right."

I pause, digesting this. "Maybe this is of Vermont, where his studio was. Maybe I'm supposed to go to Vermont." I flip to the next page while both of them attend to their BlackBerrys.

"Oh my god, Nell Slattery!" a voice calls out to me from in front of the pizza counter, and then a woman rushes forward, her blond hair flying behind her, her high heels tapping the cheap linoleum floor. "I knew it was you from the second I walked in here!"

"Don't take this the wrong way," I say, "but I have no idea who you are."

"Yes, of course, no, you wouldn't, now would you?" She waves her cotton candy–colored manicured nails. "I'm Tina Marquis. I haven't seen you since . . . well, since before. A few months before, when you called me." She makes a frowny face like this is supposed to indicate since *before the accident,* and I match her frowny face to assure her that we don't need to rehash it. Tina motions to Jamie to scoot over, and then she slides into the booth, uninvited, next to him.

"High school," I say. "I've seen you in the yearbook. High school, right?"

"Yes, darling, high school!" She has an ever so slight lilt of a southern accent, and I'm not sure if it's because she's developed an affectation or if, before Bedford, she actually grew up there. I picture her from Texas. Yes, she seems like she might be from Texas. "Anyway," she continues, "I just can't believe this! I never come for pizza, but I just got off work and my fridge is empty, so I made a quick stop in!"

"Tina"—Sam wipes her hand on her napkin and extends it across the table—"Samantha. Her friend from college. We met at . . ." She narrows her eyes, trying to remember, and for a beat I'm jealous that she can. That she'll sift around and come up with something. "Oh, yes, we met a few years ago—brunch at

Balthazar." She turns to me to say this. "You and I were having brunch and ran into her."

"Of course! Hello, hello!" If there has ever been a more enthusiastic person in the world, I haven't met her.

"Small world," Jamie says.

"And you!" Tina turns toward him. "You are the talk of the town! The *Post*! *American Profiles*!" She extends her hand. "Tina Marquis. Nice to meet you."

"So, Tina," I say, trying to lasso her in, "I called you to get back in touch?" That seems odd, doesn't seem like the old me at all.

"Oh god, no," she laughs. "As soon as high school was over, you dropped all of us like a hot stone in hell." *Ah, yes, as suspected.* "The rest of us—our crew, as we called it—got together for drinks over the winter breaks, had our summer barbecues—but as soon as you were done, you were *done*. I heard a few of them came to your party last week." She slouches in the booth, a moment of sincerity. "I'm sorry I was out of town, or I would have been there."

"Since I didn't remember you in the first place, I'll consider your apology accepted." I smile because that is what the new me would do. And should do. And what maybe I want to do anyway.

"Well, good, thank you for accepting it." She reaches over and pours some of my Diet Coke into a Styrofoam cup without asking. "But to answer your question, you called me because I'm a real estate broker."

"I was looking for a new apartment?" *Maybe that was what I was doing: kicking Peter out, starting fresh.* I look at Sam for an answer, but she's as bewildered as I am.

"I don't know quite what you were doing, to be honest," she says. "You had me taking you to all sorts of spaces: lofts, walk-ups, doormen. You were very quiet about it. Said I couldn't tell your mother—like I would!—and I couldn't tell your sister."

I flick my hand in a circle, indicating that I'd like her to get to the point already. "So you called, and I showed you well over a dozen places, and you fell in love with one of them in Gramercy— high beamed ceilings, back wall made entirely of brick, original fireplace, and then . . . well . . . then you stopped calling. I figured it was cold feet. I tried you back a few times, but then I got another interested party, and I leased it out. You left me a message right before . . . right before the crash, and we played phone tag and set up one more appointment." She grabs a pepperoni from Jamie's slice and drops it in her mouth, just as her cell phone dings in her purse.

"Excuse me for a second," she says and eases out of the booth as nonchalantly as she came. I watch her mime her order for a slice of cheese pizza to the guy behind the counter, and then, still on the phone, she grabs a pen from her purse, scribbles something on a napkin, and strides back to us.

"Call me sometime," she says, her palm covering her cell phone, thrusting the napkin toward the center of the table. She turns, grabs her boxed slice from the cashier, and is gone, her chatter a wave behind her. The door of Ray's slams, and for a second she reminds me of a tornado, like one of those cartoon characters I used to watch as a kid. I furrow my brow and try to place it. *Wile E. Coyote. Yes, that's it. A blond version of an incoming storm.* And then I remember something more—why her name was so familiar.

It wasn't the high school yearbook. No, of course not. She was on my desk calendar. *Tina Marquis.* Past meets present—a collision of time, memory, and circumstance. I must have been looking to move, but to what? For what?

"What was that all about?" Jamie asks.

I shrug and pocket her number in my bag, wondering the same thing exactly. What *was* that all about? *Everyone has their secrets,* Jamie had said just minutes before. It turns out everyone does: even me.

17

"You Can't Always Get What You Want"
—The Rolling Stones

*T*hat night I fall asleep early and dream, for the first time, of the crash. I wake at 12:47 a.m., the sheets soaked in my virulent sweat, the spot next to me unoccupied in my bed. Peter is still at work—he'll be home by 1, he'd texted earlier. Some sort of television commercial musical catastrophe, though just what that is, I don't know. I press back my doubts that are biting at my psyche, tempting my better judgment, and close my eyes, drifting right back to where I was before I startled awake.

I am on the plane. Not just any plane, but *the* plane, the doomed 757 that tossed me unceremoniously into that Iowa farm field. But for now, all is copacetic, nothing has plunged or faltered to even give so much of a hint that destiny is about to seriously go haywire on the lot of us. My mother is our flight attendant and when the pilot comes on the PA system, Jasper Aarons's voice echoes overhead. "Uh, folks, we're all set for smooth sailing," he says. "But keep that seat belt fastened anyway because you never know what's ahead." *The worst of a bad metaphor.*

Anderson is next to me—just as he was in real life—but this time, we're back in coach, not in first class—in the row that saves our lives—and I'm in the middle seat, which feels uncomfortably small and getting smaller, like a trash compactor pushing in on my hip bones, my elbows, jostling my shoulders for space. I turn to my other side and there is Rachel Green from *Friends*! She is perfect, her hair and skin luminescent. I want to reach over and clutch her because on the show, nothing goes wrong, and when something goes wrong, they gather in Central Perk and buoy each other by the time the credits roll.

The armrests on my seat are digging now into my waist, and my mom leans over, her face fifteen years younger than in real life, and offers me a drink. I order a club soda, and Anderson asks for a Bloody Mary, and Rachel declines anything at all, but rather than returning her headphones to her own ears, she instead shoves them into mine. And she is so violent in doing so, I wince—I can feel myself wince in my sleep—at the way they grate against the skin in my ear. She is listening to the Rolling Stones, whom I know from my own playlist, and for a flicker of a moment, I am lost in a New Year's Eve—a memory within a dream—with Tina Marquis and the other ghosts from high school, and we are throwing our arms into the air, crooning toward the ceiling. *"If you try some-times, you just might find—you get what you need! Oh yeah!"*

And then, just as my mother is placing the Bloody Mary on Anderson's tray table, I sense it, and then I can feel it, and then it's as if the insides of the plane are scrambled eggs: tossed and whisked so violently that I can feel my cheekbones shaking, like I might implode from within. We are being pulled downward, a vacuum, a black hole, a Bermuda Triangle that has us in its clenches and refuses to relent. The gravity pulls on my skin, thrusting my entire being backward. Rachel starts screaming, and I try to tell her that we'll all be okay, but when I turn toward her, she's now morphed into Tina Marquis, and Tina Marquis then flings off her seat belt and starts running toward the rear of the plane. As if anything can save her back there. I want to yell at her to come back, that if we stay in this row, we're somehow fated to survive, but it's too late for that. Anderson has his head between his knees, and reaches up and shoves mine down, too, and then, in that tiny crevasse between us, I say to him, "Thank you, you've saved my life."

He shakes his head because he can't hear me over the squealing engines, which sound like slaughtered pigs, and the hysteria all around us, which sounds like death. Then, as if an omen, the engines go silent, their screeching vaporized, and I know that it won't be long now, that I will wake in the field in Iowa and someone will come save me. Peter? Jamie? Rory? Who?

And then, we have impact, and fireballs swarm overhead, but just like in real life, I am alive. I am strapped into my row of seats, hanging upside down, the blood pooling in my brain, spinning stars and white lights around me. I cock my neck, despite my vertebrae begging for me not to, and peer upward, defying the forces of gravity working every which way against me.

I am not in a cornfield in Iowa.

Anderson moans and fidgets beside me, and I fight to stay conscious, fight to take it all in.

I am here, at the house, the big white house with the expansive porch where I spent that summer away from my other life. Where he spent his life away from his other life.

My muscles, still strapped to my seat, surrender—*we can't hold you up forever,* they seem to say—and my head flops toward the earth. Tan work boots with black smudges on the worn toes appear in my line of vision, and I fight—goddammit! fight for it!—to keep my eyes open, cast my neck upward.

"Hello, Nell," the woman's voice says, and I follow her long legs toward her face. "I'm Heather. It's nice to see you back again."

I finally shake myself awake again, it is 6:17 a.m. I have always been a morning person—this hasn't changed. But my brain is perpetually on now, the dial always amped toward high, and so even when rest may literally be what the doctor has prescribed, there's no having it.

The bedroom is dark. Fall has officially planted its roots: the sun pushing into the sky later each morning, sinking beneath the horizon ever earlier, evaporating those last gasps of warm air that can soothe you underneath the deepest layers of your skin. Outside, I can hear the occasional whoosh of traffic, which sounds almost exactly like a wave crashing on a beach, but mostly it's silent. No noise, no light, not much of anything. A void.

The dream still weaves in and out of me, even though I'm now alert. The Rolling Stones have wormed themselves into my ear, the thought of that New Year's party as real as anything I know. *"You can't always get what you want! You can't always get what you want!"*

I laugh at the irony—*so true*—and hum a bit of the melody before swinging my legs out of bed, happy that I have the mobility to now do so. I peel off my dank pajamas and toss them—*two points, swish!*—into the laundry basket. Suddenly, something about that motion—the movement of my arm, the snap of my wrist—feels familiar, like a sense of déjà vu.

My father. Yes. I'm remembering my father. How old could I have been? I sift through the sensors of my brain. Thirteen? I shake my head. *No, it wasn't that summer in Virginia. It was before.* Ten. Maybe I was ten. I can smell the air, a mix of paint and cigarettes, and see the glow of the easel, illuminated in the dim light of the room, in front of me. And though I may be meshing it all together—the dream and the memory and now this—I could swear that I can hear the Stones in the background, too. Where are we? My mind races, hunting for clues. Then it comes to me. His workshop. We are in Vermont, and he is teaching me the art of letting go, of giving in to randomness, of creating a masterpiece even when most of that masterpiece is out of your control.

"It's not out of your control, Nell. It might *seem* out of your control, but it never really is." He took my wrist, held it high above my shoulder with the brush in hand, and flicked it toward the canvas. Magenta paint spread like a firework. "See, my darling? Look there. You've just created a thing of beauty." He leaned down to kiss my cheek, and I could smell—can smell even now—the ash and nicotine on his breath, and then I took a giant step back, like I was about to hurl a baseball or a shirt into the hamper, and let the paint fly.

I stare at my hamper now for a beat and try to remember more—where was my mother? Rory? What of them? But there's nothing else; this must be enough for now. I reach for the phone to call Liv, but it is too early, so instead I gather up my father's notebook that Jasper has delivered two decades too late, and stride into the living room, bursting with exuberance that *something is working*. The wires are being reignited, the switches are being reset.

I step into the kitchen and dump out a liberal amount of coffee grinds into the coffeemaker. Peter has left a note under a smiley face magnet on the fridge: *Went for an early workout. Back by 7.* To be honest, it hadn't even occurred to me that he was gone.

The coffeemaker sputters to life, and I pour a dark mug, retrieve the notebook from the floor, and then sink into the couch.

I stop on the second-to-last image and turn the book horizontally, then vertically, trying to peer at it from all sides. It's unlike any of the others, like a Georges Braque that I've seen in one of the books on my shelves: shattered fragments litter the page, as if my father had drawn what his mind saw, then dropped the picture like a mirror, sending the splinters every which way. I spin the image round and round, trying to place the pieces back in their rightful place. Slowly, cloaked in the artistic noise, an eye ekes itself out, then another eye, then the slope of a nose, the hint of a lip. But this isn't Heather, I can tell that, even without knowing her. Having only dreamed her. These eyes are younger, less sure of themselves. Maybe, I think, these eyes are mine.

I reach for the phone. It's early but what the hell. A man's gravelly voice answers on the second ring.

"Hello?" I check the keypad to ensure I typed the right number. "Is Rory there?" I say. He grunts and then I hear sheets shifting, and then my sister comes on the line.

"What?" she snaps, offering neither a hello nor an explanation as to why a random guy is both answering her phone and sleeping beside her.

"Dad," I say. "I need you to level with me. Tell me the truth. I need you to tell me everything you can remember about Dad."

18

*R*ory rubs her eyes, flakes of old mascara fluttering down just below her lashes. The diner smells like fried eggs and burned hash browns, and the NYU kids in the booth next to hers—clearly still awake from an all-night bender—are laughing too loudly, throwing their youth in her face, that she can't recover as quickly as they still can, as she once could.

"Okay, first of all, you are strictly forbidden, like ever again, to call me before eight thirty. Is that understood?" Rory says, then cranes her head around. "Jesus Christ, can the waitress bring me some goddamn coffee?"

"Understood," Nell says.

"Second of all, why the urgency? You couldn't wait until, you know, a reasonable hour to decide, after two months, that you have to hear our lovely childhood stories?" She rubs her eyes again. Her head feels like a giant crater, like someone has a sledgehammer driving right into her temples. She has a flash from last night. Oh god, last night. If she thinks about it much more, she's going to hurl her brains out right here on the Formica table, with Lady Gaga singing in the background. She winces, wishing someone would turn down the music, stop the endless bleat of noise from the kitchen, from the fucking NYU kids three feet away.

"Because of this," Nell says, and pulls out a sketch pad from her purse. "Jasper Aarons gave it to me."

"Dad's friend?" Rory tries to focus, to not betray herself. Of course she knows who Jasper Aarons is. Her mother nearly had a hysterectomy when she saw him that night at the gallery.

"Yeah, I met him for coffee. He said he'd had it for years."

"What took him so long?" She waves her hand frantically for the waitress, then mouths coffee in an overexaggerated way.

"Are you okay?" Nell says.

"Hungover," Rory says. Succinct. Enough of an explanation for now. She's not sure if she should feel guilty or a little victorious. She watches Nell, so oblivious, and she knows: guilty. Most definitely guilty. One-upping Nell was fun until it wasn't fun anymore. Like now. This, here, now—this is definitely not fun. Shit. She wishes she could rewind the past twelve hours.

"Moving on from Hugh just fine, I see," Nell says. The waitress finally ambles over with a silver pot and two mugs. "Or I heard. This morning, when I called."

Rory leans closer and examines her statement for judgment—normally, there would be more than a healthy serving of judgment, but she finds none, which guts her even further. Things weren't like they used to be; Nell didn't remember what they used to be, of course, *but Rory did, so while Nell was being kinder, different, Rory kept on going like the old days. Tit for tat. Nell says she can jump, Rory then tries to jump higher. Oh, Jesus, she thinks again.*

"*Just one of those things—one off. One-nighter,*" *Rory says.* "*No one worth discussing.*"

"*Fair enough,*" *Nell says, happy to let it go.*

"*You're not going to mock me, say that I'm doing myself irreparable harm? Need to stop acting like a child and start making grown-up, responsible life choices?*" *Rory gulps down a Herculean-size swallow of coffee and exhales at the relief it provides.*

"*Why would I say that?*" *Nell answers, sipping some coffee of her own.*

"*Just . . . before. You would have.*"

"*It's not before.*" *Nell shrugs.*

"*You've changed.*" *Rory flags the waitress over once more. Oatmeal. That's what she needs. To soak up the excess tequila before it seeps into her organs.*

Nell laughs at this. "*I don't know. People are who they are. Maybe I'm just evolving.*"

"*Semantics.*"

Rory squints and assesses, wondering if Nell would react today like she had six months ago when Rory delivered the news about Peter, about Peter's infidelity. If the same acid would infuse her voice, if she'd still shoot the messenger, say that Rory must feel vindicated in telling her this because she could finally top her sister in everything. Everything! Not only was she prettier, hipper, easier to talk to, got along with Mom, but now! Now! She could triumphantly point to Hugh and hold that over her, too. Rory scoffed—well, she more than scoffed, she unleashed at this wholly ridiculous posturing, and this was when more words were exchanged: about how Nell was always Dad's favorite, and about how Rory never minded that, never minded Nell rubbing Rory's face in that part of things, either. More things were said after that. More things that the two of them would wish they could undo but, of course, could not.

"I'm trying—you know, I got that new couch," Nell says. "Think I'll get some new clothes. But really, aren't we are who we are?" Nell isn't sure what she believes anymore. She made the vow to herself to be a changed woman, but tied to this vow is the idea that the plane crash could have been a blessing. All those people died, and even though she's been given this second chance, this do-over, this make-over, the idea that this is a blessing seems disgusting almost—too trivial, too trite.

Rory grunts because she doesn't really know, either.

"So, anyway," Nell says, ordering a buttered bagel when the waitress makes her reappearance, "Dad."

Rory feels too hungover and too torn to ascend this hurdle, but she nods as if she's ready, ready to answer whatever questions come her way. She'd promised her mother she wouldn't go deep, wouldn't plunge Nell all the way back in—and besides, she and Nell had their own problems that she was more than happy to put behind them—so she sips her coffee and wonders what version of the truth she can get away with. She was the better liar of the two of them anyway. Always had been. She'd gotten that from Indira.

"I had the weirdest dream last night," Nell says. "I was back on the plane, Mom was there, Jasper was there, Anderson was there."

At the mention of Anderson's name, Rory nearly chokes on her *coffee, forcibly swallowing and trying not to demonstrate her obvious alarm. Or her guilt. Or her regret. Which of the three was it? She'd made Anderson promise to pretend like it had never happened. This morning, while he was zippering his zipper, buttoning his waistband, tugging on a shirt to cover his body that, after four shots too many, Rory had unapologetically disrobed the night before. They hadn't planned it, of course. They'd unintentionally collided at The Palms, a club downtown where she was doing her best to pretend that she didn't miss Hugh, and he was doing his best . . . well, just doing his best, Rory supposed now. This morning, when the phone rang, Nell hadn't recognized his voice, grainy, from the night spent screaming over too-loud techno music—and thank god for that, they both concurred when they awoke newly sober and absorbed the situation, mulled over the consequences.*

"What does your dream have to do with Dad?" Rory says.

Nell shakes her head. "I don't know. Something. Anyway"—she flips her hair—"okay, let's start with this: I know that you didn't always get along with him, but what do you remember about me? About the two of us?"

"I got along with him well enough. I just didn't idolize him, that's all," Rory says. "But you, no, you idolized him. You flat out worshipped him."

"Example."

Rory rubs her eyes. "After Dad left, you didn't believe it. You refused to believe it for a good six months."

"Well, that seems normal. I mean, we were kids. Who would want to believe that their parent wasn't coming back?"

"No, it wasn't just that. It wasn't normal. That's the whole point."

Rory presses her thumbs down on her temples in an attempt to beat back the shadow that the tequila left behind. "Mom would try to talk to you—I remember so clearly her trying to talk to you one night at dinner. She'd made this rice and bean dish because she freaked out when Dad left and had just gone vegetarian, and you insisted that she put out a plate for him. She refused because she thought you needed to accept that he was gone, but you kept nagging her, not even nagging, it was like needling, ribbing her—you couldn't let it go."

The waitress approaches with their breakfast, sliding the dishes in front of them, and Nell tears a piece of bagel with her teeth, her eyes focused as she tries to remember.

"So Mom kept saying no," Rory continues, "and you kept insisting that he was going to come back, and that we had to make it totally clear that we wanted him back, or else of course he wouldn't come, and how couldn't she see this?"

"And what were you doing while we were arguing?"

"I was sitting on a stool watching everything unravel. That was the difference between us. I accepted it right away. We woke up one morning and Dad's stuff was gone, and he'd left us each a postcard with a little stupid fucking drawing—which I guess was to signify his love or whatever—but I knew that it was his way of saying good-bye. I tossed mine in the garbage within a week. You? You tacked yours up to the bulletin board in your room for half the year, until you finally realized what he meant by it—that it was his suicide letter of sorts."

"Don't say it like that," Nell says.

"See, even now you're doing it—defending him."

Nell reaches over and dips a finger into Rory's oatmeal for a taste, considering the point, and then says, "So what happened that night at dinner? Who won?"

"Neither of you." Rory's teeth skate over the metal of her spoon. "Jesus, it was awful. You wouldn't give up and she wouldn't cave, and so eventually you tried to force yourself toward the oven to make a plate for him yourself, and Mom tried to block you, and you shoved her some more, and she shoved you some more . . ." Rory suddenly feels furiously ill, unsure if it's from the tequila or the story. She grabs Nell's hand.

"This scar," Rory says, running her index finger over a long vine just above the fold of Nell's wrist and winding all the way down the shallow end of her arm. "That's where you got it."

Nell pulls her arm from Rory's fingers and examines the consequence of that evening.

"It wasn't her fault," Rory says quietly now. "I mean, it wasn't intentional. She didn't scar you on purpose."

"When is it ever on purpose?" Nell asks, finally raising her eyes to meet her sister's.

Rory sighs. "Mom was just so hysterical, and to be fair, you weren't at your best. You were both delusional in your own way. You loving him too much, her hating him too much or . . . God, I don't even know what she was doing. Blaming herself? Blaming Dad? Blaming God?"

"So then what?"

"You and Mom stopped talking for a few days. You spent all your time throwing out all this painting crap, tossing cans and brushes and drop cloths in the garbage like he could see you, like you were doing

it out of revenge. You blasted your music." Rory grins a little at this. "Guns N' Roses. It was so ridiculous for a thirteen-year-old girl in Bedford, New York, but it screamed from your room and from the guesthouse for days. I don't know, it was, like, your anger music or something." She shrugs and takes another swallow of oatmeal. "And eventually, you moved on like it didn't happen—though you stopped writing music, stopped making much of it really—and Mom, in her spiritual New Age misguidance, tried to talk to you about it endlessly. It just pushed you away even further. She'd enter a room, you'd leave it. That sort of thing." Rory's nausea has passed now, the sense that she might make it out of this entanglement without narcing on any of the parties involved. "I don't know—I was only eight or nine. Too young for all of this crap in the first place."

"And me? At thirteen, you think I was better prepared for it?" Nell asks sincerely.

"You?" Rory almost laughs. "Nelly, no one is prepared for it. That's the whole problem. That's why everything is so screwed up in the first place."

19

I'm meeting an old friend today, hoping she might be able to
help me find some answers," I say to Liv, the next Tuesday. She
looks tired, less shiny than usual, and I wonder whom she shares
her own problems with. We are perched on my new red couch, side
by side, bodies angled toward each other's, which is both comfortable and still slightly awkward, the intimacy of sharing the space.

"Answers to what?"

"What do you mean, 'answers to what'? Answers to everything."

"This friend has them?" I can't tell if she's pushing me or just
generally cranky.

"Are you cranky?"

"No." She half-smiles.

"Tired?"

"Let's keep this about you. When you say 'answers,' it seems
almost too simplistic that your friend might have them."

"Isn't that what this whole pursuit is about?" I say, testily. "Getting my goddamn answers."

"Of course." She nods. "I only meant that some of them need to come from you, not anyone else. Your friend, for example, can't tell you how to feel about your miscarriage and what that meant for your relationship with Peter."

"I take it, through your therapist terminology, that you think it might actually be time to discuss the miscarriage with Peter."

"There is no therapist terminology involved," she says. "Only that it's something to consider. Something that perhaps you might want to discuss with me first before moving on to him."

"I have considered it," I say. "And I've decided that even the best relationships have their secrets. That maybe there is something to be said for some mystery, for *not* discussing everything."

"There may indeed be something to be said for it, though I can't help but think you're now mixing up your parents' relationship with your own."

I firm my jaw. "Tell me why you're cranky, and I'll keep talking."

"I do not negotiate with terrorists," she says, but I don't blink. "Fine," she exhales. "My dog, Watson, he was sick last night, and I spent most of it at the vet's. That's all. He's fine now."

"I'm sorry to hear that," I say. "You could have rescheduled."

"I'm not a rescheduler, don't like missing things I've committed to." I nod because the old me didn't seem like she broke her commitments, either. "So back to your parents."

"Back to my parents." I stand to get myself some water. "I wasn't specifically referring to them, no, but since you raised it, then, well, yes."

"So your argument is that having secrets can do a relationship good, but—correct me if I'm wrong—what good came out of their own secrets?"

"Ask again later." I set my glass down on the coffee table and lower myself back to the couch. She, intentionally or not, shifts an inch farther away. "That's the million-dollar question."

"Nell, I'm urging you to take this a little more seriously." She places her notes down beside her as if to demonstrate that she is *truly serious* now.

"I couldn't be taking it more seriously!" I say. "How could I be taking this more seriously if I tried?"

"Part of my job—and yours—is to occasionally tap into places that might not want to be tapped into. I've noticed that one thing you are very good at is blocking out something that you may not want to address."

"Well, of course I block out what I don't want to address! Why wouldn't I? In your psychological view, couldn't you argue that, in fact, this entire *thing*"—I swirl my arms here and inadvertently knock her notes to the floor—"is an effort to block out what I don't want to address?" I feel my pulse in my neck, instantly irritated at how easily she has broken this down, how simple a mark she has made me out to be. If she senses my sarcasm, she ignores it.

"Nell, look. I know you're working hard here, and I know that you're frustrated not to be making more progress. I'm only here to guide you, to suggest an opinion that may or may not be helpful."

She pauses, waiting for me to reel myself back in. "How about art?"

"How about it?"

"You've mentioned that you loved to paint, so how about art therapy? There are very conclusive studies that demonstrate how it can help in situations like yours."

I shake my head. "I never said that I loved to paint. I said that my father always thought I could be great, like him. There's a difference. What I've been told I always loved was music."

She digests this, chewing on her lower lip, which must be an old habit from childhood, not one she could shed once she got her Ph.D.

"Well, this certainly leads to a different—albeit equally important—question," she says finally. "We've spoken an awful lot about your father, much more so than about Peter or your marriage or any of the issues that, per your request, we can let rest for today. But your dad—in some ways, you seem more consumed with uncovering his past than your own."

"Isn't our time up yet?" I deadpan, and she just stares. "Okay, the truth is that I feel like the more I know about my dad, the more unanswered questions I have. And yes, I suppose I dwell on that. A lot. But so what? Isn't that what you're here for?"

"It's part of what I'm here for, yes," she concedes, and I think aha because there's something truly satisfying about proving your therapist wrong. It's the small victories these days. "But mostly what I'm here for is to help you figure out who you are *now,* not just who you were then."

"Look," I say flatly. "My dad left us, which must have been devastating. By all accounts it was devastating. And now, I can't even remember that devastation. Why can't I try to find out about it?"

"You are welcome to find out about it," she says, finally reaching down, taking a breath, and retrieving her scattered notes from the floor. "But this 'devastation,' as you put it, has defined so much of how you are. Even in the absence of it! What's wrong with that picture?"

"Ask my dad—he was the artist."

"Nell," she says, and I can tell she's losing her patience.

"Fine." I sulk. "Well, I was consumed with him once, and now I'm consumed with him all over again. Maybe this just proves that people don't change."

I gesture to the couch, as if to say, I tried! I got this enormous cherry tomato couch, but here I am, right back on the gerbil wheel, my father's absence defining me in the same way that it always did.

"No," she says, straightening her papers on her lap, then meeting my eyes. "People change. And you know that. It's the not wanting to do the work involved that makes us complacent, and it's that complacency that renders us right back where we started."

Sam cuts out of work early that afternoon and meets me in front of Tina Marquis's building in midtown. I'm early, so I have the cab drop me five blocks north when we pass a boutique that looks too hip for the old me. The new me, the one that I'd just sworn to Liv is nothing more than an ephemeral fabrication, thinks, *Well, screw that. If anyone can change, it's me.* So I shove ten dollars at my driver and stride into the store, scooping up a too-purple V-neck and an odd little beret that the salesgirl swears shaves five years off my age before she shyly tells me that she knows who I am and admires how I'm making myself over. I don't dwell on her intimation that I've actually reached an age that needs shaving off or that I did, indeed, need a makeover. Instead I assess myself in the mirror and see that the new, fabulous me very much approves. Who the hell knows if people can change?

Sam waves to me and laughs a little at the beret.

"Nice," she says, then rubs my arm.

"Just trying something new." I'm self-conscious. My instinct is to tug that insipid hat right off my head and fling it across Third Avenue like a Frisbee, but then she says, "No, really, it's nice. It's new. It's something." So I kind of pat it with my right hand, an acknowledgment that it's staying put, and we step through the revolving doors, on our way to see Tina Marquis, the friend in whom I've placed my stock to answer my questions.

"I just want to say," Sam hedges, while we wait in the elevator bank. "You know, you weren't close with her, I mean, since I've known you. When we ran into her at Balthazar, it was all you could do to bring yourself to make small talk."

"And the point being?"

"I just don't want you to get your hopes up, that's all. Maybe she knows something, maybe she doesn't. But you're practically levitating with excitement, and I just want you to be realistic."

"It's the beret," I say, as we step into the elevator. "It conveys a sense of whimsy. I can assure you I'm not levitating." I punch the button.

"Nell, I'm serious."

"I know," I say. "But I called her. *I called her,* and no one knows why. So there must be something there. There must be something important."

"Just . . . be cautious." She laughs almost incredulously as she says this, both of our eyes on the ascending lighted numbers overhead. "I can't believe that of all people, I'm now saying that to you."

Before I can register this, the doors ding open, and we step over the precipice. I look to our left and Tina is throwing herself toward us from two cubes away. Her blond hair flies behind her, her neck wrapped in a scarf, her perfect cleavage tugged tight by a magenta cashmere tee. She is my nineties sitcom character in the flesh— beautiful, crisp, a moving image of spasmodic energy.

"Nell!" she says breathlessly, like she's been running down the halls to greet us, which, I consider, she may have. "I am *so* glad that you changed your mind and reached out to me!" She holds both hands and steps back to assess. "Nice beret! Chic, chic, chic!"

I'm embarrassed all over again, that both of them have so obviously noticed my blatant attempts to step outside myself, but brush past it. "You know Sam, from the pizza place."

"So nice to see you again, Sam," Tina says, extending her hand, offering up a firm, seemingly professional handshake. I'd pegged her for an overzealous shake, a cartoonish clutch to match her caricature of enthusiasm. I cock my head, my meter reassessing.

"So how well did you guys know each other growing up?" Sam says, as Tina leads us back to her office. I scan the floor, surveying the cubicles, the busy worker bees with their heads tucked down, their glazed eyes on their screens, their headsets pressed into their ears, and see if any bells of recognition ring.

"Best friends through freshman year, less so after that," Tina says. "We . . . well, you know high school, we all went our own way."

"It's okay," I say. "I know that I changed. You don't have to be kind to spare my feelings."

"Oh, doll, it wasn't that. You were who you were. I admired it. You did your own thing. You didn't give a shit about the politics of high school."

She gestures to an open door, and Sam and I walk through and situate ourselves in two leather chairs facing her steel metal desk. Behind it, through the window, is an ample view of the skyline.

"You just had to grow up faster than the rest of us," she continues. "Didn't care about the trivialities of the cheerleading squad, the winter dance planning, the glee club." She squints and reconsiders. "Actually, you were the star of middle school glee club for a while there. Until you weren't. Stopped enjoying it so much. You fulfilled it solely for the credit eventually." She laughs. "Hell, you could have done it in your sleep."

"Did you know my dad?" I ask, without even thinking about it. Right back to the patterns that Liv implored me to reconsider. Maybe I haven't changed. Maybe this beret is just window dressing.

"Not well," Tina answers, her face dropping. "We all knew who he was, of course, but he didn't seem to be around much. After I ran into you at the pizza place the other night, I called my mom and asked the same thing because I couldn't remember much of him, and I always wondered. She said that your parents never conveyed that they were having problems right up until the moment he left. One day he was there, and the next day, gone. And then she said your mom went a little crazy." Her eyes grow to orbs. "Oh god, I'm sorry, I shouldn't have said that. I tend to have a little verbal diarrhea."

"I've noticed," I say but not unkindly. "But no offense taken."

"My mom did tell me something that you might not have known. Well, might not know now, anyway. I don't know if you knew back then." Tina rises and either instinctively or intentionally closes her door.

"What's that?"

"That there was a rumor at our high school graduation that your dad showed up."

"What? At the actual graduation? No, no, I didn't know!" *Shouldn't my mom have mentioned* that?

"Well, it was never confirmed." Tina sits back down and reaches for a pencil, drubbing it on her desk. "Just one of those things that made its way through the town like wildfire. Someone thought she saw him at Jake's Coffee, then someone else claimed she could have sworn that he was loitering—with a full beard and bowler's hat—toward the back of the gym during the processional, and it took off from there. But it was like the Loch Ness monster: never confirmed despite various sightings."

I swallow what feels like too much oxygen, and my heart feels like it might detonate inside my chest cavity. It couldn't be that simple, could it? That he was out there, watching, doing what he needed to do for himself, but still minding us, tending to us along?

From all reports, this seems entirely impossible, and yet . . . and yet. It gives me something to hold on to.

Tina reads my face. "Should I not have told you? Shit. I'm sorry, like I said, I talk too much."

I exhale and gather my breath and stare at her for a beat. She perplexes me, Tina Marquis. On the surface, she is an epitomized Barbie doll, a Dallas cheerleader by way of upper-class Westchester. But slice beneath that skin, and it's clear—from her corner office with view, to relaying just the story that I somehow need to hear—that she's also much more than that. A contradiction when I was certain that people—Jasper, Rory, my mother, Peter—were easy reads from the start. I ease back in the leather chair and consider this: that people can still surprise you.

"Thanks for telling me," I say. "Sincerely. I'd never have known this."

"Are you sure it's even true?" Sam says quietly. I'd forgotten that she was there. "You can't forget that it might not actually be true."

"But it might be," Tina and I say at the same time.

"I guess that's why we were best friends," she says, grinning, her teeth the brightest shade of alabaster white. Then she flaps her hands—grounded and flighty at once. "Anyway, let's get down to business before my phone starts ringing again. You wanted to know about the property I showed you."

"Yes. I was, well, I'm hoping that it might trigger something."

"Well, I called the current tenant and explained the circumstances, and he knew who you were. From the accident." She dislodges some phlegm from her throat. "Said he'd be happy to have you come by if you'd like later in the week. But in the meantime, this is what I have." She moves some papers—flyers, a floor plan— across her desk.

"Anything look familiar?" Sam asks. Tina's phone buzzes just then, precisely as predicted.

It is exactly as she described: a wall of cool brick, high, expansive ceilings. There are wide-open windows toward the back, with a view of the East River. Something about it feels familiar, and then I remember: my father's paintings, the water, the vibrant fresh air were always his muses.

Tina cups her hand over the phone and whispers. "Listen, I'm sorry, this is a huge client whose deal just fell through. Can we talk later?"

I nod, and hoist myself to my feet, Sam with a palm on my back in case I falter.

"Should I set it up?" Tina asks, cradling the receiver between her neck and ear.

"Set what up?"

"The apartment—do you want to stop by and see it? Will it help?"

Will it help? I consider. At this point, it's anyone's guess.

"So listen," Sam says, while we're cabbing it to the gallery. "You know that I support anything that you want to do. *Anything.* Or maybe you don't know that. Maybe you don't remember that. But I hate to see you put so much stock in this one thing."

"This is hardly one thing!"

"It's just that before all of this, you never talked about your dad. Didn't have this wild interest in chasing down his legacy."

"I ran an art gallery entirely based on his legacy. So that can't be true."

She sighs and we both point ourselves toward our respective windows.

"I'm only saying that before, you wouldn't have let this aspect eat you up."

"Fair enough. Let's let it go for now," I say, though mean anything but. *What if he'd come back for me? What if he fought every last selfish urge and regretted to his core the permanence of his mistakes? Wouldn't that, couldn't that change everything? Change him? Change the past? Or maybe I did already know that he'd come back for me, only I've forgotten it after the accident.* I shake my head, the circular noise giving me a headache. How can I know who I am when I don't even know what I knew? Don't even know what was germane and what was relevant and what wouldn't have changed anything even if I think it may have now?

Sam laughs. "You don't fool me, Nell Slattery. I can see your mind working over there. I know you too well."

"Okay, so what if I *do* want to dwell on it? What if he changed, realized how wrong he was? What if he came back at graduation and wanted to make amends."

"What if he did?" The taxi pulls up to the gallery, and Sam reaches for her purse.

"Well, I don't know," I hesitate. "It seems like that should change something—change me, maybe."

"Maybe it would," she says, "though you always insisted that people never changed." She wrinkles her nose. "I could swear, even, that you wrote a paper about it for a philosophy seminar we took our senior year."

"I'm revisiting this theory. Tina confuses me, she's nothing like who I thought she'd be."

"That doesn't mean your dad isn't who you think he was."

"Well, what about Peter?" I say, as I see Rory waving to me from inside the gallery. She's gesturing at me to hurry up, flicking her wrist in a way that I find instantly annoying, like there's no place more important for me to be than next to her at this very second. "Peter has changed."

Sam says nothing. Rather, she opens her door to exit as an answer.

"You think he hasn't?" I half-shout over the top of the cab, as she circles around the sidewalk to meet me.

"I think that he's certainly made a good show of it. Been by your side. Stayed loyal."

"Well, that's something. I mean, isn't that a change?" Rory is going apoplectic behind the front glass window. I stick up my index finger, telling her to *hold on!*

"That's the easy part," she says, before she links my elbow and we head inside. "What matters is that something else shifts, too."

"Well, that's the hitch of it all, isn't it?"

"Yes," she says. "There's always a hitch."

20

"Don't Stop Believing"
—Journey

I push open the doors to the gallery, the wind chimes twinkling hello. Thanks to the caterer, the air wafts with the perfect scent of baked puff pastry and quiche lorraine, and the music for the evening is vintage Journey, which Rory had told me yesterday is meant to be both ironic and nostalgic. When I said I didn't really get it, she snapped her jaw closed, reminding me of a tropical fish, and stomped out of the room.

"Do you know how behind we are?" she says now by way of greeting. Behind her, a waiter inadvertently clangs together two serving trays, and she and I both cast our eyes back toward him to ensure disaster hasn't struck. *Disaster. Like that could be defined as a toppled station of pigs in a blanket.*

"No, how far behind are we?"

If she senses my derision, she doesn't betray it.

"We are very, very behind. We have approximately two hundred people showing up tonight for Hope's first gallery show; we have the *American Profiles* crew coming—"

"Your idea, not mine," I interrupt.

"What don't you understand about publicity?" she says, adjusting the price placards in front of each work. "Publicity is publicity—you never got that. And now, the gallery is so hot, so in demand . . ." She does a double take. "What is that thing on top of your head?"

"It's a beret."

"Well, it looks like a sad, deflated pancake, and it needs to go." She flutters her hand. "Along with the shade of purple of your sweater. There are clothes in the closet in the office."

"What's wrong with this shade of purple?"

"For grape jelly? Nothing. For our openings?" She sighs. "You're the one who implemented the neutrals-only dress code here."

Ah, well, that explains my closet.

"Well, I'm de-implementing it," I say. "The sweater stays."

"Fine." She exhales. "The hat does not. Even without a dress code, it looks ridiculous." There's a knock on the front door, and Rory shouts, "It's open!" and Jamie and two cameramen step inside.

"I'll be in the back dealing with the bartenders," Rory says. "Try to make yourself useful." She tugs off the beret, which I have kept in place as she glides past.

"Hey," Jamie says, and kisses me hello. "Want to go over the game plan for tonight?"

I glance around. Despite Rory's instructions, I have nothing else to do. "Shoot."

"Well, it shouldn't be too hard. We're mostly doing crowd shots, interviewing some friends and family. We want to see you back in your element."

"So this is my element?" I spot Peter hustling across the street. He's early.

"For our purposes, it is," Jamie answers succinctly, impersonally, and for a flicker of a moment I'm reminded that at the heart of this, he's a reporter, on the gig of a lifetime.

The wind chimes clang once again at Peter's arrival.

"Hey, babe." Peter kisses me fully on the mouth.

"You're early." I kiss him back, and then he surprises me with an embrace. For a second, my arms flop by my sides until my brain catches up with the situation. I sink into his bear chest and inhale the fall air still hovering around him. "What was that for?" I say when he's finally untangled himself from me.

"I'm just glad to see you back in your element." His eyes mist on cue. The new, more sympathetic me is touched that he's so invested in my recovery. The old, less softened me can't help but be annoyed that it's been a few months and still he finds himself shattered.

"Funny, that's what Jamie just said to me, too."

"This place is you. Everything about it." His voice cracks.

Rory walks over and thrusts a clipboard in my hand before I can contemplate the weight behind his comment.

"You're greeting people at the door," she says.

"Isn't that your job?" Peter asks.

"Not anymore, not when I have to be the one worrying about the rest of the details." Her voice is sharp, like she's pulled a muscle.

"Shoe's on the other foot now, isn't it?" he says, and I can't tell if he's joking or undercutting her. She glares and returns to the caterers.

"What was that?" I say, flipping through the list, recognizing few of the names.

"You took care of *everything* before the accident. It consumed you—you practically lived here. You picked out the paint color, you paid the bills, you agonized over the layout of where to place each piece of art. Like I said, it was you in your element."

"Nell!" Rory yells. "Please come over here and tell them how to present the bar."

"How to present the bar? Who cares how you present the bar?" I say when I reach her. "And by the way, what is your *problem*?"

"I'm stressed, in case you can't tell. Word is out about us now—you're not here to see the tourists line up, to vet the calls that still come in from the media. *You* may be oblivious to your fame, but I can't be! And I could use your help." Since the accident, curious collectors have flooded the gallery, another unforeseen perk from surviving the worst plane crash this side of the decade.

"So tell me what to do. Jesus Christ. How have you held it together for the past two months while I've been gone?" I say.

"This is our first show since then. Press—papers and magazines and journals—will be here. This is bigger than anything we've done before. It matters." She's spiraling into hysterics now, and I can see it, how I kept everything pinned down here, partially, simply, because she could not.

"So that's it? That's all that this is. Stress from our first show? Because this seems disproportionate to just some stress for a show."

The wind chimes echo hello, and we both turn to see Anderson greeting Peter.

"Yes, for god's sake, that's all it is!" She lingers on both of them, then turns back to me. "Now please, tell them how you like the wineglasses, where you want the liquor, then go man the door. People are already arriving."

I gesture to the bartenders once she moves out of earshot. "I really don't care, whatever you think is best." Then I lope over to Anderson, kissing his cheek.

"You clean up nice," I say.

"Ditto," he answers. Peter slides his hand around my waist.

"No date tonight? I'm pretty sure that I've been reading about your rotation on Page Six." Peter smiles, a congratulation couched as a question. He raises his free hand to slap him five.

"Randy Andy!" the headline had blared just three days ago, covering Anderson's exploits with yet another model, exploits he swore to me were untrue.

"Naw, not tonight. I had invites to two screenings but, to be honest, I just wanted a night off. Away from—you know—the scene, the craziness," Anderson says, halfheartedly raising his own palm to meet Peter's. It's all a little pathetic, a little sad, this flimsy flop of their manliness. "Just wanted to be here to support the girl who saved my life." He makes a bombastic gesture with his arm, like he's a prince and I'm a courtesan, and we both smile at the showiness of it.

"And we're honored to have you," I say, mock-curtsying. "I'm manning the door," I add.

"Well, that is one area that I have much expertise in," he says. "Doormen, bouncers. I'll help."

"I'll be at the bar," Peter says. "Come find me."

"These aren't your thing?" Anderson asks him.

"I'm not the schmoozing type," he answers, then glances away. "I usually skipped these before. Not . . . not that you minded," he says to me. "You always just preferred to focus on work, not to have to entertain me."

"Well, I'm laying off the booze for tonight, man, but I'll catch you in there," Anderson says.

I pat Peter's shoulder, and then he wanders toward the martinis.

"So, things are going well with you guys?" Anderson asks, as we flank the doorway, waiting for patrons. "I mean, they seem to be going reasonably well."

"Pretty solid, actually." Things are actually pretty solid. Whether we are back in heady love, well, no, not there, but yes, *solid*. We're working toward togetherness, and my mother's prophetic words that brilliant sunshiny afternoon at the hospital are starting to fulfill themselves. I've learned to trust him again, maybe not with my full soul but with enough of it that I can envision a day when I will. Give him my whole self. So what if he didn't come to these events before? So what if I didn't beg him to be there in the first place? I steal a look around. As glamorous as it is, and certainly it *is* glamorous, part of it feels off. Part of me feels off being here.

"You think any of this matters?" I say to Anderson.

"This life, this gallery, this what?"

"This party stuff. This posturing to sell art. Who cares?"

"Collectors care. The artist cares. I'd venture that once upon a time, you cared."

"My dad wouldn't have. He wouldn't have sold any of his stuff, prostituted himself like this." *How do you know what your dad would have wanted?* I can hear Liv even without her being here. And she has a point: *I don't, I wouldn't have.* Why does it matter so much to me that I think I should know in the first place?

"This is hardly prostitution," Anderson retorts. "This is people appreciating art and wanting to bring that art into their home because it touches them. And if you think *this* is prostitution, then wait until you see my movies."

"Touché." I smile. I see Rory start toward us, then reconsider and spin on her heels toward the bar. Anderson watches her as she does so. "She's in rare form tonight," I say.

"Probably just not used to the pressure." He shrugs it off. "Like asking her to headline a movie when she's not quite ready."

"So now we've shifted to talking about you."

"I'm an actor, we try to keep it about us nearly all the time." He smiles his trademark smile, all dimples, perfect teeth. "But my agent keeps telling me, 'You gotta step up. Gotta seize the moment.' I guess that's right. For Rory, me, you. Everyone."

"Ergo, the Spielberg film."

"Ergo that." He sighs, then stutters. "You remember Stephen Calhoun from the passenger manifest?" I scrunch my eyes. *Vaguely. Jesus. I've forgotten the hundred fifty-two of them already.* "The teenage kid who was heading to Duke in the fall on a basketball scholarship? Incredible kid. He'd started a foundation helping underprivileged kids: baked dog biscuits to raise money for them."

"Seems worthy, if random."

"It was. His family got in touch to ask if I'd continue in his honor, you know, pass the torch, and keep his dream alive." Anderson leans back against the door frame. "And of course I want to say yes. I mean, that kid had everything going for him in the world, he was someone who truly could have lit things on fire . . . and yet, when my publicist relayed their message, my first thought was, 'Another favor? Who else is asking?' " He rubs his temples. "Shit, I'm a walking Hollywood cliché."

"You're not," I say, touching his arm. "We're all just wading our way through."

I stare down at the guest list. Anonymous names of who— friends? patrons?—who will soon arrive to brush next to me and engage as if nothing ever happened. No, that's not true. Some will lower their voices and their eyes will cast downward and they'll ask questions that feel too intimate, and I will freeze my smile and provide answers in such a way that I don't answer them at all.

"Excuse me, Nell?" I glance up and the reporter—the one from weeks back with the inside sources—is too close in front of me on the sidewalk. "Nell Slattery? We . . . met . . . we met last month at your welcome-back party. Do you have a second?"

"Paige," Anderson says, and she looks at him with surprise, as if she's only just seeing him there. "This isn't the time."

"What? Oh Jesus, get over yourself, Anderson," she says. "I'm here for Nell."

"This is Paige Connor, she works for the *Post*," Anderson says to me, as if he's actually announcing that this is Paige Connor, who severs little puppy heads.

"Oh, Paige, it's nice to meet you." I run my finger down the list, then hesitate. "I'm sorry, I'm not seeing you on here. I'll have to confer with my sister to get you inside." I offer an apologetic shrug. "She's running the show right now. I hope you don't mind."

"That's not why I'm here," she says, fishing in her bag until she pulls out a tape recorder, which she clicks on without asking. "Anderson, will you give us a moment?"

"No," he says, "I won't." She locks her jaw and gives him a look that suggests she'd like to inflict physical harm.

"Paige is the reporter for Page Six. We go back a few years," he says to me.

"Oh! Listen, Paige, if this is a personal query, you know that I'm open to talking with the press," I say, "but right now, we're trying to launch this show with our artist, and I have *American Profiles* here, and I've given them exclusive access until the pieces run. Also"—and I laugh here, one of those trying-too-hard types of chuckles, *ha ha*, that it feels like a girl who wears a beret might be able to pull off—"you guys haven't exactly been kind to Anderson these past few weeks. I kind of have a loyalty . . ."

"Again, you're missing the point," she says, shoving the recorder closer to me, the way that I've seen reporters do in the movies.

"Nell!" Rory yells from the back, right before I hear a splintering crash and spin around just in time to see one of our hand-blown glass vases shattering and skidding every which way across the floor.

"Oh, Jesus Christ!" I sigh. "Paige, I'm sorry, now's not a good time. Try back in a few weeks. I'll do my best to chat with you."

I glide past Peter, who is kicking the shards with the insole of his loafers, and step into the back office to unlock the supply closet in search of a broom. When I come up empty, I pull out the step stool and haul myself up toward the top shelf. I'd seen a Dust-Buster around here somewhere. I shove my hands toward the back, blind to whatever I'm grasping. My fingers work their way over papers, what feel like glossy magazine covers, but no DustBuster. They wind their way along the side and wade over something cool, sharp, gilded. I flex my wrist and yank them down: keys. Three to be exact. I step down and peer more closely. They're all identical, carved from the same set, triplets who haven't yet been broken up.

"Hey," I say to Rory, walking back into the main gallery. She doesn't hear me at first, the Journey singles amped up too loud. I step closer. "What are these for?" She's on her knees, having found a handheld broom and dustpan. She stares up at me.

"Are you going to help me or not?" she bellows. "We have five minutes until people start officially arriving, and Hope isn't even here! Can you at least get her on the phone?"

"Calm down, yes, I will get her on the phone, but these keys—are they yours?"

She stands, exhales, and unintentionally wipes her hands on her pants, leaving a film of fine dirt across her thighs. I consider pointing this out, but suspect this would only be to both of our detriments.

Rory grabs the keys and inspects them. "No, I've never seen

them before. Okay? Now, please go call Hope. Her number is on a sticky on the desk. And then please get back to your post." She looks toward the door, where Anderson is contemplating the sole of his shoe, and then she sighs in the most dramatic of ways and continues cleaning up the mess.

I wrap my palm around the key chain, letting the sharp edges pock the outer layer of my skin. These keys seem important, seem to matter somehow. I slink back to the office and sit in my chair, trying to let my brain run loose, to free-associate, as Liv would advocate. It feels almost cliché that a key might unlock something in me, but it also feels intrinsically like I have to try. That's the one thing that I miss, I realize, leaning back in the chair, closing my eyes, absorbing the coolness around me, the bustle and the music in the gallery fading to a mashed-up hum. I miss that compass. I miss my instincts distinguishing the right path from the rocky one, the one that marked smooth terrain from the one loaded with land mines. In any other life, I'd trust my gut or I'd fall back on my history. And now, I've been stripped of everything, but it's this lack of animal intuition that has left me feeling most at bay. So I rely on my mother and my sister and my husband and my therapist and even my new friend Jamie to guide me, but what is a life, after all, when you can't guide yourself?

The gallery goes silent for a moment as the CD skips to a new song.

"Just a small town girl, livin' in a lonely world. She took the midnight train goin' anywhere."

Something warm runs through me, a hit, a drug, a burst of adrenaline from my nervous system. I unclench my palm and stare down at these three beacons of promise. They are telling me something. I can feel it. I know it. I can sense it deep in the bowels of that instinct that I am so fervently trying to steer toward the surface. I close my eyes and lean back and listen until finally Rory clears her throat behind me and says, "Don't bother calling. Hope's here."

21

It has been more than three months since the crash now. The calendar has shifted yet again, time unwilling to be pinned down despite the fact that I am stuck in the hazy muddle of inertia. Miraculously, if you didn't know my story, if you didn't read *People* or watch *American Profiles,* and didn't probe too deeply into the depths of my memory, you'd never even know that I had tumbled from the clouds on that evening of the last day of June.

Today I sit in Liv's office, an emerald green sweater and a tailored corduroy blazer layered over my once-broken ribs, and I contemplate how far I've come. Even though, quite obviously since my brain is still impaired, I may not have come far at all.

"You seem distracted," Liv says.

I peer around. This is the first time I've ventured to her, rather than she to me. Her office is warm, homey, but professional, too. Behind her, there's a framed photograph of her with a yellow Lab, whom I take to be Watson, and next to it a shot of her with her parents at college graduation. She hasn't aged much, maybe some finer lines on her forehead, the circles a little more concave under her eyes, but mostly she's the same. I feel a rush of tears at this idea, that she still has her map, from A to B, that she can glance toward her framed diploma that sits on her back wall and know how she got here. Know *why* she got here.

I wave a hand, covering. "I'm okay. Tired. Stayed up too late talking with Peter. He left today for a work retreat. Maybe the fatigue is making me overly emotional."

"Talking about what?"

"Nothing. Everything. We sat on the piano bench, and I played a little, then he played a little, then we played a little together." I inhale now, getting my grip. "He said we used to do it when we were dating. It sounds silly to say, but it feels like he's wooing me again."

"So things have changed," she says. A statement, not a question.

"Maybe things have changed," I respond, less skeptically than I intended. With honest enthusiasm, actually. Because perhaps they have. Maybe Peter *is* different, or maybe we're just different because, according to all parties, *I* am different. Maybe you can't change that when you mix blue and red, you're destined for purple, but what if you alter the hue, modify the depths of the blue? Change your variables, such that both your equation and the solution to that equation shift, too. Before, in my old life, I didn't need him, and the simple fact is that I do now—mostly for the minutiae, but for the bigger things, too. And so maybe that tweak is enough. Accepting that he isn't the sole one who needed to change—maybe I did, too.

"Thereby defeating your theory."

"It's a work-in-progress theory, not something carved in stone."

"Fair enough," she concedes.

"Also, I think I found a clue. Or something. I found a set of keys in the gallery, and well, it was like I held them and I knew that they were important."

"Important how?"

"I don't know. With my dad. Or something. I felt like they were tied to another memory, another time, something that's close to the surface but that I can't pull out yet."

She makes a note on her pad now, and doesn't respond.

"Can't or don't want to?"

"Can't!" I say, annoyed at her intimation. "Why wouldn't I want to? I look around here, and I'm jealous, mind-blowingly jealous, that you can remember your graduation, your . . . I don't know . . . your classes in medical school!"

"I'm sure that consciously you do want to remember them," she says. "But I don't think it's a coincidence that nearly every memory you think you have is tied to your dad."

"Jesus, I *know* that you think I need to stop obsessing about him! But I honestly feel like he's my answer."

She looks up at me. "Why?"

"Why? *Why?* Aren't you the therapist? Shouldn't you be telling me that?" I run my hands down my brilliantly-hued sweater, as if removing excess lint, but really more as a way to show her: Look! I've focused on myself! I'm different! I've done the hard work, so why the hell won't you let me focus on *him*?

"I can't tell you that," she says plainly. If she picks up on my clues, she ignores them. "Because I don't know that I agree."

"Listen." I exhale. "Like it or not, I need to know who he was. I feel like that can unlock who *I* was."

"Look, Nell, I understand that this is difficult for you. And maybe we need to try something different—art therapy, which you expressed disinterest in. Or maybe music therapy, as I know that's a passion. Or maybe we can discuss God and your take on why you're here, why you survived."

"Well, it's not because of God." I cut her off, slicing my hand in the air.

"Fine. Point made. But the direction you're taking"—she pauses and chews the cap to her pen—"well, I think you need to decide which is more important: letting go of your past or uncovering it."

"Well, what if they're the same thing?" I retort.

"Well, what if they are?" she says back, just before her assistant buzzes her intercom to alert her for her next patient.

I mull over her point long after I've hailed a taxi and made my way home. Come dinnertime, after the microwave dings that it's nuked my macaroni and cheese, I grab my TV dinner and tumble onto the (ruby red!) couch with a fork in hand. I know that Liv isn't being unreasonable: that when you lose, very literally, your mind and survive the unsurvivable, the very purpose is to dig as deeply as you can go to unearth the core, the ultimate epicenter, and maybe this means shifting the spotlight more on myself, less on him. *It's easier the other way, though, isn't it?* I think. I've made changes, sure. I've become less judgmental. I've reveled in the newfound joy of life. I've overhauled my living room and my wardrobe, and yet . . . still. Still, I might be stuck right back where I started.

I test the noodles with my fork. Anderson feels guilt at surviving but I just feel . . . I contemplate it. I feel lost. That's it exactly. And maybe I'm so lost because I had no idea who I was in the first place. Rory and Peter and Tina Marquis and my mother have all told me who I was, who I was supposed to be, but how can they really know? How can anyone really know? Can our lives be summed up by the assorted impressions of bystanders? Ice Queen. I ponder my high school nickname. *Really?* Surely, the Ice Queen couldn't have been everything about me.

I set aside the plastic container and reach for the phone.

My mother picks up, out of breath, on the third ring. *Oh Jesus, please don't let me be interrupting their sex session.*

"Darling! Yes, hello!" she says.

"Are you busy?"

"Well," she hesitates. "A little." Tate mutters something in the background. "But I'll make time." She clearly covers the phone with her hand and says something muffled to Tate.

"Were you in the middle of yoga?" I ask. *Please, please let it be yoga!*

"We can call it yoga if that makes you feel more comfortable, dear." *Oh for god's sake, it's no wonder I'm as fucked up as I am!*

"So listen, Mom, I ran into Tina Marquis the other day."

"Tina Marquis?" My mother's voice creaks up a decibel as she tries to place the name. "Oh, the cheerleader from high school? I haven't thought of her in ages, though I guess that's not true since I occasionally see her mother at the market. It's a shame what happened."

"What's a shame? What happened?"

"Oh, nothing of consequence. Just let herself go. As if she can't still be living and loving her life in her sixties. Darling, if I have to tell you that I'm in the prime of my life, then you haven't been listening."

"Ugh, Mom, I'm listening. Can this not be about you and your weird fetishes and spirituality?"

She tuts and sounds offended. "Now, why do you have to go and be contrary?" She seems poised to unleash a diatribe, so I cut her off.

"Anyway, Tina Marquis said that Dad came back. In high school. For my graduation. Which, quite obviously, is the first I've heard of this. So is it true or not?"

There's a long swab of dead air on the other end. I watch the cable box tick from 7:33 to 7:34 and glance down to notice my macaroni slowly congealing. Finally, I hear her inhale.

"That was never proven," she says. "I really can't say."

"So it's possible."

"I don't believe so, no. I would have known. You aren't just married to a man for seventeen years of your life and don't know these things."

"But you didn't know he was going to leave. How could you know if he came back?"

"Because I would have known!" she says, her temper slowly

elevating. "I just would have. A wife knows these things. He would have told me, would have wanted to see you and Rory. He wouldn't have just blown through town without so much as an explanation for why he left!"

"A wife just knows," I say flatly. "That's a ridiculous sort of explanation. Is that to convey that I should I have known about Peter? Done something to prevent him from sleeping with Ginger?"

"Oh, now, Nelly Margaret! Don't start testing me! Don't start personalizing this! But I would have known, and this has nothing to do with you and Peter, and besides, the fact that if he came back for graduation, do you honestly think"—she pushes her breath out now, and I envision her turning a particularly flush shade of purple—"well, do you honestly think that if he were still checking up on you, after all you've been through with the crash, he wouldn't have tried to reach you *now*?"

Something sharp detonates inside of me. My heart.

"Oh," I say, because it's all I can manage. This has never occurred to me before this very moment. That my father is out there and hasn't extended himself even after . . . even after all of this.

"Oh, see, now look. I always talk too much when I'm upset!" my mother bleats. "Your sister gets that from me. I just can't keep my mouth shut. I'm sorry, I shouldn't have put that out there." She pauses. "But I've gone and said it, and really, that's probably the most cathartic thing for us both. So darling, please, let this go. Let *him* go. You are doing wonderfully and your marriage is healing, and you're back at the gallery, and life is looking so up it can't look any higher."

I nod, and then I click good-bye, which is for the best so that she can't hear my tears, either. I kick his sketchbook, the one that Jasper promised was a map back to my father's world, from the coffee table to the floor, where it splays and flops open like a dead fish.

I should have trusted that instinct, I realize. To hate him. To exorcise him from my life because, really, who needs a father once you've grown and made it on your own?

It's only later, once I've tucked myself under my sheets, that I realize how wrong I was: not that I didn't need a father, but that my instinct was never to hate him. That, in fact, it was the opposite: that I loved him so much that I was never capable of fully letting him go. I stare at the blackened ceiling, waiting for sleep to come, haunted by the notion that if I can't trust my own instincts, then, well, what else have I got?

22

"There's a Light That Never Goes Out"
—The Smiths

M aybe he's dead," Peter says when he calls me the next day from his retreat in the Berkshires, and I am weaving my way through foot traffic. I haven't asked if Ginger will be there because it seems almost beside the point, but still, a niggling part of me wonders. The old me wants to ask—*is Ginger there?*—but the new me tempers her, trying to be more confident, trying to move on from the scars of the past.

"Is that supposed to be helpful?" I press my finger into my ear to ward off the car horns. It's started to drizzle, the bleak clouds hovering too close, bearing down, threatening suffocation.

"I'm just saying. Maybe he's dead, and that's why he didn't call you when the crash happened."

An umbrella nearly takes my eye out as a fellow pedestrian

jockeys for sidewalk space, and I spin around and flip him off with my free hand. But he's already pushed beyond me, unaware of his intrusion, unaware of my overreaction to it.

"He can't be dead." I sigh, annoyed at the chilliness of Peter's suggestion but simultaneously disheartened because death seems like the only decent explanation to prove me wrong. "Even if he were the most reclusive of recluses, someone would have known. It would have been reported. We'd know."

"Well, then, this doesn't make sense."

"None of this makes sense!" I say a little too loudly while waiting for the light, and the two men next to me, hipsters in their twenties with scarves tied in perfect knots around their necks, baseball hats with ironic graphics tugged low on their faces, turn to stare. Then they do double takes at the recognition that, yes, it's me—the freak from *People*, the anomaly from *American Profiles*—and my eyes bulge back at them. *Just move the hell along, there's nothing to see here.* So they adjust their hats even lower and step off the curb, despite the still-red light.

Peter and I click good-bye, and I shove my phone into my bag, pulling out my iPod, stuffing the earbuds in. I filter through the music, looking to match the angry beat of my steps. I settle on the Smiths and keep moving.

It's been less than a full day since my conversation with my mom, and already I can feel myself coming unhinged in a way that I haven't been since the immediate aftermath of the accident. The grayish, dour me rearing her head despite my best efforts to shove her back. My mother's revelation—that after months of my trying to pin myself to my father, perhaps he never wanted to be pinned down in the first place—has set me off, a skein of yarn coming completely unwound.

Last night, after sleep refused me, I succumbed to Anderson's helpful text to "grab a six-pack and just let it go." I threw my phone onto Peter's side of the bed, tossed the sheets back, and slunk toward the kitchen. I started with the six-pack, despite my medication, despite the side effects. Truth be told, it felt *good*. To be loose, to blunt the endless chatter in my head. Armed with the alcohol, I plunked down on the piano bench and played—spontaneously, freely—until finally, yes, I adhered to the second part of the text, and *let go*. I called Jasper Aarons and left him a long, expletive-filled message about what he could tell my dad should they ever come in contact, and then I stormed around the apartment, scooping up my father's sketchbook, tearing out at least half the pages and tossing them into the garbage bin, the lid slamming with approval and finality. I pulled out my childhood pictures, excising him from my photo albums—not, to be fair, that he was in all too many pictures to begin with. But a few, yes. A posed family shot out by the woodshed. A hazy captured moment during an Arizona vacation, a drop from the nearby pool blurring the outer corner of the lens, the sun reflecting idyllically to project a portrait of the perfect family unit.

And then there was one of us that I'd missed the first time, tucked in between the pages, not in the plastic sleeves themselves. It must have been taken that summer, the summer of the white house, the one buried somewhere in my memory. Who manned the camera? Perhaps me, because the photo was of my dad, sleeping, solitary, content. In the background, I could barely make out a sliver of a painting in progress. He has a mustache and a goatee, which he appears to have grown for this occasion alone, as he's scruffy but clean-shaven in every other image, and his cheeks are tanned, his eyelashes thick and protective. There's a baseball bat on the floor underneath the couch on which he sleeps and splatters of paint, well, everywhere. His fingers, the pillows, the hardwood next to the slippers near the sofa.

I stared at the photograph, with the fourth beer blurring my edges, and cocked my head, a rage sparking through me like dynamite. Rory claimed that it took me months the first time around to believe that he had gone. I flipped my palm over and stared at the scar entrenched deep in my skin. And here we were all over again: my refusing to acknowledge the simple truths. I had fallen from the sky and my dad hadn't come to try to heal me. Hadn't abandoned his selfish need for solitude to wander out into the bright lights of the world and rescue his little girl.

Well, fuck that. Well, fuck you!

I popped the lid to the fifth beer and fell, exhausted, onto the sofa. It turns out that my theory was right all along: people don't change. Me, my dad, no one. Screw the red couch, screw the sweaters and the cute little blazers and the closet that now looked like the underside of a rainbow. Screw the new, fabulous me. Screw it, screw her, screw him.

Today on the street, I spot Tina Marquis under her pink umbrella. The rain is picking up now, and I shuffle as quickly as the sidewalk congestion and the ache in my torso allow. The change in weather makes my bones hurt in a way that they didn't before the accident, as if they're all imploring me to stay in bed, dive deep and safely under the covers.

"Sweetie!" Tina says, pulling me close by the elbow. "You're practically a drowned rat. The first rule of this weather: always come prepared."

It's impossible not to smile at her genuine, openhearted kindness, despite my mood, despite everything. I pop out my headphones. I can see why we were friends way back when.

"That's what happens when you lose your mind. You forget the basics," I say, matting back my damp hair, brushing the wayward pellets off the shoulders of my trench coat.

"So I told him that we'd be in and out," she says. I nod. This seems like a Hail Mary anyway.

"Thanks for doing this," I say. "I'm trying to put things back together, but it's starting to feel like they're impossible to connect."

"Listen, Nell." She's suddenly morose, that chameleon rearing her head. "We were best friends. And then we weren't. But we were for a long time, and if I can help you—even with some easy favor like calling up the client to show you the space you were interested in—I'll do it. That's no skin off my back."

"Well, I know you have places to be."

Tina unlatches the outside door and enters a security code into the panel on the side of the foyer.

"And I know that you're terrible at asking for help. So I'm hardly going to shirk it when you finally do."

"Always? Was I always terrible?"

She pokes the Up button for the elevator. "Hmmm, not

always. I don't need to tell you that you became, well, more independent when your dad left. But then, who could blame you?" She
shrugs, holds the open door, and I step inside. "I didn't."

"I just cut you off? Like, black and white?" I remember my
mom's words from way back in the hospital: *We all have our faults.*
Yours is that life is in black and white.

"It wasn't just me, so I didn't take it personally." She smiles, and
we both watch the overhead numbers as they tick upward. "Being
a teenager is brutal. We were all dealing with our own crap."

"What was your crap?"

"Mine? Oh, the usual: eating disorder." She looks at me, her
shoulders rising, then falling. "Bulimia through sophomore year in
college."

"Wouldn't it be nice not to have our own crap?" I say, recognizing fully that losing your memory of that old crap is precisely the
opportunity to do just that.

"The crap makes us what we are," she says, then shakes her head
and laughs. "Or maybe that's just a pile of bullshit left over from
too many self-help books."

"Maybe." I grin back. "Maybe that's exactly what it is."

The door dings open on the fifth floor.

"Just down here to the left," she says, pointing the way. I survey
the hallway. It's nondescript in the way that a lot of New York
apartment buildings are. Beige carpet, dull overhead lighting,
muted wallpaper with an innocuous faded stripe. A sad-looking
pumpkin cutout bought at a local drugstore adorns one of the
doors as we pass it by, a pathetic attempt to brighten the hallway
for Halloween, still weeks away. Tina stops in front of apartment

number 513, pulls an enormous set of keys from her purse, and tinkers with the lock until she finds the right one. The latch unbolts with a confident click.

"You loved this place as soon as you saw it," she says, our heels echoing on the hardwood through the foyer. "You said it was almost animalistic, how much it spoke to you. I remember that quote because it seemed so poetic."

I step forward into the space. It is expansive, radiating light despite the dreary, depleted day, with soaring ceilings and that original brick wall and fireplace that Tina had told me about back in the pizza parlor. The beamed ceilings resonate somewhere inside of me, and I stare upward, wondering why they look so familiar, why this whole scene puts me both instantly at ease and entirely on edge. I move toward the wall of windows, with their view of the East River. The glass is streaked with threads of rain, and below, the river looks treacherous, roiling from the storm overhead.

I close my eyes and imagine. I can still hear the Smiths in my mind, providing me a sound track, a map to what I am dreaming.

"It's not my home, it's their home. And I'm not welcome no more."

I must have first seen this place when? Five or six months ago? April. It would have been April, right on the cusp of spring. I open my eyes again and envision the river calm, welcoming, and then it comes to me.

Of course.

I remember it clearly, that summer. This wasn't in the main house, it was . . . where? In my father's studio. I know this on instinct. In my memory, the rug beneath my feet, it's the same one that's now in my living room. I am barefoot, and the fabric isn't as worn as it is today, but still it's soothing, tickling the rough skin of my arches. The Smiths, just like today, are thundering in the background, but I'm unsure if this is a crossover from my synapses or if this, too, is real. There is a picture window in front of me, swallowing up nearly the entire front façade of the workspace, and out just beyond it is a body of water. A lake? A river? It is a wildly beautiful, glorious day, and my thirteen-year-old self is itching to dive into it, so I have gone in search of my dad to come out and play. My dad . . . I search my brain as I stare out at the rain-soaked skyline and try to home in on my father. *There he is.* He is in the corner, leaning against the brick wall of his studio, pressed together like a ball, a fetus. He is sobbing, moaning, emitting sounds of an injured seal. There are pools of paint splattered every which way on the wall, a smashed easel at his feet. A lonely, empty dartboard has fallen on the floor just beyond the fringe of the rug. My childhood self watches him from just inside the door frame, and gingerly I take a step back, then another, creeping so I don't betray what I've seen. I take one step more, and my ankle gives way, rolling under itself until I, too, am crashing to the floor. A baseball bat—*the picture in my album*—spirals next to me, and I hear my dad jolt from the other room. Suddenly, he is over me, his shadow casting a pallor from the bright rays brought in by the outside sun. He is pale underneath his goatee; the circles under his eyes are etched in black.

"Get out of here, Nell," he says, his voice weary, with no malice behind it.

"Don't be sad, Daddy." I push myself to a stand.

"Some things can't be helped," he says, already turning and moving to fold himself back into the corner.

An explosion of thunder roils over the East River, and as quickly as it came, the memory is gone.

On the way out, after Tina has bolted the door and stuffed her cartoon-size key chain back in her bag, I remember my own set of keys. I dig into the front pocket of my purse.

"You seem to be an expert in locksmanship," I say, placing them in her hand. "These. In your opinion, what are they from?"

She flips each one over in her palm, inspecting them like a biologist, running the tip of her index finger over the grooves.

"They're house keys," she says. "Nothing like this is from a New York apartment, and they're too big for a safe-deposit box or locker or storage facility."

"But I don't have a house," I say flatly.

"Well," she says, just as the elevator plunges us downward, "someone does."

23

Jamie and I convene on Saturday for our next interview for *American Profiles*. The producers want to take advantage of the perfect blast of October air by shooting in Central Park.

"They want to get that melancholy stroll with the leaves crunching in the background, your face looking pensive," says Anderson when he picks me up in the town car that the show provides. He's insisted on coming, to stand by and ensure that I'm not in over my head—after all, *you're the girl who saved my life,* he says, our little inside, though still truthful, joke—and that Jamie doesn't take advantage, even though I've assured him that he wouldn't, that he won't.

"Still won't reconsider?" I ask Anderson. I know that Jamie has implored him once again for a sit-down, told him that, like it or not, he is part of this story, part of my story.

"Still won't," Anderson says. "No more press. No more unnecessary press."

"You realize you sound a bit like an ass when you say that. Like you're beating them off with a stick."

"In case you haven't read, I am a bit of an ass." Anderson shakes his head. "Or I was. I'm trying to be better. Not believe the hype. Remind myself that being the star of a now-canceled television show and a few so-so movies really isn't all that, not bringing world peace or anything."

"Though Spielberg *is* calling," I say, scooting closer, resting my head on his shoulder, letting my eyes float shut under the weight of my exhaustion. The phone rang three times last night between 1:00 a.m. and 3:00 a.m.—hang-ups each time—and I never fully ebbed back into sleep. Instead, I lay there and wondered who was on the other end: Wrong number? Ginger? *No, no, not Ginger.* My father? That last one seemed the most preposterous, but still, I wondered. At 4:00 a.m., I gave in to the insomnia, furious at myself for even indulging in the fantasy that my mother was wrong—that my dad, after all these years, was extending himself. I rose and brewed the strongest coffee I could stomach. Since five o'clock, I've been sitting on my couch, staring at my father's painting over the mantel, waiting for Anderson to arrive.

The driver drops us off at the Sixty-sixth Street entrance near the old Tavern on the Green. Three horse-drawn carriages wait in the cul-de-sac, the animals looking both annoyed and depressed, their owners smoking cigarettes on a nearby bench. The sidewalks and abutting curbs are littered with gourd-colored leaves, and the air smells like burning pumpkin, like someone on Central Park

West has fired up his wood-burning stove high enough to scent the whole city. Jamie is standing by the traverse with my mother and Rory, both of whom will be imparting their own versions of my story on air. They wave in unison, and we cross to meet them.

My mother kisses Anderson hello and pulls me into a tight embrace. I swallow what smells like patchouli oil and clamp down on my gag reflex.

"Are you nervous?" she asks. "Because I remembered something you used to do when you were nervous as a girl, in case you are, in case you need to relax." I pull back and look at her. "It's nothing, just something small. An idiosyncrasy of sorts." She bats her hands, and I can see that clearly, *she's* nervous. "Anyway, you used to sing to yourself. Made-up songs. All sorts of here-and-there melodies and lyrics. I'd come into your room on the first day of school or before a swim meet or whatnot, and you'd be staring out the window, just lost in your own place, singing."

"That's sweet, Mom." I kiss her on the cheek. I can sense how that might put me at ease, how music could have been my balm, and I'm grateful that she's offered this to me. It's not so difficult to have gratitude, I realize. Even as the new me and the old me struggle to find a middle ground, still, I can evolve somewhere in that space between them. I kiss my mother again, riding this wave of appreciation for her, for my life.

"It's not much," she shrugs. "But maybe it will help soothe your nerves."

"I'm not nervous, but thank you all the same."

I wave to Rory, who gestures nonchalantly back at me and sort of wrinkles her nose at Anderson as a way of greeting. He mirrors much the same back. There's a strange tension between them, has been since the gallery show, and I narrow my eyes and assess.

"Are you two okay?"

"Okay," Anderson bobs.

"Okay," Rory bobs, too. "Why wouldn't we be?"

My mother's cell phone rings, and she croons hello to Tate, wandering off to pet the horses while she talks. I can't help but notice the massive mound of horse shit in the driveway and watch her dance around it on her way. That's my mom. I almost laugh out loud. She can always sidestep the shit. I smile because now I can see how this might be admirable, how her optimism might have been her buoy through it all.

Anderson motions me over to a bench, casually shifting his arm around my back once we're seated.

"So, listen, before you get started, I've been meaning to talk to you about Paige." We watch the camera crews finalize their lighting and map out my blocking. We'll be solemnly strolling along the footpath between the east and west sides of the park, the better to capture both the changing seasons and our stoic expressions, the type you see on every news program when someone's life has veered wildly into the crapper: the widower gazing out with arms crossed onto an open lake; the mother of a soldier walking through her neighborhood, her worries on display in the fine lines around her eyes, her brokenheartedness showing in her jawline.

"Paige who?" I ask.

"Paige Connor. That reporter who came by the gallery at the opening. From Page-Six."

"What reporter?" Rory has ambled over, curious about what was so private that Anderson opted not to include her.

"No one you know. And she wasn't there for the show. Or the art," Anderson retorts.

"Well, you don't have to be an asshole about it," Rory says.

"How am I being an asshole about it? What about that statement said 'asshole' to you?"

"I just didn't appreciate the implicit suggestion that I'm some sort of media whore. And also, FYI, we sold every piece from the show—a new first for us."

"What are you talking about?" he says.

"What are you both talking about?" I say, watching them, their figurative fur upended, a catfight imminent.

"Nothing," Anderson says. "This has nothing to do with Rory." He shoots her a look as if to say, *Shut the hell up and keep your nose out of it,* which she responds to by shooting him a similar look that says, *Get over yours, and who invited you into our business in the first place.* "But Paige. She's a gossip reporter of the worst kind."

"Is there any less worse kind?" I joke, but it goes nowhere.

"Actually, there is," Anderson says. "My people won't even talk to her."

"Your people?"

He catches himself, then makes a retching sound. "Okay, rewind. Ignore that previous statement. The point is that Paige is vicious. She stops at nothing to break her story, even when publicists have done their best not to let her. You know: offered her better coverage in the future, or given her a scoop on someone else.

She'll run both stories. She'll burn bridges. She wants to make a name for herself."

"Is this about the fact that she's run something on you at least once a week since we've been back?" I ask. I start to mention the latest—"Andy's (Arm) Candy!"—but I can tell he's serious, so I shut it.

"No, nothing about that at all"—he zips his vest up an inch—"though it goes to show how deep she'll go. None of my friends are talking about who I've been with, what I'm doing. But she has sources out there on both of us, and she's not afraid to exploit them."

"So why was she at the gallery?" Rory says, offering a détente.

"I'm trying to figure that out. I've made some calls."

"But what's your gut telling you?" I ask, before it occurs to me that I stopped trusting my gut a long time ago, so why the hell should I trust Anderson's?

"Unsure," he says. "Only that wherever Paige Connor goes, a shit storm is sure to follow."

My mother, never afraid of drama, embraces her inner actor for the cameras. There is weeping when she speaks of our childhood, there is weeping when she speaks of the crash, there is weeping—subtle, stoic weeping—when she's not speaking, when she is simply asked to stare at the nearby tree while the camera pans away from her. I observe her from the sidelines and pang with sympathy, not because I necessarily believe all of her tears but because clearly she has suffered, and for that, I suppose, she should be allowed her due, her right to grieve, even if it's on national television.

"The Ice Queen is thawing," I say aloud, though Anderson doesn't get it and Rory is too far out of earshot to hear me.

A small huddle of spectators has gathered on the traverse to watch us unspool our melodrama, and Anderson has doled out half a dozen or so autographs, mostly to twenty-something women who push their breasts forward, even in their peacoats, and toss their hair over their shoulders when he stops to chat. He swallows up the attention but for less time than I'd have expected, and soon enough he's bored, back over to me, back by my side.

"I thought you might want to take one home for the afternoon," I say.

"Too early," he says back. "I have a newly implemented no-sex-before-six rule."

"Impressive," I say. "High bar of moral standards."

"I try," he says, and we both smile because we know that he does, that he is. That six months ago, he would have tucked his hand in the back pocket of one of the brunettes and hailed the nearest, fastest taxi.

My mother's tear ducts do manage to dry up, however, when Jamie raises the subject of my father. He'd told me via e-mail last night, that they were going to have to address it. My dad was the elephant in the media room: nearly everyone who was tuning in now knew who he was. Thanks to me, he's never been more famous. Rory confided last week that the offers she was getting on his remaining pieces were enough to fund our nonexistent children's college funds, a comment I wholly ignored, as it spewed up a wealth of issues about my pregnancy all over again. I should have raised this with Liv, how I was stuffing these feelings down my emotional bowels, but, well, it seemed easier not to. Easier to pretend that Rory hadn't said it, that my nonexistent children once very much existed, that life was stitching itself back up. If I opened myself up to more—the looming quagmire of the miscarriage and the pregnancy and what the hell I was going to do about both the baby and the marriage—well, it was like a row of dominoes: toss one over, and the rest were bound to falter sooner or later. And besides, now that things were mostly smoothed over, why upend them? Why stir up trouble when I've finally clamped the lid on it?

I lean against the cool bark of a locust tree and listen.

"Is it disappointing to you"—Jamie asks my mom, as they stop by a bench on the east side of the park and sit—"that Francis hasn't been back in touch with the family, after all that you've been through?"

My mother looks shell-shocked at the question, and I'm not sure if it's because I hadn't prepped her on the subject matter or if it's simply too public a forum to discuss such a topic. But then I realize that nothing is too public for my mother, for god's sake, so it's obviously the former. She stutters and stalls for time by blotting her mascara with a wadded-up tissue.

"I try my best not to discuss her father to the media," she says when she finds her tongue. "But I will say that, of course, I am disappointed to my deepest core that even though he is a recluse, he couldn't come out from wherever he may be to support Nell."

Jamie offers a nod, the type you suspect news reporters practice in the mirror. He is in his element now, plasticized almost, an altered incarnation of whom I know him to be.

"So there has been no contact—*none*—since the outside world stopped hearing from him as well?" Jamie presses her. He knows this will make headlines, could land him a permanent slot on the *American Profiles* team. He also knows—or I hope has at least considered—that he is asking on my behalf. That was the deal: *get me some answers, and I'll get you your exclusive.* So I watch, and I hope that he is mostly doing this for me, even though my gut—*my damn gut, shut up, I don't trust you anyway!*—nips at me, telling me otherwise.

"You have to understand"—my mother says—"what it was like to live with a genius like Francis. I suppose that part of me always felt that I was living on borrowed time with him. But I made those choices as an adult. Our children did not. So even if he wanted to come back into their lives, he'd hurt them too much for me to allow that once he left."

I feel something come unhinged inside of me, torpedoing down, deep, deeper. Next to me, Rory furrows her brow and gnaws on her index finger cuticle, then glances toward me, perplexed.

"So you're saying that, in fact, you have heard from him over the years?"

"No, no, no, no, no, no." My mother pales and starts to stammer again. "I'm saying that if I *had* heard from him, I'm not sure it would have been welcome. He probably knew that." She nods to herself, as if this is any sort of affirmation that she's convinced us.

It wouldn't have been welcome? What about her lecture in the hospital? What about these past few months, her nudging me back into my marriage, back to my husband, back to my old life?

I can't help myself. My previous moments of goodwill be damned. Hello, old me, so nice to see you again!

"But what about forgiveness?" I shout off camera. Jamie turns and looks at me, alarmed, as if to say: *This is not part of my plan.* I give him a look back saying, *Yes it is. I want my answers. You knew the deal, too.* I keep going: "What about all of that crap that you fed me to forgive my own husband for his indiscretions and that everyone has to look inside themselves and find a way to heal, blah, blah, crap cakes, crap cakes!"

Jamie signals to the cameraman to cut, but then thinks better of it, and he circles his finger around in a loop: *keep shooting.* At the base of our instinct, we really are who we are. He's the newsman on the hunt for his scoop.

I signal back to the cameraman—*quit!*—though I don't really know the industry signal, so it mostly looks like I'm trying to slit my neck, or maybe like I want to slit my mother's neck. Either way, the cameraman doesn't obey, and the tape keeps rolling while my mother digs herself deeper. *Quit! This is* not *open to a public forum. We both got what we wanted, now quit!* I jerk my hand across my neck once more, but Jamie simultaneously rolls his fingers. *Keep rolling.*

My mother, of course, doesn't quit. Once she's unleashed, she can't quit, can't tuck back her ball of emotion if she tried.

"Nell! I have done nothing wrong!" She waves her arms. "I *did* forgive your father, and if he is out there watching, Francis, darling, please, come back and help your daughter." She turns toward the camera to issue her plea, akin to a soap opera gone bad, even though she's still speaking to me. "Everything that I imparted to you about forgiveness and healing and your own marriage came from a place of true sincerity. I have worked for *years* to get to that place for myself! I only wished it for you as well."

I stare at her for a beat and then realize that, finally, she's not crying. Dried up like a well. Does that make it more plausible or less? I chew my lip and wonder. And then something else occurs to me, too: after years of running from who she was, after all the goddamn yoga retreats in the world, my mother has been running a loop. Running right back to who she was before my dad left, still filled with the same hypocritical bullshit that probably started her on that loop in the first place.

"You don't get it, Mom," I say finally, that stupid goddamn cameraman adjusting his angle for a close-up. "You're like a rat in a wheel. Running, running, running, running. And you think you've gotten somewhere. But that's the illusion of the experiment. Nothing, no matter what you think, has changed."

There, I think, triumphantly. I've gone and proven my theory: *people can't change.* And then it occurs to me, of course, that this isn't a triumph. This is a brick wall. And there's no getting around it, no matter how hard I try.

24

"Let the River Run"
—Carly Simon

*I*n his vow to become a contributing member of society and actually attempt to use this second chance to do something with his life, Anderson has agreed to host a benefit later that evening for the Humane Society.

"You don't even have a dog," I point out in the limo on the way down. Along with his promise to spread the philanthropic love, he's also staying true to his promise to curb his taste for supermodels and less than Mensa-quality actresses, and thus, with Peter still in the Berkshires, I am his date for the evening. I am wearing a wholly un-me, but entirely fabulous eggplant-hued, thigh-high cocktail dress that I bought back when I still believed that people could change. I blew my hair out, swiped a new lipstick from the makeup artists on the set, and, as Anderson noted when he met me in my lobby, cleaned up nicely. "They'll start to write about us, you know," he said. "If you keep this up, they'll mistake you for one of

those models I go home with." I knew this was his form of a compliment, so I blushed and took his hand and stepped into our ride.

"But I love dogs, I do," he says in the limo, adjusting his navy tie
and popping a CD into the stereo. "So . . . some news. I remembered something from the plane."

"Another nightmare?" I rest my hand on his knee.

"No, in fact, just the opposite." He smiles. "Remember how I
couldn't remember the bands, the bands we were listing? As a distraction?" I nod because he doesn't have to elaborate: the bands we
were listing as a distraction amid the horror of the crash. "Well, I
remembered. Last night when I couldn't sleep. This was who you'd
been listening to on the flight before I interrupted you."

We both fall silent, the music filling the space.

"Carly Simon." I grin. I know this one from my playlist. I lean
back and sponge it up, her voice resonating somewhere inside,
loosening things, loosening me.

"Music for your mood, for starting over. That's what you'd said
on the plane." Anderson pours a Jack Daniel's from the bar, while
I am rapt, absorbed in the music.

"So today . . . that was unexpected," he says, after a firm
swallow.

It takes me a moment to come to, to pull myself from the melody. Finally, I answer: "Unexpected how? That my mother still
harbors resentment for my dad or that she was able to mask it so
well for all of these years instead of putting her daughters' needs
first?"

The truth is that I tried to call Peter at the retreat to rehash it, to
make sense of it, and when I was sent to his voice mail, I tried to

call Liv for an emergency session, but I haven't heard back. So now I know damn well what he's referring to, and it's a relief to have a sounding board—whether the sounding board is my husband, or my therapist, or the guy whose life I may have saved who has helped me to save mine.

"I didn't take it that way," he says, making me a drink of my own. I shake my head no. "Take the drink," he insists. "Trust me on this. You'll need it. These things seem like fun, but they never are."

I hesitate but, bolstered by the music, by the power it gives me, I do—both take the drink and trust him, and even with that first sip, I feel my insides warming, the steeliness of my anger unleashing.

"No, I took it that she was trying to protect you, like a mother bear or whatever the analogy is," Anderson continues. "She didn't want him coming back to wreak more havoc. Maybe she *was* putting your needs first."

I take another gulp and consider this. I know that I should be more sympathetic, that these past few months should have shown me this. That there is no time in life for resentment and grudges. But I just can't bring myself to do it. I just can't get there, the new, fabulous me be damned. *My mother is that mother who wants you to think she's putting your needs first while wholeheartedly shuffling hers to the front of the line.*

"You know, she's the entire reason I gave Peter a second chance." It feels strange to say this aloud, this guttural admission that I wouldn't have thought to realign myself with the man who felt too big for me back when I opened my eyes in Iowa. That my honest instinct would have been to do entirely otherwise. "We sat outside the hospital and she swore to me that I'd be a better person if I learned to forgive him. Told me that I'd always been too black and white, that there were shades of gray." I snort and drink another sip, then thrust my glass out for a refill.

"Okay, so what if that makes her a hypocrite? In the end, aren't you glad that you listened?"

I blow out a deep bellow of breath. That part, I suppose, is true. Against all expectations, my marriage has rebuilt itself. Is it the world's greatest love affair? Undoubtedly not. Is it doing okay considering his one-nighter and that my brain has been obliterated to the point where I have no history to lean on during our crisis? Well, for that, I'd say yes.

The limo coasts to a stop before I can articulate this. Anderson grabs my hand as I step to the curb. Around us, the flashbulbs explode, blinding me for a moment, sending my blood coursing through me, my heartbeat palpable within my chest cavity.

"Shit!" I exhale, and then I feel his hand on the small of my back, steadying me as we go.

"You okay?"

I'm not, but I shake my head yes. We can't turn back now anyway. The lights are too bright, the screaming from the photographers too loud. And then I remember: it is like a giant macabre flashback of the crash. With Carly Simon still etched in my cerebral space—*"We're coming to the edge, running on the water, coming through the fog, your sons and daughters!"*—I can intuit the horrifying squeals of the passengers around me, spiraling to their imminent peril; the searchlights from up above, dilating my pupils to the point of discomfort; the chaos and the haziness in the ensuing minutes, sifting through the smoke and the debris and the moving parts all around. My breath expands within my lungs, and for a sickening minute I can't decipher which is real, this reality or the one from my past, the moment or the memory.

"You okay?" Anderson asks me again, and I see the genuine concern in his face, and because he literally has my back, *Yes, I am okay,* I say. I don't need to ask him if this reminds him of the crash site because I already know that everything reminds him of the crash site. This is why he barely sleeps, this is why he's had two Jack Daniel's in the fifteen minutes on the way to the event.

"Anderson, Nell!" The photographers are calling at us like we are cattle to be herded. A stern-looking publicist, who appears to be about twenty-four and takes her job about a thousand times too seriously, pops up out of nowhere and flares her hand. *They're not talking to the press!* She whisks us through the media circus, stopping to pose us in front of the Humane Society banner once we're through the bulk of the melee.

"Nell!" Someone catcalls to me from the end of the press line, and Anderson and I turn simultaneously to see Paige Connor furiously waving at us.

"Don't take her bait," Anderson says, refocusing, still smiling for the cameras.

But it's too late. This time, I *am* acting on instinct, trusting my gut. Whatever she wants, whatever she is looking to uncover, let her bring her worst and show it to me. I may not remember much about where I came from, but slowly I am remembering who I am.

And I'm not one to let some tabloid reporter beat me in a street fight.

"Hi, Paige," I say. "What's up?"

In an instant, Anderson is beside me. "You don't have to talk to her."

"Whatever our history is, Anderson," Paige says, "this actually doesn't concern you."

I look at him, and he shrugs, and I know that they slept together years ago, and he most likely treated her as he has so many other women in the past, and, by god, bless him for proving my theory. Old dog. New tricks. Impossible.

"You have two minutes," the publicist snaps at Paige before intently staring at her clipboard and muttering something indistinguishable into her cell phone.

"As you know, we've been covering your story," Paige says.

"As I do know, you've been covering my story." I lower my voice to a bass tone, mocking her with her gravitas that—hello! look around you!—is entirely ridiculous for the pomp and circumstance of this event. I can feel the whiskey coasting freely inside of me. Just that one glass has already wormed its way completely through. The backs of my knees throb, my blood pulsing like it's attempting to launch a mutiny through my skin.

"Well, as you know, I've been covering your story," she tuts.

"And as *you* know, I do know, so can we move on? Or are you looking for an exclusive scoop that you know I know you know."

She flushes at this, but her beady, determined eyes stay focused. She reminds me of a character from that Arnold Schwarzenegger movie I watched a few weeks back with Peter: a terminator, laser-ing her targets, then *blam!* I giggle at the idea, and turn to share as much with Anderson when Paige pulls me back.

"I can see that you don't take the media seriously, though he should have told you otherwise." She gestures to Anderson, who rolls his eyes and reaches for my elbow, ready to whisk me away and be done with it.

"I do take some media seriously," I say. "Jamie Reardon. I take him seriously. He's proven to be aboveboard, so I take him very seriously."

"Ah." She laughs at this. "Okay. But however you see it, I'm about to break a front-page story. A career-changer. A life-changer. None of this child's play 'Randy Andy' stuff that we've been doing on him."

"And what is that?" I ask. Anderson steps forward like he needs to protect me, like he can intuit the dismemberment that is about to unfurl. I splay my arm against his gut, hitting his abdomen, warding him off.

"About your marriage," she says, checkmating me in a game I probably don't understand well enough to be playing in the first place. "About your husband and the woman he claimed he loved, and how he never told you the truth but how she told Jamie, and Jamie told me, and now I'm about to tell the world."

By the time the limo drops us off at my apartment twenty minutes later, after Anderson made sweaty apologies to the publicists, and after he agreed to a hefty donation from his next paycheck, I have inhaled two more glasses of whiskey—enough, Anderson notes dryly but not unsympathetically, for a person of my weight and tolerance to sink like an anchor. Rory, along with Samantha, who flew in earlier from Hong Kong and looks like she has jousted with jet lag and lost, are waiting in the lobby of my building—on the ride home, Anderson had insisted on calling them. No one speaks as the elevator ascends to the apartment, though I can see the two of them, my sister and my best friend, locking eyes, trying to telepathically assess how best to deal with the grenade explosion.

"One of you better start talking, and by talking, I mean, like, yesterday," I say, once the door has slammed shut. Anderson makes himself useful by pouring glasses of merlot.

From the couch, Samantha starts, then stutters, so Rory waves her hand and says, "Look. We didn't know how to handle this. No one did. There's no rule book here."

"Is that supposed to be some sort of explanation? Some sort of goddamn screwed-up rationalization as to why you didn't tell me that my husband *was fucking* another woman for a year?" Tiny shards of spit fly out of my mouth.

Paige Connor had unceremoniously dumped the details on me just before Anderson grabbed me by the waist and physically removed me from the premises. She, ever so smugly, rattled off that it hadn't been a one-off, a one-night stand. That Peter and Ginger had been sleeping together for a good year, and that he left me—for her—to move in with her, to create a life with her, to love her in a way that he didn't love me. He had told me all of this before I kicked him out the first time. *He had told me all of this and still, no one had told me any of it when it really mattered. When I couldn't*

know it for myself. He came back two months later, filled to the
gills with despair at the absurdity of his decision—that of course
he didn't love her! That he was such a goddamn idiot to love her!
That he would do anything to find a way to make me forgive him.

This is what Ginger had told Jamie, and this is what Jamie had
told Paige. In confidence. With the idea that Page Six would run a
small teaser, and he would then run the ratings-grabbing interview
with Ginger on *American Profiles.* But even a scoop can be scooped,
and Jamie isn't quite the pro he thought himself to be. Paige
trumped even that.

Twenty minutes later, I don't even know where to pinpoint my
rage: at Jamie, at Rory, at Samantha, at my mother, at Peter. The list
is too long to contemplate.

"It's not supposed to be a rationalization," Samantha says quietly now. "We just didn't know what to do. All of us wanted to give
you a second chance, and even if we didn't like it—didn't like that
Peter got absolved of his behavior—we also didn't not like it
enough to ruin that second chance."

"That's bullshit," I say.

"I tried to warn you at the gallery that night," Rory says, because,
of course, she always has a goddamn defense.

"What the hell are you talking about?" I say. Anderson places a
glass of wine in the pass-through, and I drink too much, too
quickly, my larynx burning as it goes down.

"I tried to make Peter stay behind, to let Anderson take you
home, to, you know, give you some warning that I didn't approve."

"*That* is your way of letting me know that my husband was

cheating on me for a year? By acting like a bitch and bossing people around?" I am yelling now, wishing so very much that I could
forget this moment, this part of my life, too. It's so much easier
when it's all just a whitewash. Also wishing that the newer me
could be blunted toward this rage in the first place. But she can't,
she isn't, and I'm right back to where I started. "Because that's,
like, every day of the week for you, Rory!"

"Oh, give me a break," Rory says, and I can't believe for one moment that she is indignant. "We put up with you like that for years."

"Don't make this about me," I shriek. If I had it in me, I'd slug
her across those perfect cheekbones. "This is about the fact that I
have no basis for who I am without you telling me as much. And
you *didn't. You didn't tell me.* So what does that say about me?
What does that say about *you*?"

"It doesn't say anything about you," Anderson interjects.

"Don't stick your nose where it doesn't belong," Rory shoots
back at him.

"I'm just trying to help," he says, not particularly kindly.

"Look," Rory shouts. "I told you last time, okay? I was the one
who told you. Not Peter. I found out and I came to you, and you
never forgave me for it!"

"That's ridiculous!" I shout back. "Why wouldn't I forgive you
for that?"

"Because you kicked him out but he was just waiting to leave,"
she says flatly. "Looking for his excuse after a year with Ginger.
And then you turned around on me—*on me!*—and said if I hadn't
told you, he never would have had a foot out the door! Like that

makes any sense! Of course by the time he came to his senses and begged for you back, you were so angry with both of us that it didn't matter anyway. Refused to see it any other way."

"Total bullshit!" I say. The old me wouldn't have absolved him. Or maybe I would have. Maybe I got comfortable making excuses for my dad, and so I found a way to make them for my husband, too. Who knows anymore?

"I don't care what the hell you think it is! It was when everything changed—when you started pulling up everything that made sense in your life. And eventually, we weren't even speaking because of it, so yeah, you better believe that I wasn't about to rush to you now with this! Screw me once, shame on you, screw me twice"—her voice wavers here, calming—"well, you know the saying."

"I don't actually."

"Shame on me," she says. "Screw me twice and shame on me."

"Nelly, listen, we should have told you," Samantha says, the calm in the storm. "And I can only speak for myself, but I am very, very sorry that we didn't."

"The baby," I say, finally tempering myself. "Did you both know about the baby and keep that from me, too? That you knew? What I was going to do with it? How I was coping?"

They shake their heads in tandem.

"I already told you, back in the hospital—I didn't know. Like I said, we weren't speaking," Rory says.

"I swear on our friendship that I didn't know, either," Samantha echoes.

Well, that's just goddamn pathetic, I think. And then realize that

I'm thinking this about myself, at how I couldn't reach out when I needed someone most. That the self-reliance I'd just discovered in the press line wasn't the problem, wasn't what I needed. It was just the opposite: letting myself lean when I thought I could hold up okay on my own. That martyrdom was never my deficiency. Vulnerability, well, yes, that one didn't come easy.

But rather than acknowledge this revelation, I stomp over to the laptop and press Power. The screen bursts alive, the background image a shot from a vacation I don't remember with generic-looking palm trees and two strangers squinting into the sun: Peter and me, before, before all of this.

"What are you doing, Nell?" Anderson says. "Come on, let's not do this."

I wave my hand as if to say *shut up,* and then click open Peter's e-mail. My eyes run double from too much whiskey and wine, but not double enough that I can't scan for intimate details of the *year-long fucking affair* in which he chose her. *Chose her! He showed up in the hospital and made me want him, made me want his baby, made me force myself to want a life with him again. He told me about Paris, he told me how we fell in love, he told me every goddamn thing about myself when I had nothing else to believe.*

So I did. I believed him. No wonder I never chose vulnerable. Who would?

On first glance, there is nothing in his e-mail that betrays him—the fingerprints have likely long since been wiped clean, so I slam the laptop shut, scanning the room, looking for invisible evidence.

"Done? Feel better?" Rory says, and I can't tell if she's being empathetic or sarcastic.

"What is your problem?" I spin around and face her.

"What is *your* problem?" she says back. "I was asking, 'Do you feel better?' What could you have possibly interpreted from that?"

"Please, the both of you, stop," Samantha says. "There are other times to air your issues with each other. This isn't one of them."

"You're right." Rory exhales, then chews her lip. "I'm sorry."

"For this or for what you just said?"

"For both, okay? Can't you just accept an apology and move on? Must you make it harder on everyone, always?"

"I don't make it harder on everyone, always!" I reach for the wine too quickly, and it splashes on my waist, seeping into the eggplant dress, camouflaged like it was never there in the first place.

Rory gives me a steely look, and Samantha just sighs and stares into her lap. *Do I? Do I always make it harder for everyone always? No, vulnerability was never my strong suit.*

Eventually, I grow weary of their remorse and don't want to rehash another second of this mess. I ask them to leave, and Rory does with her chin still high in the air, like she doesn't have one thing to apologize for, like it might actually slay her to admit real culpability. She and my mother—I almost laugh out loud—cut from the same cloth and all of that. Samantha is more contrite, and hugs me tightly good-bye, her voice cracking under the weight of her guilt—that she didn't tell me sooner, that she hasn't done more to guide me wherever it is I need to go.

"You can't guide me," I say, despite the lessons of the hour. "This is my thing to do alone."

"Don't say that," she pleads. "That's who you were before. Alone. Independent. Even when you didn't have to be."

"Why were we friends?" I ask.

"I'm sorry?" She stutters. She is standing in the door frame, perched on the precipice between the hallway and my apartment.

"If I was such an Ice Queen, why were we friends?"

Initially, she looks confused, and then her face relaxes.

"For a lot of reasons," she says. "Because you were the girl who would tell me to stop one shot before I puked in college. Because you were the girl who drilled me for the LSATs, staying up until we saw the sun rise at that crappy diner on my block with the inedible matzo ball soup, when you knew that I wanted to get into Harvard Law School. Because when I broke my nose skiing in Utah, you not only cleaned up my bloody tissues in the hotel room, but you subsequently talked me out of a nose job." She touches a bump on the bridge of her nose. "You told me our scars give us character."

"I said that?"

"You did." She nods. "Which isn't to say I didn't make a few calls when we got back to town, but still, I've lived with it. I, at least, pretend that this bump makes me more interesting."

She smiles now, a sad smile but a smile all the same.

"You should have told me about Peter," I say.

"I know, but let's not make that everything, okay? Before, maybe you would have never forgiven me." She hugs me again and pulls back and looks at me, really examines me like she's seeing me for the first time. "Now, let's not make this everything."

25

I wake early on Sunday, having slept only two hours and hungover in a way that I suspect I've never been before, the remnants of alcohol oozing from and dehydrating my cells. I check my phone to see if Liv has returned my call, but there are only two texts, one from Samantha, apologizing again, and one from Anderson, ensuring that I haven't offed myself (or trudged to the Berkshires to off Peter) in the wee hours of morning.

I toss on a hoodie and some sweats and slide out the front door. As I make my way through the quiet streets of the Upper West Side, I can practically feel my intestines churning, like sludge through my digestive tract. My eyes are too puffy, and my hair is a haphazard ratty bun, and to add indignity to my already fairly low indignation, I am forced to slink past the newsstands, all of which plop the *Post* front and center, the paper screaming with the headline "Forget This!" There is a picture of Ginger and Peter—the

fuzziness makes me think it was snapped from a camera phone—
their cheeks pressed together, both of them grinning unbearably
cheerful grins, the glow from a TV just above their heads in what
looks like a sports bar. And then there I am, too—that sad sack of
a picture that *People* magazine ran way back when: nearly clutching my literal pearls, looking so tightly wound that I imagine half
of the *Post* readers wouldn't blame Peter for sleeping with Ginger
in the first place—the photo that has nothing to do with the new
me, even though, if I were to really look closely at both it and who
I am now, I might find some ghosts, recognize some of the old
shadows left behind.

Liv is exactly where I knew she would be. I hesitate by the park
entrance, watching her sip her coffee, fold over the page of the paper.
It feels big, brave, almost too much, to step forward and acknowledge how badly I need her, how badly I need someone. Eventually, I
amble toward the gate of the dog run, and as I unlatch it, she looks
up, casually at first, then startled to recognize the face coming
toward her.

"Nell!" She stands. "Did you get a dog?"

"No," I offer. "But I brought fresh coffee."

"I'm sorry, I don't understand. What are you doing here?"

"I needed to talk to you," I say. "I left a message at your office."

"You really shouldn't be here. This isn't appropriate." She casts
about to find Watson, who is over in the corner sniffing some
leaves. "We can find some time tomorrow."

"Look, please. I'll never do it again, I promise. I know this is
unconventional and that you have all these boundaries . . ."

"There for good reason," she interrupts.

"I'm sure they're there for very good reasons," I say. "But I'm here, and I just need fifteen minutes." I can see her wavering. "And I did bring fresh coffee."

"Fifteen minutes," she concedes, sitting back down. "And for this, I expect some seriously diligent work this week."

"I may be taking a break this week. Out of town."

She looks at me skeptically. "What happened? Tell me what happened that you had to ambush me on a Sunday morning in the dog run."

So I tell her. About Peter. About Ginger. About Paige. About Jamie, who left me a halfhearted voice mail saying he didn't intend for me to find out this way, and he hoped that I'd call him for an explanation. And about Rory and Samantha, and the destruction that comes with bottling secrets up too closely.

"So who are you most angry at here?" Liv asks when I've cut through the bulk of the story.

"Who am I not most angry at here?" I echo.

"Shouldn't it be Peter? Because it doesn't sound like he's the one you're the most upset with."

"I'm furious with him," I say to Liv, considering the truth of it. "But maybe I'm also relieved."

"About what?" She reaches down and grabs a tennis ball, hurling it toward the back of the dog run. Watson, who has meandered over toward us, takes off like a shot.

"That my instinct was right."

"What instinct?"

"That instinct I felt back in the hospital—when I saw him. He didn't feel right for me, but I tried anyway. Tried to let my mother and everyone else convince me otherwise." I shrug. "For once, god knows, my instinct was right." I don't have to mention how wrong I was about Jamie, my decision to trust him, my false sense of familiarity, like he was an old friend, a cousin, a brother. *No, no, certainly none of those.*

"And what of your mother? Rory?"

"I'm so unspeakably angry with them that I don't know what to do with myself." I hate how brittle I sound, how hateful I am, but it's there all the same. I *am* angry, I *am* brittle.

"That they didn't tell you?"

"For starters. Yes! And that they didn't treat me enough like a grown-up to sort this out on my own!"

"You realize you're contradicting yourself," she says. Watson runs over panting, delivering the tennis ball to her feet. She shucks it back across the run. "You're angry that they didn't tell you, and yet you're angry that you didn't trust yourself in the first place to do it on your own."

"Listen, I'm pissed off at a lot of things! You can't tell me that I don't have the right to be!"

"I'm not telling you anything," she says, then takes a long sip of her coffee. "Let's get back to the free association we did in our early sessions."

"I kind of want to *talk* about what just happened," I say.

"Yes, I get that. But first, you came to me today, so I make the rules. And second, the point of that free-association exercise was for you to explore those instincts that you've disregarded, spit out whatever is in your gut, and then consider it, rather than stuffing it down where you'll never hear from it again."

"We're back to my walls."

"We were never past your walls."

I sigh. "Did I tell you that my nickname in high school was the Ice Queen?" I ask, and she shakes her head no. "Well, it was. Evidently. Or so I've been told." I think of the Beatles' song for which I was at least partially named. *It's a song about the loneliest woman in the world!* Jesus, I think, what chance did I have?

"And what does that say to you?" Liv asks.

"It says that I've long been an expert in, as you say, stuffing that stuff down into my gut."

"And now?" Watson is back with his saliva-covered ball. This time, I scoop it up from the ground and toss it as far as my once-broken body will allow.

"And now," I say, "maybe it's time for a change. Maybe it's time to pull up whatever was stuffed down and unclog my intuition."

"I thought you said that people can't change." She looks at me now and smiles.

"Don't listen to me." I smile back. "Don't you know that I've lost my mind?"

"God, I haven't road-tripped it since sophomore year in college, right after I dropped out," Anderson says, situating himself inside the driver's side of the SUV we rented at Hertz on Monday morning. The car smells like old cigarette smoke masked by lemon air freshener, and under other circumstances, I might have complained and demanded a new one, but this is not before, and as Samantha said, I am trying not to make this about everything.

That when you tumble from the clouds and slay the odds of surviving, maybe the little things can't matter as much. So I strap on my seat belt, holding my breath, and eventually my senses adjust and I stop noticing what was so offensive—the stomach-churning mix of nicotine and manufactured citrus—in the first place.

"Where'd you go," I ask, "on your trip?"

"Packed up my old Volvo and shot from Poughkeepsie to L.A. with my fraternity brother." He laughs, remembering whatever it is that he's remembering—the crappy hotel rooms, the waitress he bedded from the truck stop, the flat tire outside of Salt Lake City. "Jesus, I should call my buddy and say hi." He shakes his head and says, more to himself than to me, "I haven't spoken to him in forever."

"I can't remember if I've ever road-tripped it," I say to him. "So we'll call this virgin territory."

"And Rory? Is she coming?"

"No."

He nods, getting it. That there are some things to let go, and others not to. There are lines to be drawn, and maybe this is my line. Maybe, even though I did indeed tumble from the clouds and slew the odds of surviving, it doesn't mean that I can't feel bruised when sucker punched, turn the other cheek and refuse to look back.

"Don't be angry at her forever," he says, turning the key, the engine responding with its hum.

"Says the guy with the emotional gravitas of a fly."

"Says the guy who never let himself get too invested because it's easier not to," he says. "But easy isn't always better." I can tell that

he is thinking of his old roommate, and how life was less complicated back then. Just the open road and the prospect of Los Ange-
les. And he is thinking how he'd like so much to pull into a truck
stop with his old friend right now and not deal with the complications and the grief that this life has brought to both of us. What
had Samantha said back in the hospital? *Sometimes, I wish we
could be twenty-one again.* Only at twenty-one, I wasn't who I
wanted to be at all.

"So why not call your friend? It's not too late."

"Maybe I will. I lost track of everyone once things took off for
me," he says, clicking the blinker and turning out of the garage
onto Broadway, then navigating over toward West End and the
highway south. "Where exactly are we headed?"

"South. Just drive south." The truth is I'm not entirely sure
where we're headed. Charlottesville. That I know. The rest, I'm
winging. My phone buzzes in my back pocket, and I shift to pull
it out.

"Jamie," I say to Anderson, then click the Decline button, the
country-western ring that Peter had customized for me swallowed
up in an instant.

"I'm not going to say, 'I told you so,' in case you were waiting for
it." He smiles.

"You can say it regardless."

"But I'm not. You trusted your hunch, went for it. You didn't
know. It was like sheep to the slaughter. He and Paige, they just
knew better."

"But my hunch wasn't right."

"That doesn't mean that it was entirely wrong, either." He veers onto the highway and flips down the sun visor. "He helped you get what you needed. Answers, whether or not they were welcome."

"Well, once you get past the various ways he manipulated me, I suppose this is true."

"So get past it," he says. "There are other things anyway. Don't give him your energy when you need it for so many other things."

I squeeze his shoulder. "My own personal Buddha."

"I'm trying," he says, "you know, trying to be that better person we swore we would be." He glances over his shoulder to change lanes. "And what about Peter? Word from him?"

I exhale. I so very much want to make this trip not about Peter, not have anything to do with Peter. If I could, I would pretend that he didn't exist entirely, that I hadn't betrothed myself to him, that I hadn't carried his baby though no one was the wiser. In fact, I realize, I would very much like to forget him in the way that my amnesia has made me forget everything else. The irony isn't lost on me, nor is the fact that Liv would be telling me that my desire to forget him is the very problem in the first place.

"No, no word," I say quietly.

In fact, Peter will return to the apartment tonight to find the stack of his e-mails—I'd gone back to his laptop after promising Samantha that I would let it go—and discovered them deep in the bowels of his deleted files. His disgusting, love-professing, sex-stinking e-mails—printed in a concise stack on our dining table. He will find his closet empty—in a frenzied state of what Anderson deemed "terrifying, tornadic Zen" on Saturday night—I stuffed the bulk of his clothes down the garbage chute in the hall, and he would find a concise note in my handwriting, a pathetic summation of this whole debacle: the past few years of our marriage, the past few months of my life.

> *Dear Peter:*
>   *We're done. I'll be gone through Thanksgiving. Be gone when I'm back. That will give me something to be thankful for.*
>
>   *Nell*

My phone rings again—that grating country-western clang—and I remind myself to change it. My mother. Rory has surely reported the carnage back to her by now.

I press the phone to my ear, immediately regretting it.

"I have been trying to reach you since yesterday!" she says, a little too hysterically. "Rory told me what happened, and I want to come into the city and talk about this."

"There's nothing to talk about, Mother," I say. Anderson tweaks the radio down a volume peg, but I wave my hand at him, telling him to turn it the hell back up. This won't take long. "And besides, I'm not in the city."

"Well, where are you? I'll come there, to wherever you are!"

"I'm on my way south," I say. Enough of an answer that she'll know, she'll intuit it.

There is a long pause in which I imagine her screaming inside her brain, and I smile at the idea, of giving it back to her as good as she gave it to me. Even though I know that I can't make this about everything. But as with Rory, yes, there are some things I need to make it about.

"How can you possibly think this is a good idea?" she says, finding her voice. "This can't end well, and you shouldn't go chasing skeletons who don't want to be chased."

"This isn't about their skeletons," I say. "It's about mine. About getting the answers I should have asked for a long time ago."

"Look, Nelly Margaret, I think that you're fragile and unbalanced right now with the news about Peter, and *I really do not think this is advisable!* Have you spoken to your therapist about this? Thought about the consequences?" She is spiraling now. "Because these things can't be undone! I've been there. Why won't you listen to me? These things that you're doing, they'll change everything! And you have no idea what that means, what that's capable of."

"Mother, don't you get it?" I say, when she has exhausted herself, knowing full well that she both gets it—that's the part that haunts her—and doesn't get it at all. "The change, the blowing everything wide open: that is the point entirely."

My body, despite being virtually healed, can't stay frozen for too long, so we break for the afternoon outside Washington at a roadside diner that Anderson says reminds him of his college trip.

"Only then, we'd order six beers and split the cheapest toast and eggs, and call it our meal for the day."

"Other than the cheap toast, what's different?" I say, scanning the menu.

His forehead wrinkles as he mulls this over.

"I'm trying"—he sets down his own menu—"trying to grow up. I think it might be time."

"Don't be ridiculous. Twenty-eight is way too early to grow up," I say, then grin.

"Another fair point. One more, and you'll turn me into a monk for life."

The waitress whose hair is overly crimped and who has saggy breasts and a sad-looking face that reminds me of a basset hound wanders over to take our order. She does a double take at Anderson the way that people do when they recognize you but can't decide if they should publicly acknowledge it, and her cheeks turn even pinker under her unnatural swath of wet n wild blush.

I have the French toast, Anderson the waffles and fruit bowl, and then I pull out my father's sketchbook. After I nearly destroyed it, tearing out the front half of the pages, I've barely even taken notice of it. I laid in wait, hoping that other people would deliver some sort of answer, some sort of salvation that was never going to come. Now, it's time to dig deeper, peel back the skin on my own, even if it means incurring some scars.

Scars give you character, Samantha had said. Or I had said to her, and she then said back to me when I needed to hear it most. I flip over my palm and run my finger over the imprint from that night when I finally accepted that my dad was gone and wasn't coming back. What other wounds had he carved into me that I couldn't yet acknowledge?

"Have you made any sense of it?" Anderson nudges his chin toward the drawings.

"Not yet, but I feel like it's the key to something, to where we're going." I giggle self-consciously. "God, that sounds ridiculous."

"I went through a phase in my early twenties when I believed in all of that crap—that we're all connected, that there's a yin to every yang."

"So you think this is crap?" I'm not offended.

"No, certainly, some things are connected, sure, but if I hear one more person tell me that *this happened for a reason,* I think I'm going to kill someone."

"It makes people feel better." I shrug, though I remember the vow I made to myself, to take this seriously, to spin myself into the fabulous me, or maybe even more accurately, the happier me. I'd settle for the happier me. "To try to tell us that there's sense behind this. Liv even wanted me to discuss God."

"God." He laughs, and doesn't even need to add, *Who's that?* "I think I'm backing out of the Spielberg project," he says after a beat.

"That's insane. No one backs out of a Spielberg project."

"In light of everything, it seems silly. Dressing up and acting out someone else's words."

"Don't be idiotic," I say, turning a page in the sketchbook.

"It's not idiotic! I don't feel like pushing myself right now. I want to . . . I don't know, breathe! Drive to Virginia with the girl who saved my life!"

"I thought the whole point of this second chance *was* to push ourselves." I can hear myself, chastising him like a mother would a child. "Don't turn your back on something you're actually pretty good at just because you worry you're not up to the task. And don't use me as an excuse for it, either. And breathing. What does that even mean anyway?"

"I never said I didn't think I was up to the task. I said the task itself is meaningless." He grabs a Splenda pack from the kitschy sugar holder and starts flapping it back and forth. A nervous twitch.

"Weren't you the one who told me, on that night in the gallery, that art isn't meaningless? That it resonates and that's what's important?"

He wrinkles his nose, trying to remember. "Look, it's just so much easier not to take it."

"To flush a decade's worth of work down the toilet because it's so much easier? Who ever said anything about this being easy?"

Before he can answer, two brunettes in pencil jeans and turtle-necks bought in the children's department swarm the table, breathy and wide-eyed at the prospect of meeting Anderson Carroll.

I listen to their over-the-top fawning, and then excuse myself, sketchbook in hand, to the bathroom. They slide into the booth exactly when I leave, a seamless transition that barely gives Anderson pause. *He's never turning down Spielberg,* I think, waiting outside the restroom door, *even if it's not easy for him.* I hear the toilet flush behind the door, and I flip the page to the drawing that mesmerized me the first time: a shattered face, a child's. The eyes—something about them is familiar. They're not Rory's. They're not mine.

The bathroom door swings open, and a disheveled-looking mother with a ratty ponytail escorts out her toddler, clutching his tiny little fist, navigating him back toward their table.

I watch them for too long, until the boy is settled back into his highchair, until he has knocked over his orange juice, and the mother, in her exasperation, has snapped at him to finish his eggs so they can get going already.

"Are you going in?" A woman taps my shoulder behind me, and I startle.

"Excuse me?" I say.

"The bathroom? Are you going in? 'Cause I really need to go."

"No, no, go ahead of me," I usher her in with a sweep of my arm, and she scurries past, bolting the door.

The baby. I have to deal with the baby. What I was going to do—get my answers. My intestines clench, and my appetite is strangled along with them.

"I'll be in the car," I say to Anderson, on my way to the parking lot. "When you're done, come find me." I trudge outside and cast my neck around at the landscape, like the answers might be tucked behind the pickup trucks, the minivans that litter the lot. *No, I* think, *not here.* If there are any answers to be found, I'm going to have to look a little harder to find them.

26

"Into the Mystic"

—Van Morrison

There is little to no reception on the car radio, barring an old-ies station that every once in a while breaks up into static even though the car is unmoving. For the tail end of October, it is a glorious day. The fall leaves, in this desolate spot outside the nation's capital, are bursting from the tree limbs: ruby red, golden yellow, a veritable feast of riches. The air smells like firewood, like nutmeg, and I wish, so very badly now—with the window down, the sun's rays pressed against my cheeks—that *I could just remember*. Remember what it was like to inhale a fall day as a kid, remember dressing up for Halloween, or gathering gourds in my mother's garden for an autumn feast. You don't realize until there is an absence of it, but your memory is the foundation of *everything*. Your marriage, sure, there is that. But of so much more than that: your family, your self-perception, your ideals about the future. And here, in the driver's seat of a rented SUV on my way to my father's mistress's home that I can't recall, I am gutted by the fact that it might never happen: I might never remember those soccer games from the falls of my childhood, of whether or not I sucked on frozen grapes, and whether or not I was a decent midfielder, and whether or not my dad showed up to cheer me on the sidelines. Who, really, are you, if you don't know where you come from?

This entire time, I'd counted on that: those little shards of memory easing their way back in. But what if that's it, there are only slivers, nothing in its entirety? The idea of failure weaves into my psyche, sweat pulsing from my underarms. What if this trip yields nothing? What if my father's sketchbook means nothing?

I open his book once again in my lap, my fingers tracing those familiar eyes, the emotion behind them both resonant and haunting.

Think, Nelly, think! Who is this? What does it mean to you? I try to force the circuits in my brain to connect, to somehow rewire themselves and magically grant me, after months of fumbling in the darkness, a light.

I ease the seat back and shut my eyes, trying again, trying harder, trying to knock down the walls to whatever it is that I'm protecting, refusing to let back in. *What else is there left to lose?* Nothing. There is nothing else to be taken from me, so by god, this is me at my lowest. I implore my will to relent. *Relent.* Because from here, there is nowhere else to go.

The static on the radio blares then fades, and then the music is back, swarming the car, swarming me. It's a song that Rory has thought to include on my iPod, so the melodies, the harmonies are already part of me, the lyrics like a vision: Van Morrison, rusty and croaking and wonderful.

"When that foghorn blows you know I will be coming home, And when that foghorn whistle blows I got to hear it, I don't have to fear it."

Something sparks within me, and it spreads like a flame of joy throughout my veins. And then I can see it, I can remember it— the music from both now and before, melting together, a swirl of past and present, memory and reality, now and then.

"Hey!" I hear a voice, startling me. Anderson is outside the open window.

"You're already done?" I ask.

"It's been half an hour." He pokes his head closer. "What have you been doing?"

I stare down at the sketch, to the one thing that I've been running from maybe this entire time.

"Oh my god," I say, peering closer, and then, yes, I remember. "I know where we're going. Come on, get in. I don't need directions. I know the way."

Behind the house, there is a dock. This was what my memory had unlocked for me. This is what my ears—nearly disconnected from my brain—had sifted through the black noise for me.

I am in a pink bathing suit, with a stripe of flowers running up each side. My legs still are skinny, gangly, my hips haven't yet formed a full curve, my breasts are mostly small buds. There is a glaring red scab on my temple. My arms are scrawny and bruised on the biceps, like the tomboy in me who maybe played tackle football with Rory that summer. There is a boom box on the dock, its volume turned up to full tilt. Van Morrison is singing "Into the Mystic," just like he was in the car, his voice both aching and tender, from a mix tape that I have made for the summer. Journey, the Police, Jackson Browne, Van Morrison. They're all on there. *Of course.* It's so obvious, I nearly want to throttle myself for not seeing it sooner—that the music was the key. Always.

"Come in!" a voice shouts from the water. "Last one to the raft owes the other a Coke." I look out and see a rash of sandy hair bobbing and weaving, arms lapping each other in perfect form. So I take off at a full sprint, hurling myself into the cool, dark lake, pushing my legs as fast as they can propel me under the silent water until my lungs demand air. I resurface and see him already up there—squirming up atop the wooden raft moored fifteen feet away.

"You owe me a Coke!" he yells, smiling, his dimples cratering into his cheeks.

"Over my dead body," I shout back, sipping the lake water, spitting it back out as I paddle closer. "You got a head start. That's cheating."

I'm nearly at the raft when I hear someone calling me from shore. I turn and tread water, my pigtails wrapping around my neck like damp snakes.

"Nelly! Come on!" Rory whines. "You weren't supposed to get wet again! You have to come in now."

I turn and look back at the boy, his face a shadow of what it was just thirty seconds before.

"Come on. Now!" she yells. "Mom's here. And she's ready to take us home."

"Seriously? You just listened to something . . . and remembered? And now you know where we're going?" Anderson says.

We're nearly there now—thirty miles or so outside of Charlottesville. I remember the roads, the smell of the fields, the pastures, and though I can't pinpoint why, I know how to get there.

"Can you just drive faster?" I say, partially because I can't articulate it myself, partially because it doesn't matter: I do know, I saw something, and I want to get there as soon as possible to confirm it. Dr. Macht had expressed this way back when, almost four months and a lifetime ago, he explained that maybe there was a block, a straitjacket that I'd sewn myself into, and now, maybe I can find a way to set myself free from it, too. Everyone has told me that I'd always been a musician, always had that gift ("You got that from me!" my mother had said), but my father had pushed me toward art. And then when he left, I'd pushed it aside completely, barring the small gasps of bliss from the radio, a few binges of karaoke with Samantha, a stolen moment with Peter when we first fell in love.

And perhaps now, it's the key to finding my way back. To what? To who I was before. To who I can be after.

"So is everything back? All of it, all of your memory?"

"Not everything." I shake my head.

"But you're close," he says.

"Maybe," I concede, watching the whoosh of the trees blend

into each other as we speed by, wondering who the boy was, if he was my first love, if he loved me back. *You owe me a Coke!* What else did we owe each other?

"It's strange that your mom wouldn't have just flat out told you the address, told you about this place," Anderson says after we've fallen into silence for a bit, the wheels and the engine our background noise. I turn up the radio, that same oldies station following us down the highway. "Wouldn't she have thought to look here for him, your dad?"

"Who's to say that she didn't? That she didn't find him, that she didn't know?"

"True enough."

"Who's to say anything at this point?"

He goes quiet at this, and then quickly glances toward me.

"You think I'm wrong?" I say.

He shakes his head. "No. No, not wrong at all." He wants to say more but thinks better of it.

"I don't know," I say, a non sequitur of sorts, talking mostly to myself. "He loved this place."

On the radio, the DJ who has the evening shift clears his throat on air, detailing tomorrow's weather, then reading a kitschy advertisement for a local car dealership. "Here's your next set of oldies, coming to you commercial-free thanks to Dwayne's Custom Chevrolet," he says.

I don't even recognize the tune until a minute or so in, right when the chorus is about to break. It's following me, this song, this curse, this birthright.

"You know my parents named me for this song," I say. "About

the loneliest woman in the world. My dad, for a while, as cliché as this sounds, well, John Lennon was his muse. Until he outgrew that phase. But by then it was too late. I was already named."

"I don't believe that," Anderson says. "No parent would do that to a child."

"Ah Buddha, there you are again. It's true. I looked it up on Wikipedia."

Anderson laughs. "So no one has told you that you can't believe anything you read on there?" He glances over to me. "Maybe he just really loved the name and then wanted to look cool by dropping the Beatles into it. You know, coolness by association."

"You might know a thing or two about that," I say.

"I might. We artists are afflicted with the desire for coolness by osmosis." He reaches over and touches my arm. "Besides, it's only a song."

"But what if, as ridiculous as it sounds, it was my destiny? Who names their kid after the loneliest woman in the world?"

"So what if it *is* true. Parents do worse things," he says, and we both nod, an acknowledgment that indeed they do. "And besides, I thought we decided that we don't believe in destiny, that things don't have to happen for a reason. That that's all total bullshit." He looks over at me now and smiles.

"But what if it's not?" I don't smile back.

"Yeah," he says, "but what if it is?"

Anderson kills the engine in the driveway. A solitary light near the front door casts just enough of a glow to barely make out the house, which is dark but doesn't appear deserted. There is a red-and-green Indian blanket strewn across the bench on the porch, trash cans outside of the garage, a rake leaning up against the side wood paneling: all signs of life inside.

"So you're just going to go up and knock?" Anderson asks.

"Yes." I exhale. "I am just going to go up and knock."

"Listen." His voice catches, and he folds his hand over mine. I tear my eyes from the front porch to meet his.

"What?" I say when he falters. "You okay?"

"It's nothing." His hand is off mine now, and he waves it through the air, dismissing whatever has gone unspoken. "We'll talk another time."

"Okay."

"Remind me," he says, "in case I forget."

"You're not going to tell me you love me, are you? That I've finally ensnared the ungettable Anderson Carroll?" I am still staring at the porch, wondering how I am going to find the strength to ascend it. Now, with this banter, I'm just buying myself time.

"No." He laughs. "There are things to talk about before I profess my love for you. Just remind me, okay?"

We fall quiet.

"Want me to go with you?" Anderson asks.

I wobble my head but force a weary smile. *No. People have clanged too much in my ear as of late. If I'd trusted myself earlier, maybe it wouldn't have all become such a mess. This, I'll do alone. Not because I have to go alone, always. But because this time, I must.*

I collect my breath, which is moving quickly through my core, my heart accelerating along with my trepidation.

"Good luck," Anderson says, leaning over, kissing my cheek. "I'll be right here if you need backup."

I click the door open. The Virginia air is surprisingly cool, with a bite that nips my cheeks and a scent of dead pine. The gravel gives way under my feet as I steer toward the house, each step crunching beneath me toward what I can feel in my bowels is my destiny, what this whole thing has maybe been leading up to.

The house itself, even in the dim light of night, is exactly as I remembered it, exactly how I painted it, and just before stepping up onto the front porch stairs, I pause, lean back, and stare. The paint is peeling around the second-floor windows, and the black shutters are tightly shut in the attic, but other than that, it is as if I am thirteen again, remembering for the first time, remembering all over again.

It's amazing, I realize, the details that your mind can store: lyrics to every song you've ever known, even if you haven't heard it in twenty years; scents that can place you right back at your sweet sixteen or your first Christmas spent with your husband; small details—a run of notes in a melody, a hint of cinnamon in your apple cider—that embed themselves in your brain forever. Unless, of course, you're tossed from the sky, and your memory is tossed with it. But even then. Yes, even then, some of those details remain. Bread crumbs to help you make your way back.

The porch boards creak as I ascend the stairs, my hands trembling from a dangerous combination of adrenaline and nerves. I turn to glance back at the hopeful face behind me. Anderson peers out the car window, and I can see him nodding his encouragement. Suddenly, something shifts, and I hover over the porch railing, wondering if, for a fleeting second, I might puke. But then I gather myself and push up the final two steps to the front door.

There's no bell, so I grab the knocker and rap three times.

Nothing.

I don't even realize that I'm holding my breath until I hear myself exhale loudly, my entire torso shaking, like I'm exorcising a demon. I wait another ten seconds, and still nothing, so I turn on my heels, the weight of defeat, of the fact that this *whole concept was utterly foolhardy, totally ridiculous, like it could have been as easy as this! Why did I start listening to myself now when I've more than proven that I have no fucking concept what I'm talking about!*— and start back to the SUV. But then I plunge my hand into my pocket and remember: the keys. Found on the top shelf of the gallery. They gave me hope, they gave me a glimmer, a sense that I might be able to tie a bow on this just yet. They are what set me off in the first place. I can't have come all this way and not at least try.

I pull them out, assessing which one to slide in first, even though they're all identical, when I hear it: the latch unbolting on its own, and I stare up to face the reaper of what? My past, my present, my future. Yes, all of these. The foyer light inside flips on, and then the porch light, too. I squint, trying to adjust to the changes.

A man, handsome in a rugged way, with crinkles around his eyes, and tanned cheeks even in dying days of October, swings open the door. His face goes slack when he sees me.

"Oh my god," he says. "You came."

27

*S*he looks exactly like he remembers her from nineteen years ago, though he wonders if this is accurate, since he's seen her on the news, seen her wary face in People *magazine. Maybe he's mixing up what he remembers and what is reality, he thinks, once she's seated on the couch, sipping the coffee that he's brewed at this hour, and trying not to stare. But it's been two decades. It's hard not to.*

"So you live here," she says, "not my dad?"

"Yes," he says, for the third time. He's read about her amnesia, so he knows that it shouldn't be as jarring as it is, but everything, the lot of it—her showing up, her void of memory—well, he might be as shell-shocked as she is.

"And these keys?" She sets down the coffee and jangles a familiar set of keys in the air. "You sent them to me?"

He nods again. They've been over this in the very first minute she arrived.

"Yes, back in March." *He clears his throat.* "With a note, too."

"I didn't find a note." *Her brow creases, like this might be the most perplexing thing in all of this. That she didn't find a note.*

"I sent one." *He shrugs, then wishes he hadn't, hoping he's not coming off as cavalier.* "I remember writing it, telling you that my mother had died, that she'd have wanted you to know that, and know that the house was still here and that you were always welcome." *He sighs.* "I never heard back from you, and, well, I wanted to be in touch when I saw you on the news, but I took your silence as a sign that you didn't want to hear from me. Didn't want to revisit that chapter, which, I mean, just to be clear, I don't blame you for."

Shit, he thinks. He knew he should have followed up. Shouldn't have let his own crap stop him.

"Your mom is Heather."

"Yes," *he says.* "You remember her?"

"Kind of, vaguely. In a dream . . ." *She stops to think, wrapping her arms around herself, like she's still cold from the outside air.* "I don't understand, though. I have so many questions."

He eyes her, wondering how much he can share in a singular conversation that won't send her off the deep end. She seems different than who she used to be, though really, after what she's been through, who wouldn't be?

"Your friend, in the car, should you bring him inside?"

She startles, like she's forgotten, then stands abruptly, rattling the table with her knee, and upends the coffee onto the rug.

"It's fine." He waves a hand. "You go get him, I'll clean up. I'll get more drinks—I think I have some Coke and wine in the fridge. It's all I have. I wasn't expecting visitors on a Monday night."

She angles her head, faltering for a moment, staring at him in the way that a child does a zoo animal.

"Cokes." She says it like she's hypnotized.

"Yes . . . Cokes. I have some cans in the basement."

"You—you're the kid from the dock."

"I'm sorry? I'm not following." He steps toward her and guides her back to the couch. She is frail—he can feel that when he moves his hand over her hip—and paler than he remembers. Her eyes have faded—they have a gray hue behind them that wasn't there. Her cheekbones are sharper, which makes her nose look sharper, too.

"Earlier today, I heard something—a song—and remembered you," she says. "Of you down at a dock, racing me to a raft, owing me—or rather me owing you—a Coke."

His face glazes over for a moment, and then he grins, widely, like maybe he did when he was thirteen, too.

"Yeah, that was me." He laughs. "You almost always lost, though not for lack of trying."

"And we"—she hesitates, her forehead wrinkling in thought—"I'm sorry, were you, like, my first boyfriend?"

He lets out an honest-to-god guffaw before realizing that she isn't joking, then buttons himself back up. "No, I'm sorry, you really don't remember at all?"

"No." She sits back on the couch, still watching, waiting for her answer.

"Okay, then," he says simply, sitting down beside her. "We were *hardly boyfriend and girlfriend.*" He clears the phlegm from his throat. "*I don't know how else to say this, but, in fact, I'm your brother.*"

If she is astonished *from the revelation, she doesn't betray it too much. Wes sees her wince, then her face goes totally ashen, and then, for a moment, he thinks she's going to pass out.*

"*It's a lot to take in, I know,*" *he says.*

"*This is the tip of the iceberg,*" *she says.*

"*Listen, it's a big thing, what I've just told you, and it's okay to kind of want to fall apart.*" *He watches her, wondering if she'll cry, thinking that in the same circumstance, certainly, he would.*

"*I've done a lot of that lately,*" *she says.* "*Falling apart.*"

"*And?*"

"*And what?*" *she says.* "*And now, I'd like to put myself back together.*" *She squints and sees it then, the connection—that, in an odd sense, in the right light, he looks like Jamie. The blond hair, the creamy skin. Yes, of course, she can see it now. No wonder she had trusted him. It wasn't that her instincts were so off, it was that they were blurred, misguided. She considers it a moment more: it wasn't just that. No, she wanted to take that leap, be entirely different from who she was before, so while she can point to the connection—that Jamie shares an odd resemblance to her newly discovered brother—she shoulders some of the blame, too. Not blame, really. She shakes her head, deep in thought. Responsibility. She gambled. She wanted to roll the dice. She did. She lost. There needs to be an ownership in that.*

A knock on the front door jolts them both, so Wes rises to unlatch it.

"*I'm sorry,*" *Anderson says.* "*I was freezing out there.*"

"Come in," Nell waves. "Meet my brother."

Anderson does a double take as Wes extends a hand.

"Half brother. And let me go get us drinks."

Nell stands slowly and trails Wes to the kitchen, halting abruptly in the precipice, staring up at the painting over the farmhouse table.

"Your dad's?" Anderson says, the same question that was posed so many weeks back in Nell's apartment, back when she reentered her new life, frozen, skeptical, alone.

Déjà vu, she thinks, only now armed with the hindsight that comes with standing on the ledge, taking a leap.

"No, not his," Nell says, before Wes can answer. Because she already knows. "It's mine."

You left it behind *when you guys left so abruptly," Wes says, rolling out the wineglasses, pouring the cabernet too close to the rims.*

"It's of the same dock, isn't it?" Nell asks. She's gazing at it wide-eyed, unblinking. Finally, she reaches for her glass and swallows fully, leaving just a puddle toward the bottom. Like a ripple, Wes does the same, the wine loosening them almost immediately. Anderson watches them but sips slower, more deliberately.

"Your interpretation of the dock," Wes answers, which seems self-evident, given the gray overtones, the wood planks that look more like daggers than anything ever originating in nature, how the water appears menacing with shots of light radiating in ways that the sun could never create. "When you left, I begged my mom to send it back to you, because I knew how much it meant to you, but she wouldn't let me. Well, I mean, she made it clear that we couldn't be in touch.

That your dad had gone back to your family, and whatever was left behind was"—he hesitates, trying to articulate it—*"well, whatever was left behind was a necessary casualty. The cost of their warfare."*

"She put it like that?" Anderson asks.

"No, my words, not hers." He rises to refill the wine. "All of them—my mom, our dad, your mom"—he gestures toward Nell with the corkscrew—"it was like playing a giant game of Battleship. Sunk sometimes at our own expense. That's how I remember putting it to my mom when you guys left: that she sunk my battleship. Well, that and a long string of swear words. I was angry through the entire fall."

"It's sort of a depressing piece for the space," Nell says. "Or, maybe it's just depressing that I'd paint something so bleak at thirteen." She exhales. "Jesus."

"Bleak or not, I liked that it reminded me of how things were before everything changed," Wes says.

"Changed for good," Nell says, a period to his sentence.

He looks at her, perplexed for a moment, and then half-laughs.

"You're here. So nothing is ever changed for good, Nelly."

She half-laughs back in response, and because she is trying to prove this theory correct—that there is nothing and no one that can't be undone—she listens to her instincts and believes him.

28

Jesus, I have had too much wine. The second glass was perfect, but the third was too much, and now the walls are moving, and the ceiling is cresting like a wave. I can see how quickly this can become habit, an easy slope to slip down into a numbed abyss, and I no longer blame Anderson for desensitizing himself to what feels like nerve endings that are too raw.

It's eerie: this room. It smells like vanilla potpourri, and the walls are covered in stark portraits, like Victorian death paintings, of people I don't recognize. They used to do that: paint someone after he died, eyes closed, the pallor already drained from his cheeks. I lie in bed, trying to ignore the macabre stares, and wonder what my own death portrait would look like: Who would draw it? How would I be remembered?

Wes has the house to himself, and it's too big for one person. He hasn't done much with it since his mom died. As he made up the bed, he mentioned that this was where Rory and I slept when we came that summer, the one that started me down this spiral. I stuff my head under the pillow and try to remember those days whispering late into the night, but of course there is nothing.

I slide out of the covers and off the bed. The floorboards moan when I tiptoe down the stairs, the kitchen light still on, the wineglasses dirtied and left on the table. I grab my jacket off the back of the chair and take a long inhale at the painting, jarred at how dark a thirteen-year-old can be. Jarred, really, at how dark I've been all along. *Eleanor Rigby. Ice Queen.* The shadow chasing me my life through.

I chew on my lip, the alcohol making me lucid in the way that alcohol can. This shadow, it feels like too heavy a weight to carry. Like it has drained me, sucked out life's possibility. I want to slice it away, cut it from my existence, and emerge from its cocoon to see what else there might be. I tried before, with the new couch and the new sweaters and even that new beret. But there is more: that's window dressing, nothing substantial, nothing substantive. I stare at the painting and consider this: maybe it's not that we can't change—that we can't shed the inheritance of our destinies—it's that to do so, we have to be brave enough to risk exposing ourselves, with the understanding that we might not like what we find. Maybe it's just that the only way to evolve is to force yourself into the wind when you'd so much rather take shelter. *Yes,* I think, *maybe that is it.* Maybe I can walk into the wind, with Anderson, with Wes at my back. Maybe now, I am strong enough, brave enough.

I sigh and shove my arms into my coat. My mind is tired from digesting. After so many months of digesting, digesting, digesting, I just want to cut the rope, even with this bait dangling so close I can nearly swallow it whole.

I swing the front door open, and the blackened outside air hits my face like a salve. I ease my hand along the wood siding to find the porch bench.

"Hey," a voice says, and I jump.

"Jesus! You almost gave me a heart attack," I say, my eyes slowly adjusting to the darkness, making out Anderson's figure on the bench.

"Couldn't sleep?" he asks.

I shake my head.

"Me neither," he answers, "though what else is new?"

I plunk down next to him and curl into his underarm, which smells a little like Speed Stick.

"I'm a little drunk," I say.

"And I'm actually a little sober," he says. "I stopped at one glass."

"There's a first for everything." We both laugh.

We sit there, with only the air between us, for who knows how long. I can hear his heartbeat through his chest, slow, steady, calming, and for a moment, I wonder if he's nodded off, finally finding sound sleep. But then I hear him sigh, and before I can think clearly, I turn my head, cradle his cheek, and kiss him, the alcohol my armor, protecting me if I royally fuck this up but illuminating things like I've never before seen them. He's momentarily surprised, but then softens, and though I know he's done this with a thousand girls before me, I close my eyes and pretend that this is fate, that the plane crashed, and that my husband cheated on me, and that my father screwed me over, and that it has all led up to this one moment, this moment that can change everything. I taste the cabernet on his tongue, and the firmness of his lips, and just as I am pretending this could go on forever, he gently pushes me away.

"Wait," he says, then runs his fingers over my face, like he isn't about to ruin everything. "This is too messed up." He stutters for a moment. "I wanted to tell you before. I tried to tell you before— in the car, but now, before this goes any further, I need to tell you about Rory."

I wake up with a jackhammer of a headache, my temples scolding me with every pulse at last night's overindulgence. With my side serving of humiliation at mauling Anderson, it is enough to make me want to down a bottle of Tylenol PM and call it a day, a week.

"It's not like I own you," I said last night, when that cabernet was still floating on my taste buds, when I could still feel his heat electrifying my nerves. *It's not like I had a claim on you! Ha, ha! Don't be ridiculous!* I said, though my intestines were broiling, and the anger was rolling through me like a cannonball. *But still!* Was it too much to ask for a little loyalty from someone around here?

"Frankly," he mumbled, "I'm a little surprised you made a move on me. We adore each other, Nell, but maybe we're confusing things." By *we,* I was certain he meant *me.*

And so I said, "I'm pretty sure that you have women throwing themselves at you all the time, you're a little bit of a man-whore, aren't you, so I can't believe you're surprised." Which was a dig, of course, because I was so pissing mad that I'd made such a fool of myself, but he deflected it, because at its heart, it was also true.

So he replied simply, and maybe a little sadly, "Nell, I think we're all pretty messed up right now. I mean, you left your husband twenty-four hours ago. And anyway, you're the one true friend I have now—*you're the girl who saved my life*—maybe we shouldn't risk it."

This morning, I roll over with my eyes still crusted shut, my mouth tasting like petrified grapes, and throw my arm over my face. I can feel the sheet marks on my cheeks, the burn of the old cabernet on the back of my throat. There is an incessant noise coming from downstairs that is making my veins throb, so I peel the covers off, toss my coat over my sullied clothes, and wander toward it. It sounds like disharmonious church bells until I realize that, in fact, it's the doorbell. I check the grandfather clock in the hall. It's 9:15 a.m. Anderson and Wes must still be asleep from the late night, the wine.

I push a glob of sleep from my right eye and roll my tongue over my teeth, wishing very much that I'd thought to use a toothbrush in the past day.

"Coming!" I stage-whisper. "Coming, coming, coming!"

I unbolt the lock, which Anderson must have flipped when he came in at whatever hour he finally retired, and swing the door open, a cool gust coasting in as way of greeting.

"Well, thank god!" my mother exclaims, her wrist bangles

jangling as she flares her arms. "I found you in time to talk some sense into you and bring you home."

She glides past me without invitation, and just as I'm about to slam the door tight, I notice Peter lingering just beyond the porch, and then Rory two steps behind. My mother, my goddamn mother, just can't leave well enough alone. Not then, not before, not now. Nothing changes, even when it does.

I refuse to talk to any of them, and instead half-dress, and grab my music and headphones and bolt out the back door before anyone can reprimand me for doing something other than what it is they want me to be doing. Making amends with my husband. Apologizing to my mother for pursuing a history she wanted to long ago leave behind. Ignoring the fact that my sister had to one-up me in a game that I was no longer participating.

Well, *fuck those expectations!* I think, as my feet crunch on the near-dead grass down the slope to the water. *Maybe they should walk a mile in my shoes, where there ARE no goddamn expectations because you have no idea what came before this, no idea what lies ahead.*

Before I surrender to the pulse of the music, I pause and absorb the setting, letting the atmosphere sink into me like maybe I once did when I was thirteen. It's eerily quiet out here—the occasional bird chirps, the occasional tree stirs, but other than my breath and the impact of my sneakers, there is nothing. Total silence. A coma. Back at the house, I'm sure that there is a cacophony of overzealous, sensational noise. My mom in pretending that her New Agey methods can temper this storm; Rory exploding at Anderson that he unfurled their secret; Anderson defending himself in a sincere, albeit actorly fashion.

Poor Wes.

The hell I've unleashed on him. Until I remember that he sent me a letter, offered me his keys—though in the confusion of it all last night, I forgot to inquire why: Why, after all this time, did he do so? Why didn't I reply back then? I add these to my list of unending questions.

I reach a footpath enclosed by a thicket of trees. It's steeper here, so I slow my pace, sidestepping down, hooking my insoles on the coarse roots that poke up through the soil. And then, without warning, the trees give way to an untouched, beckoning, Eden-like body of water. I freeze for a moment. I realize that I've stopped breathing, and that while I should be exhilarated at its beauty, what I sense instead is dread, fear, an undercurrent riding through me issuing warning that nothing is exactly as it seems.

Still, I force my lungs to find my breath and push on, down to the dock, which juts out fifty feet into the placid, unmoving water, the fog from the morning still hugging the low-lying posts that sink into the lake. The planks echo into the still air when I start down them—*thunk, thunk, thunk*—and I start to laugh at the melodrama of it all: it feels so much like a horror movie I've seen on cable recently, like someone might run out of the woods with a buzz saw and hack me in two. I reach the end, remove my sneakers, and plunge my feet in. It's frigid, and I lose sensation in my toes almost immediately.

I pop the headphones into my ear, pressing them in to vacuum out even the stoic silence of the woods and ignoring the pain of the icy water that is radiating up to my ankles now. I lie back, close my eyes, and allow myself to imagine where I was once upon a time, at thirteen, when nothing was what it seemed and before even that illusion was taken from me, too.

29

Wes finds me there long after my toes have turned so dead-person white that I finally caved and tucked them beneath me, a flimsy attempt to warm them after instilling intentional damage.

I hear him coming from behind me—*thunk, thunk, thunk*—but don't turn to greet him, so unsure as to whom it could be. My list of grievances with my supposed loved ones is long. *Peter? Please kill me now. My mother? I might drown her in this lake. Anderson? Ask again later.*

But then Wes taps me on the shoulder and says, "Hey," and whatever is cramped up so tightly inside slowly uncoils, and I turn, blocking out the weak October sun with my right hand, and force a weary smile.

"I slipped out before they realized I was gone," he says.

"I'm sorry to bring the circus with me." I pause the music. "Obviously, I didn't realize they were coming."

"No one ever does."

"I'm sorry? I don't follow."

"Family. They never give you much warning. That's all." He gestures toward the iPod, stating the obvious: "Music."

"Rory gave this to me right after the accident." I shrug. "Old songs from my old life. They're starting to spark something, bring things back."

"You were always good with that—making up songs to make fun of me, little lyrics to jab me when, you know, I'd kick your ass swimming out to the dock." He smiles, and so do I. "So," he says after a pause, "what do you want to know from me?"

I laugh, in spite of myself. "I'm done with people telling me their stories. Turns out, everyone has their own perspective of your life, but that doesn't mean that it's the right one."

"You were always wise beyond your years. But I'm certainly happy to help. To, you know, fill in some blanks, if you can't come up with it on your own."

I grin at his kindness, and we ebb into silence, the trees settling in around us. I stare at him for a beat while he loses himself to something across the lake, and I can see it now, see it clear as this Virginia air—that those bluish hazel eyes, even with the ever-so-fine wrinkles that too much sun and two decades can bring, even with the flop of burnished blond hair that sweeps over his forehead to mask them—that those eyes are the same ones my father had drawn in his sketchbook. That they were watching over me, and that maybe my dad was sending me a message, even if that message was obscured through his murky encryption. It was his wayward code to let me know that someone was out there, that someone had my back, even when he couldn't. My father couldn't have known that the book wouldn't make its way to me. My father couldn't have known that when it finally did, I'd have lost the ability to remember what the message was about in the first place.

Or maybe not. I reconsider. Maybe none of this is as complicated as I'm making it. Maybe my dad just wanted me to have a piece of him once he was gone, his final act of infamy, and maybe I need to stop affixing everything, every aspiration, every goddamn breath on who he was to me, what he meant to me, and how I can ever capture both of those things again. Maybe, simply, it was his apology—for asking me to live up to expectations that I could never meet, for not cutting me from those expectations when he understood the toll that they were taking. For not freeing me to make the music that burned inside of me.

"Okay, so one question: Why send me the keys?" I say finally, and Wes subtly releases himself from whatever thought he was lost in.

"The two of us had a pact," he says, brushing the hair from his eyes. "When your mom came and took you that summer, we promised each other right before you left—while she was downstairs waiting, and my own mother was going bat-shit crazy at your father for letting things spin this far out of control—but we made a pact." A laugh forms somewhere deep in the back of his throat. "You'd just read *Flowers in the Attic,* and when things got really haywire in those last days, you were convinced that we had to stick together, so we did that typical angsty thing of pricking each other's fingers and rubbing our blood together."

"Rubbing blood together can never be a good sign."

"I know—weren't we the cliché." He smiles. "But anyway, we rubbed our fingers together and promised to watch out for each other, to figure out a plan to be a family somehow." He shrugs. "Then Dad eventually moved back in with you guys, and then he went off the reservation until a few years ago . . ."

"Until a few years ago?" I interrupt. "You've seen him?"

He pauses. "Before my mom died. She must have known how to contact him or known someone who did. He just popped up on Wednesday afternoon shortly after her diagnosis. I wouldn't have been here—I run a graphic design company in town—but Mom wasn't feeling well from the chemo . . ."

"Cancer?" I say.

"Isn't it always?" he answers, then picks the cuticle on his ring finger with his teeth. "Anyway, he rang the doorbell and then used his key to let himself in—I guess Mom never thought to change the locks or maybe she didn't change them on purpose, knowing that he still had a key—and I swear to god, it was the most surreal moment of my life: Francis Slattery standing in my living room as if he hadn't been AWOL for the past two decades."

As Wes is telling this story, my lungs feel smaller and smaller, tighter and tighter, like someone is suffocating me just slowly enough that I can recognize that I'm asphyxiating but quickly enough that I'm helpless to do anything about it. I wave both hands in front of my face.

"Please, stop." I gasp for the clean lake air.

He looks startled for a moment, until he realizes that I'm running out of oxygen.

"Shit!" He moves to rub my back. "I'm sorry! Is this too much? Should I not be telling you this?"

I focus on my breathing, too embarrassed to admit that the realization that he came back for *her* but not for *me* has knocked the literal wind out of me.

Screw you, Father! I can't believe that I've chased you all this time, and you couldn't be bothered to chase me back. Not even for a plane crash and amnesia and the entire godforsaken disaster area that my life has become! It was exactly what my mom had predicted, exactly what I refused to accept, even in the wake of mounting evidence. And here I was, still chasing him. Screw you, new me! Screw you, old me! Who else is left for there to be now?

"Just go back," I bleat. "Go back to what you were telling me before, about us, about why we lost touch."

"Okay," he says and hesitates, giving me a long once-over, his hand still forming concentric circles between my shoulder blades. He glances toward the house, wondering if he should go for help.

"I'm fine," I say a bit more forcefully. "Please, go on."

"Well, okay, so we made this vow to—god, this sounds so young and naive—but we made this vow to stay family."

Naive? I think. *It sounds kind of nice, nothing short of a miracle.*

"And this was before e-mail, before Google," he says. "Our parents weren't speaking, much less letting us speak . . . I wrote you letters for a while." He runs his hands over his face, and I readjust the scarf around my feet. Slowly, blood is starting to pool back in my toes. "Anyway, a year goes by, then another, and then, I just figured that life pulled you out into it, and it certainly had me by the balls—college was not my shining moment—I got suspended sophomore year, and then arrested my junior year for selling weed."

"Weed? Speaking of clichés."

"Tell me about it." He grins.

"Jesus, are we screwed up."

"Not anymore," he says.

"Speak for yourself."

"Fair enough, but yours are due to extenuating circumstances. It's not every day that you survive a plane crash and lose your memory." We laugh together at this—at the truth of it, at the sadness of it, at the inanity of it. "So anyway, after all of that, so I let it—let the idea of us as a family—go."

"And yet you sent me the keys."

He sighs, heavy and purging. "My mom died." He shrugs. "That changes you. Like, literally triggers something in you. And then I found your painting in the attic. It seemed like a good time to reconnect, to try to build something." His voice drops. "I didn't have anyone else, you know? The keys were an open invitation to coming back."

"I wish I could remember why I didn't respond."

He raises his shoulders and lets them drop. "We had a complicated situation. I'm sure that part of you blamed us for the fallout."

"You're very levelheaded, you know. I can't really believe that we're related, not when I'm surrounded by all of this insanity."

"Ah yes, speaking of which, your mother is currently in our kitchen about to blow a gasket." He chuckles. "The dressing is different—last I saw her she was decked out in her best late-eighties tracksuit—but Jesus, isn't she exactly the same."

"Funny," I say. "She'd say that there's not much about her that hasn't changed."

"That's the thing about self-perception," he says, before rising to leave me be. "It's a bitch."

"I thought that was karma."

He squints and assesses. "Who's to say it's not both?"

30

"Ramble On"
—Led Zeppelin

O nce I found the song—sought it out on the iPod, and forced myself to listen—once I heard the song and remembered it—it seems impossible that it didn't come to me sooner. That the music was the key to finding the moment that set everything into motion.

A bud of anguish builds inside of me, not just for what happened that day, but that I sacrificed so many months of my childhood running both toward it and from it. An animalist cry spills out from the underpinnings of my belly. *How long had I let him define me? Even when, as an adult, I pretended that he hadn't.* I grab a wayward twig and chuck it out to the water. It floats for a moment before inexplicably sinking. *Forever. It seems that I had let him define me for just about forever. Whichever version of myself I was embodying at whichever moment, really, weren't they all in reaction to him?*

The song is still playing on my iPod—Zeppelin's "Ramble On" stuck on Repeat. I turn away from the water and see it: my dad's studio. It's off to the left of the dock, tucked beneath the line of trees, with a clear view of the lake, which he claimed provided him serenity, but really, who the hell knows what ever provided him serenity? Booze? Sure, that. Cocaine? Occasionally that, too. But his deepest secret is that I think his pain, his anguish, the depression that he so sunk into, *embraced even,* is what provided him serenity. At thirteen, this was impossible to realize. But now, two decades later, it is impossible to miss.

I'd wandered into my dad's studio that afternoon. Wes was at the dentist for a chipped tooth he'd gotten during Little League practice—an errant bat went flying—and Rory was inside napping off a sunburn. Without my mom around, no one tended to things like if we drank four Cokes a day or if we thought to apply sunblock, so just yesterday, she'd fried her shoulders like pork rinds. She cried all through dinner, and Heather broke some aloe from her garden and tended to it, but my dad excused himself to his studio and didn't return. Rory's wails gave us all headaches, but it was only my dad who couldn't tolerate it. The rest of us forked at our pasta, and knew that those were the consequences of living rule-free. You got to drink four Cokes a day, but sometimes you burned the hell out of yourself.

So I was bored. On the dock, two decades later, I still can feel the listlessness running through me. I'd come down to spend the summer with him—*I'd chosen him!*—and he was never around, and when he was around, he was mostly snappish. That day, with Wes at the dentist and Rory asleep, I picked grass and threw it for a while, watching it flutter from my palm back to the ground, but then resolved to go see him, breaking one of the few rules that had been imposed. *Don't interrupt him,* Heather had said early on. *Not when he's working.* The three of us—Wes, Rory, and I—bobbed our heads in unison and understood the gravity of crossing this line, and then we ran outside in our pajamas to watch the fireflies.

But today felt different. I'd hardly seen him in days, with the exception of last night's short-lived dinner, and I was thirteen and testing my limits, pushing up against what was expected of me, and goddammit if I didn't want a little bit of his attention!

He was working with the stereo on: blaring Zeppelin so loudly that the guitar split my ears.

"Mine's a tale that can't be told, my freedom I hold dear. How years ago in days of old, when magic filled the air."

He didn't hear me when I came in, even though the door squeaked, and I kept shouting, "Dad, Dad?"

I snuck in closer and closer, and even then, he didn't see me, or didn't choose to see me. Finally, I reached out and tapped his elbow, which was frozen in midair, his forearms splattered with paint, his brush still aloft. I knew I was crossing some sort of boundary, I *knew* that I was popping the bubble of his private seclusion, but I just wanted him to turn around and see . . . me. That the color I'd gotten yesterday across my nose had already turned to freckles, that I'd braided my hair into long pigtails just like I used to as a kid, that I smelled like honeysuckle because Rory and I had spent the morning wading through the back bushes, embracing the freedoms that we didn't have back in New York with our mom.

Instead, I tapped his elbow, and he spun around, dropping his brush, and there was blackness in his eyes. Even now, on the dock, I can remember that so acutely, that he was practically dead. Dead inside anyway. That his dark space had gone bleaker, which didn't seem possible, knowing his spells, but that it was indeed possible. His pupils were dilated to saucers, the rims around the whites of his eyes pink like salmon, the circles under them black as soot. *He can't see me,* I thought, *he can't see anything.*

I realized my mistake, my brazen foolishness, almost immediately, but by then it was too late. Like disturbing a rattlesnake. Once you step on it, it's not like you can pretend that you haven't.

"What is the rule we have?" he erupted. "What is the one *fucking rule* we have, Eleanor Margaret Slattery?" His breath burned my cheeks. It was laced with bourbon and beer and god knows what else. He grabbed my biceps and lifted me, and that's when my regret of interrupting him turned to fear. That he was so unhinged, so out of his mind in his depressive trance that he might actually hurt me. He started shaking me, slowly at first, and then faster, faster still, until I was flopping around like one of Rory's Raggedy Ann dolls, and I started crying, and then begging for him to put me down. I could feel his fingers worming into my skin, pressing against my muscles, bruising them almost instantly.

I was sobbing when he finally—and violently—threw me against the couch, like I was so disposable that I was a pair of socks.

We both froze for a second as reality sunk in, and I saw a flicker of humanity return to him, at the gravity of what had just transpired, that neither one of us could go back in time and erase it. *Oh Jesus, do I wish that I could go back in time and never come down to his studio, that Rory wouldn't have gotten sunburned, that Wes wouldn't have chipped his tooth. Then I wouldn't have been so bored, wouldn't have thought to break the one rule I knew that I shouldn't have.* But then he turned his back, flicked the stereo on just a touch louder—"*Gonna ramble on! Sing my song!*"—and grabbed the brush, which had fallen to the floor, marring the Oriental rug.

I finally found my breath and ran, as fast as my thirteen-year-old legs could carry me, down the rest of the hill, feet flying out beneath me, pebbles casting themselves away underneath. I was peeling my shirt over my head, preparing to launch myself head-first into the balm of the water, when my ankle snapped under. Nineteen years later, I can still hear it: that pop, the searing tweak that radiated up the side of my calf, and then I was falling, spilling over myself mostly by accident, but also in my grief. The planks of the dock got close, then closer, and then the pain in my ankle gave way to an acute, anguished burning in the side of my temple, right where my head impacted the corner of a two-by-four on the dock. And then I felt the cool sensation—just for a fraction of a second— of my body plunging into the water. And then, I stopped feeling anything at all.

31

I find Wes in the kitchen. I tiptoe inside so as not to alert my mother or Peter or Rory that I have come up from the lake down below. Wes is typing on his laptop, his fingers flying furiously, the wrinkles on his forehead crinkling like a paper fan. I slide the glass door into place behind me, and he pauses abruptly, looks up, and smiles. And then, as if he knows me too well after so many years apart, he holds his pointer finger to his lips, rises, and ushers me to the back porch.

"Zeppelin," I say, as if I need no other explanation.

"He had it on all summer," Wes says back.

"And the lake, the water . . ." I gesture inside to the painting.

"You never truly trusted it," he says. "You loved it, you forced yourself to love it, but you always took a while to warm up to it. Every summer."

"But I'm a good swimmer," I say.

"I'm not saying it was rational." He shrugs.

"That day," I say, turning to meet his eyes. "That day when I went under, you found me, didn't you?"

He grimaces, then nods. "I got back from the dentist and went out looking." He unconsciously rubs his jaw. "My face was still half-numb. Jesus, can you believe I remember that? That my face was still half-numb from the Novocain?"

"Who knows why we remember the things that we do?"

"Ah." He wiggles his finger. "The easy way out, the metaphor to your problems." He picks up the iPod, sticks an earbud in his ear, placing the other one in mine. We listen to Zeppelin together until he says, "I subscribe to the theory that we block out what we don't want to see, but it's always there, buried in our brains, waiting to be called up again."

"Is this some sort of Big Brother intervention?" I turn toward him, and the bud drops out, hanging between us. "Are you saying that I've unconsciously buried a wheelbarrow of crap because it seemed easier?"

"I'm saying that I think we all wish we could forget those last few days that you were here. So it's no surprise that you managed to."

"But it was among the first things that also came back to me."

"That's not particularly surprising, either." We stare out into the fading fall landscape of his childhood home, and he removes his earbud, refocusing. "Anyway, yes, I found you. You'd fallen into the water somehow on your back. Thank god. If it had been the other way . . ." He trails off, then collects himself. "I pulled you out, and checked your pulse, and you were still breathing, just unconscious, and so I ran to Dad's studio to get help, but he'd locked the door by then. I knocked for a good three minutes until I realized it was pointless, so I ran to the main house to get my mom."

I lean over the balcony now, waves of nausea cresting over me, and I wrap my palms around the railing to ensure that I don't spiral over.

"My mom called an ambulance," Wes says, "and by then, you'd come to. They did some tests at the hospital, determined it wasn't anything more than a bad contusion. But the bruises on your arms—Jesus, they were these massive, purple welts, like tattoos or something—they didn't really show up until we were headed home or else they'd have never sent you back with us." He hesitates, wondering how to sum it up. "So that was that."

"So that was that," I echo.

"Dad didn't even know about it until he finally came up to the house long after dinner. You were already asleep, but I was still up, watching TV. My mom confronted him, and insisted on calling your mom, who promptly—and rightly—demanded that you guys come home immediately. She got here, I don't know, a day or so later. Of course, Dad reacted to the news in the only way that seemed fitting for our family—with visceral cries of pain that were so loud, I remember flipping off the TV, heading up to my room, and stuffing a pillow over my head."

"And when I woke up the next morning," I say, filling in the blanks, it all rushing back to me now, "he made us pancakes, kissed the top of my head, and we all acted like it hadn't happened."

Wes bobs his head. "It was his surest path to forgiveness."

"Ours or his?"

"Both, I guess. We learned what we know from our parents"—he waves a hand—"or something like that."

"Jesus, that's depressing."

"When he came back, when my mom was sick, it was the same thing all over again. Hat in hand but no real acknowledgment of his sins in the first place."

"How long did he stay?"

"Off and on for a few months. I didn't ask questions."

"And then he left?" It's an assumption phrased as a question.

"And then he left," he says. "He and my mom made their peace, and she begged me not to hate him, and I swear to god, she believed it, she truly, honestly loved him. And because she was dying, and because I was so far past hatred by that point, I promised her that I wouldn't. We never heard from him again."

"Not even when she died?"

"I don't think his forte was showing up during a catastrophe," he says plainly. "He was never a man to rise to the occasion—good or bad, despite whatever his devout art-collecting followers believe about him."

And yet, I worshipped him, too. Ignored all of those signs, all of the neglect, because when he loved you, for those rare glorious moments that he gave himself to you, it was all you ever needed. A drug in and of itself.

I think of that rumor that Tina Marquis passed on, a real-life, high-stakes game of telephone. Could he really have come back for something as simple as my high school graduation? Would he really have been there to mark the occasion, when all other evidence points to the contrary? No, probably not. Just another hallucinogenic that I swallowed up and hoped to somehow make a reality.

Behind us, something stirs in the kitchen, and we both turn in unison to see my mother gaping at us from behind the glass door, like we're zoo animals. Her standard-issue muumuu has been replaced by age-appropriate dark-rinsed jeans, a robin's-egg-blue oxford, and a tasteful (*tasteful!*) violet neck scarf. Her skin is blotchy and her eyes are swollen, and part of me breaks in half for her, because I can vaguely remember who she was before all of this came undone, and how difficult it must have been for her to swirl herself into someone she thought was entirely different than before.

"She did come get you," Wes says softly. "I know that she's had her share of screwups, but through everything, she was actually the grown-up who always came to get you. Figuratively or not."

I start to agree—the new me would want to agree with him, until I remember that she has held on to secrets for so long that they must be part of her, integral to her very being, like her blood or her liver or her heart. And that part of me that breaks for her seals itself all the way back up.

Before I can articulate an answer, there is a distorted crash from behind where my mother stands, out toward the front of the house. She swivels toward the noise, then rushes toward it, and Wes and I, after a moment's hesitation, do the same. It's a family trait, of course, rushing forward toward disaster.

"**What the fuck, man?**" Peter is yelling from the front porch. He is on his ass, barreled over, and nursing what appears to be a bleeding lower lip. He touches it gingerly, then winces. "Seriously, man, what the fuck?"

Anderson has backed off toward the corner of the porch, his left foot resting on the toppled bench, his arms folded, assessing the situation like this is some sort of movie shoot, and he is waiting for his close-up. His ever-so-perfect stubble frames his locked jaw. *Oh my god,* I realize, *he thinks that he is fighting on my behalf. Like I need him to fight on my behalf!*

"Jesus, Anderson, what happened?" I manage.

"*He* confronted *me,*" he says, throwing his palms in the air. *Hey, don't look at me, I'm innocent.*

"What's your problem with Anderson?" Rory says from behind me. She scoots beside me, and here we are all, gravitating around this mess.

"This asshole convinced her to leave," Peter says, steadying himself and rising. The back of his hand never leaves his lip, and I can see the bright spread of blood washing across his wrist.

"What the hell are you talking about?" Anderson says. "Like I had anything to do with it!"

"He had nothing to do with it, Peter! Didn't you get my note? Didn't you see the *Post*?" I say. *Is he the one person on the planet who doesn't read Page Six?* "If you want to blame someone, blame yourself."

"You didn't want to leave until he started hanging around, started being there when I couldn't," Peter says, and for the first time in, well, ever, I start to pity him. Is this what we were like before the crash? Making excuses? Deflecting blame? Working so hard to avoid the obvious that the work itself became more exhausting than anything else? "I tried, you know! I tried to be there every step of the way until you got better."

"I haven't gotten better!" I gripe, and then I realize that maybe I have. Maybe I *have* gotten a hell of a lot better, and I've only been holding on to my amnesia because I've been working hard to avoid the alternative. The memories. The journey. But I am standing here now, strong, capable, and perhaps it's time to accept where I've been, what I've gone through, what comes next. I step toward Peter, who looks so small now, cowering up against the front porch beams. "Besides, you're forgetting," I say, my voice quieting, "I kicked you out the first time, too."

"But you *forgave me.*" He starts to cry now, knowing that it's over.

"Don't you get it?" I shout, and everyone startles, even Anderson, who has been practicing his best menacing brood, even Rory, who is shifting her weight back and forth, debating the details of what exactly has transpired between Anderson and me and what this means for her own confessions. *Too late,* I think. *Too late for all of that. For everything.*

"Don't I get what?" Peter says, and I can see in him that he really doesn't. That none of them do. Only Wes. They don't get that I can remember now, that I've figured out how to guide myself back into my cerebral space, and that, despite their best efforts to stop me, I'm going to dredge it all back up.

"I know that you're full of shit!" I say. "I know that I didn't forgive you, that I never intended to forgive you!"

His eyes grow to orbs, and mine do, too. To be honest, I didn't even realize that I had indeed remembered this detail—that, like Wes suggested just a moment ago, the history was tucked in my brain, waiting to be cajoled out. I can recall it so clearly now— Rory telling me about the disgusting mess, Peter professing his love for Ginger, his showing up on that one night when I was nursing my sadness with wine, and how we fell into bed together. And how I recognized, almost immediately, that taking him back was a cataclysmic mistake. And then there was baby . . . oh god, *the baby—yes, I was going to keep it and raise it on my own.*

I spin around to see the faces of my family who have led me too far outside of this pasture. "Don't *all of you get it?* What this has taken from me? What *all of you* have taken from me?"

They stare back at me, and I can see that they don't get it at all. And then I am crying, real and hard and purging tears. Mourning the months that I wasted after the crash trusting them, tuning my ear toward them, when I should have been listening to my own inner beat instead. Mourning, too, my own culpability in this: that it was so much easier to listen to them than do the heavy lifting that was actually required. If I'm to blame them, I must also blame myself. Though that does little to soothe anything, to make anything any better.

"We were trying to help," Rory offers.

"Bullshit," I say. "You were trying to help *yourselves.*"

"Nelly," my mom interjects. "Please."

I shake my head at her—*do not even think of saying anything else*—and wipe the snot from my nose, before I turn to flee down the steps and out to the dirt road, away, for once, from catastrophe. As I fly down the steps, the sides of my ribs flare, a quiet reminder that I may have healed, but somewhere inside of me, there are still plenty of scars.

32

I find a quaint little coffee shop about thirty minutes later in town. In my haste, I hadn't thought to bring my wallet, but the cashier, who wears a waitress uniform with the name Mimi sewn on in blue thread, gives me a once-over and says, "Hey, I know you. You're Francis Slattery's kid."

"Yeah, I've been on TV." I sigh, scooting out a chair, its iron legs scraping the tile floor. I think of Jamie, and how he duped me, and then I consider that part of me wanted to be duped. To believe that Operation Free Nell Slattery could be as simple as I thought it could be. That somehow pouring my trust onto this relative stranger could offer me answers that really only I had. I'll call him when I get back, I resolve. Tell him that I wish him luck, even though we'll never be friends, that he'll never earn a morsel of my loyalty again.

"Yeah, I've seen you on TV," she says, pouring me a mug of

black coffee without my even asking. "But I remember you from when you summered here, too."

"You do?" I say, squinting my eyes, wondering *just how old is she anyway.* She can't be more than midfifties, with a round head of brown hair that looks like she wears a shower cap to bed. Her breasts are too large for her smaller frame, and her skin is leathery, but in a way that suits her. Mostly, despite all of these things, she looks content. *Content. How far do I have to go to find that? I tried everything, it seems: embracing my childhood, running from it, pretending it never existed, and yet still. Content? No, I never found that.*

"You and Wes, you were always causing some sort of trouble," she says, cutting off my thoughts. "You were in town a lot, rode your bikes in for ice cream."

"And my dad? Have you heard much about him lately?"

"Oh, darling, that ship has sailed." She takes a grungy-looking rag and starts wiping down the other tables, though I'm the only customer and, given the dead air swaddling the rest of main street, there won't be many others this morning.

"I know." I sigh. "But figured I'd ask." I sip the coffee, and it burns my tongue.

"I saw him here a few years ago," she says, reopening the conversation I thought she'd just closed. "When Heather was sick." She winces ever so slightly. "God rest her soul. No one deserves that."

"Cancer or my father?"

She stares at me for a beat too long, and I hope that I haven't offended her.

"Oh, child, the cancer! Heather and your dad—*and* your mom—well, they were grown-ups, and they knew what they were getting into."

"And what about the rest of us?"

In my mind, I can still feel the water ebbing over me, the cold, murky water from that day on the lake, how it lapped up against my cheeks, how it nearly suffocated me and pulled me down to the bottom. God knows what lay on the bottom. And part of me knows that I was unconscious, that I *can't* really remember those blackened moments because my brain had all but turned off, but another part of me wonders if maybe I can. If, like so many other things, I'd just spent years blocking it out, building that wall because, as a kid, what other choice do you have? My father didn't rescue me, and then, months later, he drowned me all over again by leaving. Really—*Eleanor Rigby*—did I stand any chance?

I gulp down the coffee too quickly, and I feel its heat all the way into my guts.

Enough of that for now, I think. Anderson had told me as much. That it is only a song, not a destiny, and maybe it was just some stupid Wikipedia entry in the first place. Something we all took as lore but wasn't any more real than anything else. Why must my father's abandonment have to trail me forever? Maybe this was the cork that needed to be popped, and now that it's off, everything else—the memories, the instincts, the trust in my own self instead of everyone else—will follow.

"And what about the rest of you?" Mimi echoes, her dirty dishrag slowing to a stop as she considers the question.

"Yes, what of the rest of us? The kids who were damaged in their wake? What of us? Did we deserve that?"

"I suppose not," she says, her bosom rising and falling. "But eventually, kids become grown-ups, too, and from there, the world is whatever they choose to make of it."

I'm on my third cup of coffee when I hear Wes's Land Rover before I see it. The muffler must have fallen off, so it comes clanging down the road, echoing through the glass storefront of the coffee shop, until he careens into a parking space just across the street. A dinky little bell rings overhead when he enters, and a sole couple who has ventured out for pumpkin muffins, young retirees who look like former investment bankers who made a few million and then figured *what the hell* and bought a farm, turn and give him a little nod.

"How'd you know I was here?" I ask. I'm picking at a scone, thinking of way back when with Jasper, at Starbucks, and soaking up both how much and how little can change. Despite your best efforts, despite everything.

"Mimi," he says, then gestures toward her. She toddles over with a full mug and a croissant.

"Wes"—she greets him—"the usual," and slides the plate across the table.

"Is it okay that I'm here?" He tears the corner off the pastry and places it under his tongue, looking just like I imagine him to be as a kid, and the memory of who he was, who we were, is so close on my brain, so acutely begging to come out, that it's as if I can physically feel it lighting fire to my gray matter. It doesn't yet, but I trust that it will.

"It's fine," I say, "though Mimi's a pretty good therapist."

He laughs. "One of the best."

I think of Liv and how I have to call her, but that also how, one day soon, I'd like not to think of her so much, not to have my sentences begin with phrases like "my therapist." How one day soon, accountability to myself will be enough to keep me in line.

"The keys," I say. "Why send them?"

He chews on the croissant for a moment, then swallows. "As a gesture, I guess. After Mom died. That, as cheesy as it sounds, we had the power to reopen the doors, despite the mess that our parents made of everything."

"Do you miss him?" I say, out of context but not really.

"Who? Our dad?"

I nod, pushing my scone away.

"No, not really. I let go of him—or the idea of him—a long time ago."

"So you've never wanted to find him, track him down?"

He considers this for a long time, watching a pickup truck loaded with dead branches amble down the street, stopping for the red light, then skidding out too quickly when it finally turns green.

"Not really," he says finally. "I guess I always felt like he gave us what he could, and when he couldn't any longer, he didn't. And of course, I spent a few years being royally messed up by it."

"Ergo, the weed arrest."

"Ergo that." He chuckles. "But I got tired of wondering, tired of wasting so much goddamn energy on a guy who didn't deserve it. Sure, yeah, wouldn't it have been great to have him there at base-ball games and college graduation and *blah, blah, blah.* But he was always with you guys, most of the time anyway—he only did sum-mers at our place, and even then, a few weeks here and there for the most part, so I guess it was just one more thing on top of the other." He sighs. "I don't know, at what point do you start owning your own life?"

I smile. "That's exactly what Mimi just told me."

"We raise them smart around here." He smiles back, and we fall into a bubble of comfortable silence.

"I'm thinking of selling the house," he offers, after we've drunk nearly half of our coffees.

"Your mom's house? Really? How could you?"

"I don't know, not a lot is left for me there. I have an apartment near the university. The house is too big for me, too much mainte-nance. What's the point in trying to deal with the upkeep? It's just history, that's all it is."

As he says this, something small but tangible snaps in place, the cork moves just a little farther out of the neck of the bottle, and I remember. Yes, I remember asking Tina Marquis to show me that apartment because I was determined to leave Peter, not to simply let him leave me—no matter what I told Rory. I wasn't going to pretend that the smoking ruins he's created could be rebuilt, not in the way that my mother pretended as much in her own marriage. *My dad deserted her, deserted us,* and I am paralyzed with this realization: that *she never left,* not even when his own hands inflicted purple welts around my arms, not even when he spent his summers with a woman whom he might have loved more. So I asked Tina to find me a new home, and then what? What was I going to do? I focus and grind my teeth just a bit, and Wes, rightfully perceiving that something was shifting in me, interlocks his fingers with mine and doesn't let go.

I was going to start making music again. Raise the baby and make some music. Of course. Playing the piano. Writing. Singing. See what that could do for me, what direction that may lead. *That is who the new me really was, really is.* Yet because I remain my father's daughter, I chose a studio that mirrored his. And that's why Rory and I were fighting: not just about Peter and that she was the one who told me. But that I was going to leave her to pursue something that could have been mine, that I could have claimed rightful ownership to, rather than peddling the wares of a man who made it all too clear that he didn't want to be owned in any capacity.

Jesus. I feel sick. Even while I was trying to untangle myself from him, from how much he defined me, I never really did. With the studio, with my innate comparisons of my marriage to theirs. With the years I delayed in getting back to the one thing that I loved more than anything other than him. *Even in my attempts to run away from him, I snared myself back in his net.* And now, for the past few months at least, I've done it all over again. Working at the gallery. Listening to my mother and accepting my too-flawed husband because I didn't trust myself to stand out on the high wire and walk across it on my own, without a safety net below.

I unlace my fingers from Wes's and push my chair back,

standing upright and feeling my legs steady beneath me, ready to take ownership of what is mine. My life, my name, my memory.

"*Eleanor Rigby . . . waits by the window, wearing a face that she keeps in a jar by the door. Who is it for?*"

Of course it's only a song. How was I ever foolish enough to think something otherwise?

33

"Forever Young"

—Bob Dylan

My mother is waiting on the front porch when we pull up. I slam the Land Rover door shut, and Wes does the same—*bam, bam*—the sounds of the metal doors reverberating through the quiet country air like gunshots.

She starts to rise when she sees us, like she's actually going to greet us as if this were some sort of homecoming, but for once in her life she reconsiders and flops back on the bench, which has been righted after Peter and Anderson's earlier melee.

As I get closer, I can see that her eyes are bloated, the skin around them puckering like cauliflowers, and they are pink and watery and guilty. She opens her mouth to speak, but I flare a hand up quickly—*don't*—because I do not, not for one second, want to hear another excuse from her.

Wes scoots around me and heads inside with a squeeze of my shoulder, and I stop, there on the front steps, and jut my chin, wondering if words can ever be enough to clear the debris from the fallout, to say what needs to be said. After a lifetime of carrying around the weight of her—of all of the grown-ups'—sins, of the debt that mired us, what is there even left to do to move toward healing?

She clears her throat. "Before you say anything, I sent Peter home. Rory took him to the airport."

"And?" I say, like I'm supposed to thank her for this when I didn't ask her to bring him here in the first place. Didn't ask her to stick her head into *any of this in the first place,* until a wiser voice reminds me that, in fact, I did. Back in the hospital, when I didn't know where to lean, I leaned on her, and asked indeed. So maybe the lines are blurred between black and white, family and foes, instinct and self-preservation. The new me and old. And also, my responsibility in this and to her and my loved ones.

"And I'm sorry," she says, hiccupping like a toddler.

"For which part?" I contemplate sitting next to her but it feels like too much of a concession.

She gnaws her upper lip and blinks, and for a split second I think she's going to delve back into her plasticized, spiritual guru self. I can see her debating it, slipping under that mask because under that mask, she never had to reveal her true self. The woman who stayed with him despite my purple welts. But then she surprises me.

"Look," she says in a voice so guttural I barely recognize it. "I screwed up. I screwed up from the minute your father first met Heather, and I didn't stop until now."

"And you're only realizing this now? Because of everything that's happened?"

She shakes her head, staring down at the painted white porch. "No, *no*. I've pretty much known it from the start. I just didn't know what to do about it, didn't know any better. And he was everything I had, back then, when they met at some party for the artist crowd. I was just . . . I didn't find out for a few years. He always told me he was in Vermont at his studio." She loses herself to something, then circles back. "And by then, well, I was desperate. You'd already been born, and I had no career, and our lives rose and set around your father, and so when I discovered that he was screwing other people, well, I mean, what else was I supposed to do?"

"What else were you supposed to do? Are you seriously asking me this question?" After everything, is she really asking me *this*?

"Well, sure, now, today, you guys are all very I-am-woman-hear-me-roar, but it wasn't like that back then. And besides, he promised that he wouldn't leave. Not *leave* leave. I mean, not leave *us*. Just for a few weeks in the summer because, well, there was Wes, and then you sometimes went with him and seemed content. He had his terrible moments."

"Clearly an understatement." I instinctively reach for my upper arms, and she knows exactly of what I speak, her eyes welling.

"I drove down and got you as soon as I could," she says, her voice breaking. "Of course I knew that he had his moods, but never once . . ."

"You know what I hear? I hear a whole slew of excuses. I hear a mother who didn't do right by her daughters twenty years ago and who didn't do right by one of them this past year, either." I am suddenly seething, rage boiling viscerally in my guts, that she could sit here and still not own it, *still* not see the weight of my inheritance. Even though I know that I'm better than this anger, even though I know I need to let it go if I'm ever going to find it in me to move on. "I'm seeing a mother who didn't learn from her own goddamn mistakes! Who instead urged me, when I was most vulnerable, to repeat them! To take my own dickish husband back, for god's sake!"

"You don't get it!" She stands now and squeals. "It wasn't just me! It was you, too!"

"Don't make me complicit in your games! Don't tell me that I knew what I was doing when you told me to forgive him because I was, for all intents and purposes after the crash, a goddamn newborn! How can you hold me accountable for my decisions when I had no information—except what you told me—in making them?"

"No, no," she says more quietly now, retreating and sitting back down. "I meant with your dad." She sighs and regroups. "After I picked you up that summer, you refused to talk about it. Refused to even acknowledge it. And you were so very, very angry with me for ruining your time here, for making you leave. So angry."

I narrow my eyes and try to remember—how much of this is coming through her own filter?

Bits and pieces come to me: of the drive home, of the hot pleather seat in the station wagon on the back of my thighs, of Rory sitting up front and tuning the radio from station to station, the static of the in-between moments fraying my already frayed nerves. The bruises were ripe by then, so I'd tossed on one of Wes's long-sleeved lacrosse shirts, like concealing the welts meant anything. I stared at the back of my mom's head, at the wisps on her nape that dragged beneath her ponytail, and wished her dead. Dead in the way that only teen girls can. *I wish you dead!* I'd watch the hairs fly around from the open window, Bob Dylan singing dissonantly between us—*"May your heart always be joyful, may your song always be sung, and may you stay forever young"*—and come up with the various ways that I could maim her.

"Go on," I say to her today, the seeds of her truth finding their way into me.

"I tried to make you go see a therapist, which, at the time, was almost unheard of." For a moment, she can't help herself, and she so easily slides back into her old persona. But she realizes her mistake, clears her throat, and continues. "But you were having none of it. You retreated to the guesthouse and painted and painted—music blaring just like he used to, like you were, I don't know, sending him a message, compensating. And then your dad did come back—one day, a few weeks later, out of the blue, he shows up, and you ran out to the front lawn, swallowing him up. Instant, total absolution on your half. Both of you pretending like nothing happened."

"And then?" I ask, though part of me remembers what comes next. Part of me, if I were to dig far enough into my cerebrum, could tell her the story myself: that my dad stayed for a few months, fighting his fight against whatever demons eventually consumed him, and that when he did leave, I kept pretending—that he would come back, that he loved me more than he loved himself, more than he loved anything, and that when I finally understood that he wasn't and that he didn't, I underwent a transformation of my own. Stopped believing that the lines could be blurred, stopped seeing in color, started living in black and white. Stopped painting (for him), stopped making music (for me), stopped absorbing joy, stopped absorbing much of anything. Until the plane crash reset all of that.

I scurry my head. *No, it was before that.* Own it. *Yes, this I will. It was back when Wes sent me the letter, the keys. That's when everything got set in motion, when I stopped following the hard lines like a subway rat. I left Peter. I contacted Tina Marquis. I pursued my passion for music. I relished the joy from the plus sign on the drugstore pregnancy test.* The crash hadn't changed me—I had. *I had.* I'd been reawakened, stepping out from the shadows into the heated light of day.

"I was going to keep the baby," I say, and her head snaps up, a vein throbbing in her temple.

She mistakes this as a question. "I don't know. You didn't tell me you were pregnant." She chokes back a noise that's somewhere between a muffled sob and a laugh. "You probably didn't trust me with it, knew that I'd bring you home and make you drink holistic tea for the next nine months."

"No, I was going to keep the baby," I say, more firmly now. "I was going to leave the gallery, and keep the baby and aim for a new life."

She digests this, her eyes welling. She finally allows herself to speak.

"Well, you were certainly going to leave the gallery. You and Rory had stopped speaking over it. Things were tense enough between you two already."

"So I've figured."

"Don't be mad at her about it," she says, detecting my

undertones. "For starters, she never condoned my urging you to stay with Peter after the crash, and the gallery? You guys had worked so, so hard on it, that for you to up and decide to leave without so much as an explanation—well, it was hard for her to understand."

"How could she have been okay earning our keep off Dad's name for all of those years?"

She stands, wearily, placing her palms on her knees and pushing herself up, then moving to me like she has aged thirty years over one night.

"Your dreams are your dreams," she says. "Sometimes you compromise yourself to get there." She drops her chin just a touch, then gazes out across the landscape. "Show me someone who isn't guilty of that, and I'll show you someone who never dreamed in the first place."

When Rory returns from the airport, she comes and sits with us after it's obvious that neither one of us is abandoning the front porch for the duration of the morning. I'm curled over the front steps, my mom back on the bench, the silence wafting between us in what some might call a peace. I want to reach over and smack Rory when she slides up next to me, but then a wiser, more forgiving voice, one without the ragged corners—the *new* new me— realizes that, *well, what's the goddamn purpose?*

"Are you going to hold Anderson against me forever?" she asks.

"No, not forever," I say.

"Then you *have* changed," she says, and we both smile tired smiles at her point.

I hear my mom exhale behind us.

"I should probably be honest with you both now. Your father did come back for your high school graduation, Nell. It wasn't just the town rumor."

"*What?*" Rory and I say in unison, turning to face her.

She averts her eyes. "He knocked on the door one day and asked to come in for coffee. You were at tennis." She nods toward me. "And I can't remember where you were, Rory." She sighs and runs her hands through her hair. "I told him no. I said—and I remember it to this day—*'Get out of this house, get off of my property, and don't you ever, ever try to get in touch with us again.'*" She flops her hands. "And I hated myself so much because I'd tried so hard to go against that anger, to make myself over into someone kinder, more compassionate. But I couldn't stand the thought that he came back on his own terms, and that—and this I understood, finally—he would leave again on his own terms, too."

Beside me, Rory is pale, and I feel like this should stick more, like I should *care more,* that after this quest, after this whole endless search—really a lifetime of a search—this is what it's come to: that he was there, and who knows, maybe would have been there, *be here,* again—if circumstances had been different. But they weren't, and he wasn't. And that's all it can be for now. I stare out at the deadened lawn, the dormant trees.

"Please don't hate me," my mother says, and I can hear her crying behind us, which sounds both pitiful and remorseful.

"I don't," I say.

"I know where you can reach him," she says, this time really sobbing, the weight of her guilt releasing her. "If you want, I do know how you can reach him."

I rise now and gaze at her, then at Rory, then crane my neck and inhale the expansiveness of this house and the gravity of everything that has happened here and beyond.

I step across the creaking steps and glide past her, the screen door slamming as an exclamation point.

"No," I say from behind the metal door. "I have had enough with old ghosts. Let's finally bury them so we can all just find our peace."

Come the next evening, everyone heads for the airport, though Anderson and I linger behind for the road trip, neither of us quite set to hurl ourselves midair just yet. Wes drops them at their flights, while Anderson and I load up the car—packing it up without ever really unpacking in the first place. But ensuring that we don't leave anything behind all the same.

Wes is going to sell the house—he made his decision earlier in the day, when we took a final walk down to the dock, past my father's studio, which has sat vacant, a vessel, for years now. I'll probably sell the apartment up in New York, too. Maybe call Tina Marquis and ask her to show me something totally unexpected, something that might resonate with the new me who is yet unwritten, the me without the heft of my birthright weighing me down. Or maybe I'll leave New York entirely. Point myself in a direction where I can make music again, feel the notes inside of me, listen to how they can move me. I don't know. This has to be what I can do for now. Embracing the change and the shades of color that it brings into my life.

"You sure you're okay with driving back with me?" Anderson says. It's dark now, and we're both zipped into our jackets, the temperatures dropping with the last light of day. The fallen leaves smell of evergreen, the branches cackling, the few remaining birds and squirrels keeping us company with their busywork. He leans against the hood of the car. "Because look, I get it, I get that I screwed up— messed up everything by doing what I did with Rory."

I wave my hands. "Don't."

"No, let me." And because I'm living in the softer moments of who I wasn't before, I do. Let him. "I promised to have your back, to do anything to thank you for saving me, and I lost track of that."

"We all lose track of things sometimes," I say, pressing back against the hood next to him.

He shakes his head. "It was more than that. I just . . . I just couldn't step outside myself, even when I wanted to. I couldn't stop myself from self-destruction, despite knowing better."

I nod and rest my head against his shoulder because I know. Who hasn't known better and who hasn't crossed a threshold anyway? My father, sure. But my mom, sister, husband, and yes, me, too.

"I just want you to be able to rely on me. Always," he says.

"I'm the girl who saved your life." I smile.

"You are indeed. There's no replacement for that."

"I think you should do the Spielberg movie." I right myself and look at him now.

"What? No, I told my agent to pass."

"Call them back, convince them that you made a mistake." I stare at him, the lanterns from the porch our only light, and honest to god, he looks like a movie star, like he never fell from the sky alongside me, like we never lost ourselves to everything along the way. Both before and after. I lost myself long before I lost myself to that crash. I lost myself at thirteen, and then again every year since when I refused to shovel through the muck, digest it, own it, and let it all go. But I can now, can shovel through that muck to hopefully tunnel through to the other side.

"I don't know," he hesitates. "There's something nice about not, about staying here, parked in the backwoods of Virginia with the girl who saved my life."

"But there has to be more," I say. "I think it's time to go out, live our lives, and try not to duck behind the shadows anymore. Your drinking, my hard lines. They're crutches, you know?"

He bites the inside of his gum and assesses. "And then what?"

I laugh because I can barely remember the past, much less predict the future.

"And then, hell if I know. But I'm pretty sure that's as good a start as we're going to give ourselves."

He wraps his arms around me, and I sink into the barrel of his chest. For tonight, I let my new self trust my instinct to lean in and let him hold me up. And then tomorrow? Well, there is music to be made tomorrow, and it is bright, beckoning, wide-open.

Acknowledgments

A writer is only as good as the people who hold her hand along the way, and I couldn't be more grateful to the amazing team at Putnam for holding mine. I'm not sure that I have the right words to properly express my admiration and gratitude for my editor, Marysue Rucci, so I'll just say this: how fortunate I am to have found you, and how appreciative I am that you pushed me to be a better writer when I didn't realize that I had it in me. Thank you, thank you. Ivan Held, Kate Stark, Lance Fitzgerald, Alexis Welby, Chris Nelson, Lydia Hirt, and Diana Lulek: my deepest and unending thanks as well.

Thank you to Elisabeth Weed, my Jerry Maguire: you had me at hello. (Because saying "you complete me" would be creepy, even if true.)

Thank you to Laura Dave: my critique partner and the other half of my brain. Also my dear friend who makes me laugh every single day.

Thank you to Jon Cassir, Jessica Jones, Crystal Patriarche, Lucinda Blumenfeld, and the team at Parents.com, all of whom have been such advocates and friends.

Thank you to my husband and children, who remain my biggest cheerleaders.

Finally, thanks to you guys, my readers. I am so, so grateful that I get to make up stories and that you all take the time to read them. You push me to keep going, to keep improving, and not a day goes by that I don't realize that I'm the luckiest woman in the world because of all of you.

Readers Guide for

THE SONG REMAINS
THE SAME

by Allison Winn Scotch

Discussion Questions

1. The book opens with a playlist, *The Best of Nell Slattery*. What songs have profound meaning in your life?

2. Each member of Nell's family has his or her own agenda in helping Nell "re-create" her past. Do you sympathize with any of their motives?

3. Nell's amnesia gives her the opportunity to reassess her life and start over. Imagine yourself in Nell's shoes. Would you rather have a blank slate or know the truth about your past?

4. We accompany Nell from her first confused moment, when she wakes up in the hospital, to when she discovers big secrets about her family history. How do your feelings and perceptions of Nell change as she uncovers new facts about herself and as her personality is revealed? How does the author's willingness to show Nell in both good and bad light create a more vivid portrait of her character?

5. Nell's father named her after the character in "Eleanor Rigby," and she struggles with the notion that her life is destined to follow the same lonely path detailed in the famous song. Have you ever worried that a label placed on you by another could similarly control your destiny?

6. Nell tries to use her memory loss to her advantage, to reinvent herself and her relationships with the people closest to her. To what extent are these reinventions successful? What obstacles does Nell face when attempting to make these changes?

7. Throughout the course of the novel, Nell makes some decisions based on what she (thinks she) knows and some decisions based on gut feelings. Which is more successful for her: knowledge or instinct? Which do you find more reliable in your life?

8. Most of Nell's memories are triggered by music. Are there any sounds, tastes, scents, or sensations that remind you of specific memories?

9. Nell decides not to reconnect with her father after coming to terms with his absence. Do you agree with her decision to bury "old ghosts"? What would you do if it were your decision? Why do you think the author allowed us to draw our own conclusions about Nell's father's silence, and how does that choice affect our reading experience?